HEARTBREAK ON A DEADLINE

DANIELLE PALLI

ISBN: 978-1-7367982-8-7

Thank you to my friends, family, and fans, who have been so supportive of my work. Special thanks to my friend and publisher, Cindy Readnower, for her ongoing help in all areas of publishing, beta reading, editing, and keeping a finger on the pulse of book marketing. Thank you to Lisa Ramirez for being my sensitivity beta reader. Thank you, Graham Mack, for helping me bring my characters to life in the audiobook. Shout-out to Kelly and Kim and everyone at Main Street Travel for helping me plan research trips to Ireland, England, Scotland, and Italy. And, as always, thank you to my husband, John Palli, for being my partner in love and life and for his unwavering support. I am grateful.

CONTENTS

CHAPTER ONE

THE HURRICANE
VIDALIA OLIVEIRA—SEPTEMBER

My goodness, I will never understand why they call it a "Hurricane Party." For me, hurricanes are terrifying, and sitting one out is anything but a party. While the rest of the world imagines us "hunkered down" with a fruity rum cocktail eating salty snacks while playing *Cards Against Humanity*, the reality for those of us living on the Gulf Coast of Florida is quite different. Hurricanes are ruthless, violent, and downright scary.

I should know. I witnessed my first dead body after a Cat 4 storm one humid September evening. It changed my life—forever.

"What was that?" I asked nervously of my then-boyfriend, Tod.

Tod, God bless him, was tall, lanky, and had a mess of golden-blond hair, blue eyes, a sculpted v-shaped chin, and about as much sense as a baby chimpanzee. He was born "Todd" with two Ds but decided in his teenage years that one D was much cooler, and he'd been signing his name with a singular D ever since. These days, I have my own ideas as to what that D should stand for.

"I dunno," he shrugged, sucking back a can of Bud Light.

We heard a scratching noise above the living room, followed by the ominous sound of something getting dragged back and forth across our roof.

The storm grew louder and more insistent as the winds picked up. The rain overhead pelted angrily over our modest Parrish home. It was as if we had offended it somehow.

"Palm fronds? Tree branches or some other debris?" I suggested nervously.

"Vidalia, how the hell should I know?" Tod grew defensive, as if not having the answer was a slight to his intelligence.

Just then, the lights went out, sending a cold shiver up my spine. Fortunately, I had a flashlight at the ready and clicked it on.

"Geez!" Tod put up his beer-less hand to block the light. "Could ya not shine that damn thing right in my face?!"

"Sorry," I apologized, shining the light away from him, up toward the ceiling. It was then I noticed something else. A light grayish-brown stain began spreading across the otherwise white plaster.

Tod noticed it too.

"Aw, great." He slammed his empty beer can on an end table, sending our frightened rescue dog, Skinny, rushing at warp speed to his crate, where he promptly curled up tight like a fortune cookie, hiding in the corner. "I need a roof leak like I need a hole in the head."

I glanced at poor Skinny, our recent tan-and-white Terrier mix adoptee. "Keep it down, you're scaring the dog," I pleaded. "Even more than the loud storm outside, apparently." I ignored the fact that Tod referenced the house as "his" and not "ours."

"Oh." Tod pursed his lips in a way that wrinkled up his nose as if he'd caught a whiff of something awful. "Excuse me," he huffed.

Tod glanced at what I can only assume was my deflated expression.

His face fell, and his demeanor shifted. It happened so quickly that I can't be sure if it was real emotion or fake. Had he become so practiced at his facial expressions that I no longer saw what he was, but only what he wanted me to see? Before I had my answer, his voice cracked.

"Aw, I'm sorry, sweet pea." He reached over and touched my arm. "Guess I'm a little spooked by the storm, same as you."

I placed my hand on top of his and smiled. "It's okay, honey bear. We all are—including Skinny." I gestured my head in our dog's direction.

As if on cue, the scraping noise kicked up again, along with a loud popping sound, as if our house were in a popcorn machine. That could only mean one thing—shingles were being ripped off our roof in the hurricane. I dared not share this with Tod, not now that I'd gotten his emotions settled.

"Did you hear that?" Tod jumped, eyes growing wide. He grabbed my arm so tightly, I could feel his fingernails biting into my skin.

"I'm sure it's nothing," I lied reassuringly. "Why don't we climb into bed early and ride out the storm?" I wriggled my eyebrows at him suggestively, adding a little extra twang to my light Southern drawl for emphasis. I knew he liked when I did that. Wincing slightly, I then (with some difficulty) removed his clawed fingers from my arm.

"Aw, I'm all for climbing into bed with you, sweet pea. But given my nerves, I'm not so sure I'm up fer … you know." His eyes wandered downward toward his belt before eyeing me up and down like a piece of prime rib.

I smiled sweetly. "I just thought we could curl up with a book and a flashlight, and maybe I could read to you for a bit."

"Or, I could read to you," Tod offered, a hint of defensiveness again, as if I thought he didn't know how to read. (There was a modicum of truth to this.)

"I've got a book of love poems, Shakespeare. Care to read a couple to me?" I smiled. (My God, walking on eggshells around his fragile ego was tiring.)

"Lead the way, Cleopatra," he grinned.

I took his hand and led him toward the bedroom. "Hey, Skinny?" I called. Skinny lifted his head. He'd only been with us for a month, but he was quick to catch his name. "You comin'?"

Skinny leapt to his feet and hauled ass to our bedroom, nearly knocking Tod and me over in the process.

"Did ya have ta invite the dawg?" Tod whined.

"'Course I did," I defended. "He's scared too."

"I'm not scared," Tod insisted.

"Of course you aren't, honey bear." I closed the door behind us.

I tried to be optimistic. Relationships have their ups and downs, don't they? But in my heart of hearts, I knew this was the beginning of the end.

CHAPTER TWO

HEARTACHE'S LAST REVENGE

SIBLEY BLOOM—TODAY

"Hey, hey!" Yolanda knocked on the doorframe of my open office. "Team meeting in five, Sibley!" she reminded me.

"Be there in a sec," I answered, placing a pencil between my teeth and gathering up a notepad and manila folder with ideas for next month's feature. I used my free hand to close out the windows on my laptop, lest prying eyes wanted a sneak peek at my latest spread. In the office, I was known as the "magic maker" because, somehow, our little magazine had survived more than fifteen years in the biz, both in print and online, despite numerous others folding up shop in the digital age. I always seemed to pull the perfect "gotcha" piece out of my top hat, just in time for another revenue-boosting issue.

I shut my door and swished my way to the meeting room, wearing an oversized but comfy ankle-length yellow skirt and white sweatshirt, brown ankle boots on my feet. That's the thing about being the "magic maker." It meant I didn't have to abide by the dress code. As a staff writer and senior editor for a small, metaphysically minded magazine, the pay was crap. I almost think that my private corner office and autonomy with my dress and working hours was some sort of apology. It was—

My internal musings were interrupted once I reached the meeting room …

Everyone was looking at me … why?

"Sibley, welcome!" My boss, Reed, greeted me as if it were my birthday and I'd just discovered my surprise party. (It wasn't—in either case.) True to his name, he was tall and wiry with broad shoulders that didn't quite match his thin hips. Top-heavy, it always appeared as if he'd fall over from the weight of his upper body at any moment. Reed spent too much time in the tanning booth at the gym, with bulky arms hiding underneath his form-fitting black T-shirt. He always wore an adjustable, sliding-knot Orthoceras fossil necklace and used words like "safe space" and "compassion" a lot.

I glanced around the room apprehensively, not unlike my new room-mate Vidalia's rescue puppy, Skinny. Afraid and all but shivering, I sat down, willing my hands to stop trembling. Something was wrong.

Next to Reed sat Bertram, a fragile young lapdog who agreed with everything Reed was about. Bertram was in sales. He had polish. Not a hair of his thick, dark hair out of place. His teeth were whitened into a shade that doesn't exist. I'm fairly confident he breathed Botox, and his nails were manicured and buffed (including his cuticles). I looked down at my own gnarly cuticles and pursed my lips. I didn't want to be like Bertram, per se. But I recognized that my appearance lacked a certain *je ne sais quoi.*

At Reed's opposite side was his viper executive assistant, Krystal with a K (and pronounced "Kris-Stahl," not like the word *crystal,* and heaven help you if you get it wrong). Krystal was so petite, blond, and pristine that you'd swear she'd just escaped from a Mattel Barbie play set.

"Hi, Sibley." She looked up from her laptop, her legs crossed with her top leg swinging nervously back and forth as she tapped the edge of her long, neon-pink fingernail on the table beside her laptop in synchronicity. Krystal had a slight lisp that got more pronounced when she was innocently asking a question that might get her in trouble or apologizing for screwing over her teammates in some way. Like the time she convinced them to take a voluntary pay cut during one economic downturn, only for Bertram to later let it slip that she and Reed had somehow had enough funding to give themselves raises. She was also good at shouldering out the competition. "I hate to speak ill of a colleague," she'd whisper to Reed. "But I don't think they are truly *Positive Enlightenment Journal* material."

I'm fairly confident Krystal and Bertram are having an affair, even though they are both, reportedly, happily married to other people.

And then there was Yolanda, my friend, a self-described "big, bold, and beautiful" fellow staff writer and calendar editor. (Most of us had more than one hat to wear.) She had dark ebony skin and large round eyes often accented with bright blue mascara and generally preferred bright floral maxi dresses. Today, her dress was complemented with gold dangle earrings made up of random shapes that hung long enough to almost touch her shoulders.

Next to her sat my other favorite coworker and friend, Phoebe. Originally from Malaysia, Phoebe's family moved to the U.S. when she was only three years old. Now, in her mid-forties, she juggled work while raising two teenagers. As managing editor and lead graphic designer, she was technically higher rank than Krystal, and a fireball of energy packed into a small, five-foot frame with long, dark-brown hair streaked with gray and all-knowing piercing eyes. But Phoebe had this uncanny ability to hold the space with power and poise while still allowing Krystal to assert her importance.

I aspired to become more like Phoebe. I sat opposite her. She smiled at me, almost apologetically. Why?

"Hey, sorry I'm late," a deep yet personable voice announced. Asher Starling had arrived. While my beat was all things love and light, Asher was the dark side of *Positive Enlightenment.* His job was to "keep it real" and uncover the hoaxes, cults, conspiracy theories, and fraudulent psychic mediums through in-depth research and reporting. While I was writing about a psychic mom and daughter hosting drum circles on Siesta Key Beach, Asher was exposing staged alien visitation sites where the visiting creature turned out to be a down-on-his-luck convenience store owner who was hoping to turn a quick buck. Asher also doubled as our in-house photojournalist.

I envied Asher. I promoted fluff, while he saved people from themselves. He took the remaining seat next to me, wearing gray dress slacks and a white button-down shirt, opened just at the neck with its sleeves rolled up. You could see a hint of an undershirt beneath it.

I had mixed feelings about Asher. He's the only other staff writer for *Positive Enlightenment* who, like me, has been here since nearly the beginning. I remember being introduced to him that day, when the boss that predated Reed (now retired) was starting the magazine. I had been there for just under a month. I could swear that Asher's eyes lit up for a split second as our hands touched the moment we shook hands. It quickly faded, however, when he noticed the modest silver sliver of a wedding band, that I was still getting used to, wrapped around my left ring finger. I had only been married a week and just back from a whirlwind honeymoon.

While I settled into a life of pleasant monotony, I got to observe Asher's life with vicarious fascination, dismay, and—if I'm being honest—a bit of envy. It wasn't as if he had a woman on each arm or a "girl in every port," so to speak, but while his life was spent hiking the Dolomites and clubbing until all hours, my free time was spent cooking dinner, doing the laundry, and explaining to my Neanderthal husband why it is important for women to have an equal place in the workforce—a good two decades after most of the rest of the male population had figured it out.

But the "Sibley Bloom" story—my story—is still a common one in some parts of the world …

Boy meets girl. Boy sweeps girl off her feet—then puts her on a shelf only to take her down and play with her once in a while, or if he needs her to do something like the laundry or make dinner. Thomas knew a good thing when he spotted Sibley sitting on an outdoor swing in the park, reading a novel. She was smart, she was beautiful, and … she was his.

But Thomas didn't know the phrase "there's such a thing as too much of a good thing," so while Sibley got into writing and began working for a local metaphysically minded magazine, Thomas got into their next-door neighbor, Gemma. It was a short-lived romance, and Sibley conceded to forgive him, but only because he swept her off to Nevada to get married in a show of commitment (and before she could change her mind).

It was only after fifteen years of marriage and a fair bit of gaslighting that Sibley discovered Thomas hadn't really changed that much from the boy she first met in the park that day. Sure, his blond hair had thinned a bit, and he now had a pronounced bald spot, not to mention a little extra flab around his midsection. But that did nothing to change his self-perception. To him, he was just as young, just as clever, and convinced he could charm the pants off any woman—and did so many times over the course of their marriage.

It was only when Sibley found a pair of red lace panties tucked in his pants pocket during laundry day that she finally voiced her suspicions. After all, she didn't own any frilly panties—they were too expensive, and Thomas didn't think that was a practical use of money at all. Yet apparently, he admired them on other women.

So, with just over fifteen years of marriage at an end, and Sibley well into her thirty-eighth year, she was starting over—

"Sibley?" Reed snapped his fingers at me. I hated when he did that. So condescending. "You're doing that thing again."

"What thing would that be?" I asked, as Phoebe passed me a strawberry muffin from the basket she'd brought with her from a night of baking.

Something bad was about to happen. I could feel it. Why else would Phoebe try to placate me with pastries?

"Never mind." Reed waved his hand. "I've got an exciting proposition for you." He smiled.

"Oh, Reed," I joked. "My divorce has only been made official this week. Surely you're not asking me out on a date?"

Reed paused for a long moment, just long enough for me to wonder if I missed the mark. He usually had a fairly good sense of humor. Reed was gay and had been happily married to his life partner for over a decade.

"Oh!" He chuckled and feigned a smile. "Funny!" Somehow, I didn't believe him. "In fact, Phoebe, why don't you let Sibley in on the plan, since it was your idea?"

Phoebe's eyes grew wide as she shot me a *please don't kill me* look. "Well," she began nervously. "The original idea was, well, given that you had your heart broken and just went through a painful divorce … " She paused and swallowed hard, eyeing me for any hint of a reaction. My stomach and heart were turning inside out, yet I didn't give her one. "And given that we're heading into the holiday season, arguably the toughest time for people in your … situation." She paused a second time, wringing out a napkin that once held a muffin in it. The crumbs spilled onto the table, along with bits of the shredded paper. "Perhaps we could run an ongoing feature, starting with Halloween for the November issue, Thanksgiving for December, and Christmas and New Year's in January, all culminating in the largest feature for Valentine's Day in February. What do you think, eh?"

"I don't follow," I finally choked out. "What does this have to do with me?"

Phoebe's lower lip quivered. "I just thought that as part of your healing journey, and given that we are a holistic magazine, you might explore some unique and interesting places that foster a sense of community and personal growth." Before I could protest, she shot her palm up. "At the magazine's expense, of course. You know, right?"

"So, you want to turn my failed marriage and heartbreak into an ongoing feature?"

"You could help a lot of people," Reed interjected. "They could be inspired by your recap of each holiday as a single woman." He began messing with the Orthoceras fossil necklace as if conjuring the right words. "And I wouldn't say 'failed marriage.' Perhaps it was a successful relationship that simply ran its course. The two of you learned what you needed to from each other in this lifetime, and it was time to move on."

"Really?!" Yolanda sat upright, shooting Reed an *oh no, you just didn't* look. "The man cheated on our girl—repeatedly! What did she have to learn? Other than maybe to be careful who she trusts." To me she said, "I'm sorry, Sibley. I told them I thought this idea was whack. I feel like we just ambushed you, somehow." Yolanda flopped back in her chair and crossed her arms.

Krystal tugged at Reed's sleeve and whispered something in his ear.

"You're right!" Reed smiled. "Krystal piggybacked off Phoebe's idea with a bang-up one of her own. Tell 'em, Krystal."

Phoebe's ears perked as she eyed me and Yolanda, shrugging her shoulders. This was news to her.

"How would you feel about New Year's Eve in London and Valentine's Day in Paris?" Krystal fanned her hand out in front of her.

"Why not throw in New York for Thanksgiving?" Yolanda added flatly.

"We couldn't line up advertisers willing to participate in New York," Krystal answered, never missing a beat. "At least … not yet. I'm working on it."

"It would be like your version of *Eat, Pray, Love*," Reed smiled knowingly. "A journey to rediscover … Sibley."

"I'm supposed to journey alone to all of these exotic places—"

"Some local," Reed interjected. "A Halloween or Day of the Dead in Bradenton might be interesting. Perhaps a couple of days in Cassadaga?"

"And … what? Just write about my feelings?" I cringed. This was getting more humiliating by the minute.

"Not exactly." Krystal began to circle the table like a shark looking for the best moment to attack. "What if you get right back on that dating horse?" Krystal suggested. "We already have a few men willing to—"

"Wait, what? No!" My eyes began tearing up. "I'm not ready to be set up on dates, and certainly not for the world to see!"

"It's not as dramatic as all that." Reed patted his hands in the air as if lowering the energy in the room. "We would set you up on four casual dates—companions, if you will—to accompany you on each of your excursions."

"What's the catch?" I squinted at Reed.

"No catch … but if you happen to fall in love by February, that would go a long way toward increasing magazine sales. You could pick the 'best of' for Valentine's Day—"

"No, no, and no." I protested, literally stamping my foot and crossing my arms like a child.

"Sibley, it's not just about you," Bertram suddenly chimed in. Up until now, he'd spent the entire time tapping messages into his cell phone. I didn't even think he was paying attention. "Sales have been down for the past two years. We need this. We need … you."

"But look at me!" I gestured. "I'm not exactly front-page *Vogue* material. I'm more of a small banner ad on the Macy's website, with me in comfy PJs and a cup of cocoa."

"Yeah," Krystal clucked, eyeing me up and down. "We will definitely need to work on that."

Yolanda sat up, about to land into Krystal. Phoebe's hand shot out, grabbing Yolanda's arm before the young woman said something she might regret—something that could get her fired.

I let out a long sigh. "Just give me a minute to think," I demanded.

Suddenly, the room fell silent. Bertram went back to focusing on his phone. Krystal pretended to get distracted, pointing out something on her computer for Reed to review. He nodded, with feigned interest. Yolanda's eyes bored into the side of Krystal's head, while Phoebe's attention darted between keeping Yolanda cool while trying to gauge my face for a reaction. As I sank back into my seat, I was suddenly aware of the one other person in the room … Asher. I glanced in his direction. His hands were folded and resting on the table, long legs crossed at the ankles as he calmly sat in silence. He forced an awkward, toothless smile, his lips pursed together, once he discovered that I noticed him.

"You've been awfully quiet," I whispered. "No thoughts on the matter?"

"Plenty," Asher whispered back. "But none of them matter. I trust you to decide what's in your best interest."

"Hmmm." I furrowed my brow. That's a first. Most people just assumed they knew what was best for me, and I usually had little say in the matter. "I tell you what," I answered finally. "Give me a copy of the itinerary, and I'll let you know if—and that's a big if—I'm on board with this—"

"Don't take too long," Bertram cut in, eyes never leaving his phone. "We have to let our advertisers know by the end of this week so we can finalize the terms of our agreements." Reed elbowed Bertram in his upper arm.

"Ow." Bertram winced. Reed's eyes bore into Bertram's, and the sales manager fell silent.

"Take the weekend to think about it," Reed said warmly. That was his *I'm a great listener and here for you* voice. "This could give our little magazine the boost it needs to make it another year. But that's not what's important. More importantly, it will help you move on to the next great stage in the life of Sibley Bloom."

I picked up my manila folder and notepad, sticking the pencil I brought behind one ear as I stood. I hadn't even gotten to pitch my own ideas for the calendar. That was a first.

"Just get me the itinerary today. I'll give it some thought and get back to you with my answer on Monday."

"Oh." Reed addressed Krystal. "Make sure Asher has a copy too."

"Why would I need a copy?" Asher asked, surprised.

"Because you're our photo journalist, of course. Wherever she goes, you go too."

CHAPTER THREE

BAR FLY
VIDALIA—TODAY

"What about him?" Yolanda asked curiously. "He's kinda cute."

"Married, hon," I answered, wiping down the bar with a hot towel. Spotted that one from a mile away.

"Really?" Phoebe chimed in, fascinated. "How can you tell, eh?"

It was a girls' night out at the Bar Fly, except I got called in last minute to fill in for someone who was ill. It was a relatively slow night, so Yolanda, Phoebe, and Sibley decided to stop in for a drink, giving me a little time to catch up between customers.

"Easy," I replied, plunking down an Old Fashioned in front of Sibley, along with a tall glass of water. "He's got a school ring on his left hand, a pressed dress shirt with a starched collar, and pants that have been clearly hemmed."

"I don't follow," Yolanda answered, smirking at us. "Look it." She gestured toward Sibley. "I can tell from her expression she doesn't buy it either."

"Because, my naive friends," I sighed, "if he took his wedding band off, it would leave a white mark. Hence, putting his school ring on his opposite hand." I leaned in for emphasis as the three of them hung onto my every word like a sinner on Sunday morning. "Look at his right hand, though."

"It has a large white mark ... where his school ring used to be!" Phoebe gasped.

"Exactly." I winked. "And how many men do y'all know in this day and age who press their own shirts and hem their pants?"

"Eh, I'm sure some do that, or visit the dry cleaners?" Yolanda offered, accepting the sweet tea I placed in front of her.

"Maybe in the big city, darlin', but I doubt they would in Bradenton!"

Yolanda gasped. "Looks like he's heading in our direction. Do you think he heard us?"

"Above this racket?" I gestured around the room with one finger at the five flat-screen TVs, the sound of a rowdy bunch playing billiards and darts in the back, and "Heartache Tonight" blaring from an outdated jukebox.

But the man in the finely pressed suit was definitely headed in their direction. He sidled up beside Phoebe, running one hand through his thick black hair. "Get you a beer?" he offered. "Heineken, maybe?"

"Well, I don't usually accept drinks from strangers. You know, right?" Phoebe answered coyly, lowering her eyes toward the floor.

"Maybe just this once, eh?" His voice deepened as he leaned a little closer.

"She don't accept no drinks from strangers 'cause she's married," Yolanda barked a warning. Yolanda, typically a brilliant writer, let her grammar slip when she got annoyed.

"Really?" The man's eyes grew wide. "Are you happily married, eh?" he asked.

"Well, the nerve—" Yolanda slid off her stool.

Sibley grabbed her arm. "I'm sure Phoebe can deal with this on her own."

"Ecstatic," Phoebe whispered, winking at him.

Sibley and I exchanged glances, laughing as it hit us both at the same time. Phoebe and the stranger joined in.

"What in the hell is going on?" Yolanda complained. "What am I missing?"

"Yolanda, Sibley, Vidalia, may I present my husband, Amir," Phoebe laughed. To her husband, she asked, "I thought it was a boys' night out tonight. What happened?"

"Yeah, the guys are next door at the pool table. But I—" He picked up Phoebe's hand and began stroking it. "Happened upon the most beautiful woman I have ever seen, and have been sitting over there for ten minutes, my mind *bertanya-tanya* about best ways to approach her." He gestured toward his now unoccupied seat in the distance. Phoebe blushed. After more than two decades of marriage, he still had that effect on her. "What say we ditch this joint, and I take you back to my place, eh?" He wriggled his eyebrows suggestively.

"Well, I don't normally go home with strangers," Phoebe bit her lip. "But maybe I'll make an exception just this once." She grabbed her purse from the bar top and leaned toward the girls. "Don't wait up." She winked.

I smiled to myself knowingly before an impatient man at the end of the counter flagged me down. Why do people interrupt during the best parts of my work night?

"That was weird," Yolanda wrinkled her nose.

"I think it's sweet," Sibley praised. "A little role-playing to keep the romance alive."

"Well, what would I know about romance," Yolanda complained. "Don't get me wrong, I love my Bert, but his idea of foreplay is—" she deepened her voice for emphasis—"So, you wanna?"

Sibley shook her head and sipped her Old Fashioned. Just the right amount of smoke. I could tell by the way the corners of her mouth turned up in a smile. I was a gem of a mixologist.

"So, about today," Yolanda asked. "You gonna take the assignment?"

"From what it seems, I don't have a choice," Sibley complained. "If I don't do it, the magazine is screwed and we're all out of a job. At least, that's the way Reed makes it seem in the near future. But if I do it … well, it could tank and we'd still be out of our jobs."

"Hey." Yolanda touched her arm. "You always have a choice. Don't buy into Reed's guilt bullshit. You taking the assignment or not is not going to be the deciding factor in making or breaking us. You need to think of your own emotional well-being."

"Aww." Sibley leaned her head on her friend's shoulder. "I love you, my friend. You're the best."

"What'd I miss?" I returned to my station, refilling small cocktail napkins that no one but me seemed to notice dwindling. (Darn lazy barback.)

"We're talking about Reed guilting Sibley into using her heartbreak to fuel our next big story," Yolanda explained.

"Oh, that guy." I shook my head. "Not sure he's a narcissist, per se, but he sure ticks enough of the boxes to have narcissistic tendencies. I'd have to watch him more closely to see if he has an avoidant attachment style. That would help." I leaned my chin in hand, elbow on the counter, contemplating Reed's attachment style. It was meant to come across as intellectual, but I'm not sure I pulled it off.

"You're not a therapist," Yolanda and Sibley chimed in, almost in unison.

"What?" I complained. More like whined, actually. "I listen to people's problems all day long. That's what bartenders do! And I give great advice, if I say so myself."

"Still not a therapist." Yolanda shook her head. "I should know. Mine doesn't give me great advice. She don't give me no advice at all. Just asks questions about my childhood trauma and how I need to heal the past to move forward. But how can I heal in the past tense?!" Yolanda slapped the counter for emphasis.

I nodded knowingly. "Just give it time. Trust the process."

"Hmph." Yolanda sucked down her iced tea. "Still not a therapist."

CHAPTER FOUR
CONVERSATION WITH ASHER
SIBLEY

I received a text message from Asher that I must have missed while hanging out with my gal pals at the Bar Fly. I read it as I punched in the key code to the apartment I currently share with Vidalia. *Just read the itinerary,* it said. *Whatever you decide, I support you. I'm on board if you wanna take the assignment. If not, that's okay too. Let's talk.*

I struggled to get our front door open, pushing on what appeared to be a few items of mail that had been slipped through our mail slot while we were away. I sighed. I almost never received mail. Vidalia, on the other hand, got more mail than Santa at Christmas, everything from bartending magazines to *Psychology Today*. All I got was a postcard ad offering to reduce my fine lines and wrinkles for a low, low price.

Screw that, I thought. I've earned every one of my age lines and battle scars … most of them thanks to my ex.

As I carefully collected Vidalia's mail and set it on the living room table, I caught a glance of the proposal Reed had sent home with me. Letting out a sigh, I picked up the folder.

Last month, Vidalia ended her relationship with Tod. For some inexplicable reason, he kept the house, even though they were equal partners.

Vidalia never let on why she let it go so easily. With me separated from Thomas and planning my divorce, I rented one of the only low-cost apartments I could find in Bradenton—one that didn't require first and last month's rent to move in, just a small deposit. I managed to find one with two bedrooms, with the idea that, if all went well, I'd turn the extra room into a home office. I didn't expect Vidalia to move in with me, and given her emotional state upon arrival, I didn't ask too many questions.

After slipping off my shoes and changing into the most comfortable set of blue cotton pajamas that I own, I settled onto the couch with a glass of grapefruit-essence-infused seltzer by my side. I opened the folder and began to read …

It didn't take long for my face to flush and my nerves to rattle. I picked up my cell phone and fiercely thumbed my reply to Asher: *Just looked at Reed's proposal. I know it's the weekend, but are you up for a chat tomorrow? Perhaps around 10 a.m. or so for coffee?*

I wasn't sure of Asher's availability, as I knew he'd just started dating a woman he'd met at the gym … Chloe, I think, was her name … worked in merchandising, or some such. Honestly, Asher dated a lot. So, it was hard to keep track. Although, as someone who'd been in the same relationship for nearly two decades, I'm not sure what's considered a little or a lot. I just know … more than I.

Moments later, he replied: *Yes to both. Where should we meet?*

Asher flagged me down as I entered a little Taiwanese tea house near my apartment. When Asher asked where to meet, I'll admit I was a little at a loss. Until Thomas and I had reached a legal agreement, I was reduced to what little I had in a personal savings account. Which, arguably, wasn't much. Therefore, it was a rare treat for me to go out—unless it was to the Bar Fly, where Vidalia always insisted on treating.

"Hey," I answered awkwardly, glancing around at the minimalistic design. The tea house had a few simple bucket seats, some with a metal base, others plastic, with cushions of varied fabrics and colors on top, surrounding small wooden tables. There were even a few flat, faux leather couches in the corner for more casual conversation. Asher had chosen a table for two by the front window.

He stood as I made my way over to him, only sitting after I took a seat across from him, hanging my purse on the back of the chair and setting Reed's proposal on the table.

"I hope you don't mind," he apologized. "I ordered you a cup of the Assam tea. I don't think I've ever seen you drink coffee in the office. Was kinda surprised when you suggested it."

"That's perfect," I was surprised. I'm not certain that, even after fifteen years of marriage, my ex-husband ever paid attention to what I drank in the morning. "I suggested coffee because … well, I seem to remember that's what you drink. Most people, actually."

"I thought I'd live on the edge for once," he laughed. "I'm trying the green bubble tea … happy to swap yours out for something else, if you prefer."

"Gosh no," I replied. "You guessed right. Simple is better for me."

"I have an order for Starling," an attendant from behind the counter called.

"Ah." Asher stood. "Back in a jiffy."

With chin in hand, I leaned an elbow on the table and gazed at the traffic and passersby outside. Funny how your entire world can get upended in a moment.

Once my co-worker had returned and we'd settled in, we each took out pens and began marking up our individual copies of the itinerary. The premise had me feeling like I was a contestant on a reality game show.

"Reed has me 'accidentally' bumping into a shamanic practitioner outside a metaphysical shop in the Village of the Arts during the Festival of the Skeletons parade honoring *Día de los Muertos*." I was incredulous.

"He even wrote in how I'm supposed to feel—'charmed by his spiritual centeredness and uncanny ability to see into my very soul.' Can you believe this crap?"

"Sadly, I can." Asher shook his head. "My whole beat was uncovering the charlatans in the metaphysical world. I'm ashamed that the CEO of our magazine has become one."

I leaned across the table and whispered. "Is revenue really that bad? Why would Reed stoop to this level?"

"I dunno," Asher confessed. "Bertram and Krystal are always wearing the latest designer clothes and hottest tech. And Reed manages to have the time and means for jet-setting around the globe for months at a time."

"And furthermore," I tapped the back of my pen on the table. "Did you see where he has me going after this? London … Paris! How can the company afford this?"

"I'm led to believe that the places you're covering are paid for by advertisers and sponsors of this—" he glanced at his itinerary—"'International Holistic Conference,' held in London this year. And all the side trips … Stonehenge, the London Eye, Notre Dame … along with … ooh, look at this … an overnight at the Akashic Spa and Resort with a complimentary stone massage included. Well, isn't that nice?" Asher put one hand on his hip and nodded. I couldn't tell for certain whether he was impressed or this was his idea of a joke.

"Hey, I'm all for doing a write-up on the conference, the hotels, the day trips and restaurants. To me, it's an all-expense-paid holiday." I took a sip of my Assam tea, the aroma tickling my nose. I wriggled it and sniffed. "It's the romantic dates with men I don't know, where my feelings and reactions are written like stage direction, that I don't like. Did you see this?" I flipped to page three. "'While my thoughts returned to the mild-mannered Bodhi, from our meal together at Cassadaga Spiritualist Camp, I could feel myself energetically pulled toward Jack after our time together sipping champagne and taking in the breathtaking view overlooking London—'" I dropped the paper angrily. "If Reed is going to write the whole thing for me, why even go? I can just do a Google search on the rest."

Asher stifled a laugh. "That actually sounds more like Krystal. She fashions herself a writer, but there's a reason she's not."

"How will anyone trust us if we are dishonest with our readers?" I complained. "And furthermore, how could I live with myself? Besides, who are these men that are supposedly falling all over me? I'm not exactly model material!" I immediately regretted that last statement, lest Asher think I was fishing for a compliment.

"Well, that's covered on page one, don't you see?" He leaned over and pointed. "If they are able to get the Magnolia Day Spa to provide you with a cut and style, plus mani-pedi, and Saks Off 5th to supply a couple of outfits, I'm sure you'll look—" Asher cleared his throat uncomfortably. "Fine."

"Hmm." I wrinkled my brow.

"What is it?"

"The itinerary spells out a great reveal. At the end of my final feature, I'm to have found true love again … as if I ever had that in the first place. How's that gonna work?"

"If I know Reed, he'll ask you to play along for a few months and then break up amicably," he sipped his tea. "If timed right, you'll be ready to date again for a summer fling."

"Very funny … I don't like any of this. It doesn't even specify how much time I'm supposed to spend with these men. That part seems rather open-ended. And where are these guys coming from, anyway?"

"I wish I didn't know the answer to that." For the first time since we arrived, Asher shriveled in his seat.

My eyes pierced into his. "You have to tell me."

Asher sighed heavily. "After you left on Friday, Krystal went around the room asking for candidates from friends, people we know attending the London conference. Bertram even suggested we roll that into the pitch to sponsors … they could match you up with someone single from their business for a little extra attention."

"I think I'm going to be sick." I pinched my lips together. An attendant behind the counter glanced in my direction, concerned. I smiled and took another sip of my tea.

"I hate to add insult to injury, but there's an extra section to my itinerary."

"What?"

"Who do you think has to photograph all of this? While you're on your romantic adventures, I'm supposed to catch romantic moments … photos for print and web, and video shorts for social media."

"Oh, Asher," my heart sank. "I know you just started dating someone too … Chloe, I think? It's sucky to have to leave her during the holidays."

"Well, I wouldn't worry about her," he confided. "She's made it clear on many occasions that we're 'keeping it casual,' and that she's 'seeing other people.' She quite likely has other plans already."

"Oh." I paused. Thomas and I were sort of thrown together all of a sudden. And before him, I guess the dating rules were different. I generally dated one person for a bit. If that didn't work, I dated someone else. I don't even know what it's like to juggle multiple prospects … I guess I'll find out. "Well, on the plus side, we're spreading things out over four issues, but most of this happens mid-December through the first week in January. Day of the Dead and Thanksgiving in Florida … or to New York for the Macy's Thanksgiving Parade—if they can line up advertisers in time. England and France are all scrunched together. While we'll be there for Christmas and New Year's, we're fudging on Valentine's Day since we fly back early January. Maybe you'll at least get to be her Valentine?"

"Perhaps." Asher seemed unsure, evident by his knee bouncing with nervous abandon under the table.

I changed the subject.

"Well, I appreciate that you'll be there, anyway." I smiled in what I hoped was a display of friendship. "It's nice to have the support."

Asher's expression brightened. "Happy to be there. We can't have our 'magic maker' floundering on her own in a strange city, now, can we?"

"Now, I just have to get Reed to agree to my terms," I concluded, placing my pen overtop the outline of my trip in what I hoped felt definitive. "It's gotta be authentic. Blind dates? Fine. Chronicling my journey? Fine. Finding some spiritual epiphany? I can roll with that. But I draw the line at pretending to swoon over anyone, just to boost magazine sales."

CHAPTER FIVE

NADIA

VIDALIA—SEPTEMBER, AFTER THE HURRICANE

As long as I live and breathe, I'll never forget the look on that man's face.

It was two days after the hurricane. Tod called some of his cronies to climb our roof and assess damages. Up until about five months ago, Tod worked as a concrete and general contractor. But a fall-related spinal injury put him on disability. In my humble opinion, he overdramatized his pain when the insurance people came to visit, but that's neither here nor there. The point is, after we heard the strange noise above the ceiling, we needed some answers. Our biggest fear was that we'd need a new roof due to storm damages. And roofs don't come cheap in Florida.

The man's name was Manny, and his face was white as a ghost.

"Erm," he coughed, putting his hands on his hips and sucking in air as if he'd been underground for days and was struggling to breathe. He tapped his boot on our doormat as if summoning the gods for just the right words.

"What is it, man?" Tod slapped Manny on the arm with a laugh. The two of us stood almost shoulder-to-shoulder at our front door. "Cat got your tongue?"

But I knew better. "Manny," I asked gently. "Are you okay, hon?"

Manny's eyes rose to meet mine just before he doubled over, dry heaving for a moment in an involuntary reflex. He put his hands on his knees and braced himself, sucking in a few labored deep breaths.

"Yeah," he answered finally, standing tall and puffing out his chest, pulling his red cap from his head by the rim and tucking it under his arm as if in a place of worship. "It's just that … " He coughed again. "I think we found the source of the noise you heard a coupla nights ago."

As if on cue, the sound of emergency sirens could be heard in the distance. Moments later, an EMS vehicle arrived, along with a team of local police officers.

"Detective Gerard Jameson here," an average-sized, thirty-something man with bulky shoulders emerged from one of the police vehicles now stationed in our driveway. "Did someone here report a body?"

"A body?!" I blurted out. "No—"

"Yes," Manny corrected. I looked at him incredulously. "I was the one who phoned."

"Well," the officer eyed me suspiciously before turning toward Manny. "Where is it? In the house?"

"No," Manny corrected again, pointing upward. "On the roof."

"The roof!" Detective Jameson was taken aback. "Any chance of life?"

Manny shook his head. "I seriously doubt that, sir." His face dropped. "I'm gonna wager that it's been up there for a while. Think it might be a woman, based on the hair and skirt. But I can't tell fer certain."

"How in the hell did she get up there?" Jameson asked.

"Damned if I know," Manny answered. "That's what I called you for."

Jameson nodded, motioning for two other officers to come forward. "Can you help two of my guys get up there and see?"

"Surely," Manny nodded gratefully. The sooner this was someone else's problem, the better. He shivered. Not sure he'd ever seen a dead body before. Come to think of it, neither had I, outside of my nana's funeral. I wasn't eager to start.

Tod was oddly quiet.

Three hours later, we got the news. That's pretty darn fast, if you ask me. The woman was Nadia Perdita, a music teacher at a local elementary school. Six months ago, she requested a leave of absence, effective immediately, citing health issues (according to the school). It was believed that she went back to stay with her family in Tennessee while undergoing treatment. For what, we couldn't be sure.

So, how did she end up stuck on our roof during a hurricane? The police didn't know. But we were politely advised to stay put until they could figure it out.

This didn't sit well with me at all. Particularly since I happened to know that Nadia was Tod's ex-wife. In point of fact, she and Tod went halfsies on this house together. When they divorced last year, he sought to buy her out. I remember because when he and I began dating, he mentioned having ended "the shortest marriage in history," and that they were still working out the details of their separation. He assured me it was all amicable, though he seemed annoyed that she insisted on keeping his last name. He convinced her to change it back to her maiden name.

Now, I'm not sure.

He asked me to move in with him in March. We'd only been dating for a few months, but he was so sure that I was the one and that we were meant to be together, that, before long, he had me believing it too.

After all, I'd never had anyone ever be so smitten with me.

So, I said "yes" and here we are.

Fast forward to six months later, and I am filled with serious regrets … and a dead ex-wife on the roof.

"Of all the shitty timing!" Tod complained later that evening, pacing back and forth across our bedroom floor. Skinny stood, wagging his tail tentatively each time Tod passed, as if it meant attention for him.

It didn't.

I placed the copy of the *DSM-5* I was reading on my end table. I was trying to understand the difference between distinguishing Borderline Personality Disorder from other mental health issues, but having trouble.

Yes, I recognize that I'm not a therapist … something my friends are fond of pointing out. But the human mind fascinates me to no end.

Or maybe I was just really trying to figure out what the hell was going on in Tod's brain.

"What do you mean, darlin'?" I asked, trying to be supportive.

"What do you think I mean, Vidalia!" He put his face a little too close to mine. "Think!" I felt a little spray from his saliva as he spoke.

"I need you to calm down, sugar bear," I answered sweetly, calmly. "You're scaring me."

The rage in his eyes felt so intense, I could almost see flecks of fire in them. He eyed me wildly for a moment. Then, as if something clicked in his brain, he shifted. It was so abrupt, it was as if I was speaking with a different person.

"I'm sorry, sweet pea," he continued to pace, running his hand through his hair. "I just thought I was done with that bitch long ago!"

"What?" I squinted at him. "You mean Nadia?"

I'm not an expert in matters of the heart … or much of anything, for that matter. But in my book, if someone you loved dies—even if you don't love them anymore—there's still some sadness, a modicum of compassion.

"Who do you think I mean, sweet pea?" He tilted his head, thrusting his chin forward and slowing his words as if my comprehension skills were lacking.

I swallowed hard, choosing my response carefully. "Aren't you curious how she died?"

He paused a moment. "Not really."

"Are you sad she's gone?" I pulled the covers up carefully, as if protecting myself from the fallout of that question.

He peered over his shoulder at me with a look I will never forget. I almost thought he saw her in me … or maybe mistook me for her, somehow.

"No, sweet pea. I'm not. I'm just sorry that hateful woman got stuck on our roof. Can't seem to get rid of her, no matter how hard I try."

Chills ran through me, though I wasn't entirely sure why. Somewhere, in the back of my brain, was a niggling little voice. It yelled a single word at me … *run.*

CHAPTER SIX

CHLOE

"You're going to London for New Year's and Paris for Valentine's Day?" Chloe's voice was a mix of excitement and resentment, simultaneously. "And you didn't invite me?"

Asher had invited his "keeping it casual" date over to his house for dinner. He prepared an eggplant Parmesan with a side burrata salad, both of which he knew she liked. While he would have preferred red wine, he knew that Chloe had a particular fondness for Pinot Grigio, so that's what he got.

"I just found out about it at work yesterday," Asher explained, taking a bite of the eggplant. Not bad, he thought, if he said so himself.

Chloe seemed less impressed, pushing a tiny cherry tomato around her plate absentmindedly. "And when were you planning on talking to me about it?" Her voice developed a distinct nasal quality when she was annoyed.

"This is me talking to you about it." Asher sucked in a breath and let it out slowly. "And since we're 'keepin' it cas'—your words—I wasn't even so sure you'd mind."

"Well, when you have plans for Halloween, Thanksgiving, Christmas, New Year's, and Valentine's Day, and not one of them include me, I definitely mind." She nibbled a bit of her eggplant.

"Not exactly," he explained. "Day of the Dead in the Village of the Arts is the first week in November, so we could technically spend Halloween together. Thanksgiving is a daytime event, so we could plan for something in the evening—"

"Not really interested in those," Chloe mumbled. "But you'll be in England during Christmas and New Year's and France for Valentine's Day."

"Not quite," he corrected again. "The trip ends the first week in January. So, while I'd be away for the first two, I would be home before Valentine's Day."

"But you've still got an early Valentine's event planned in advance in Paris, right?"

"That is correct."

"Hmmm." Chloe pushed more of her food around her plate.

"Do you not care for the dinner?" Asher asked. "It's okay, I won't be offended."

"No, it's fine," she answered quietly. "I just had Italian last week when I was having dinner at Taverna Toscana with—" She caught herself. "Well, last week."

"Ah, I see. I just remembered you ordering the eggplant rollatini some time ago and thought this was a safe bet. I'll consult you on the menu next time."

"Oh, silly." She smiled, reaching across the table and touching Asher on the hand. "You don't ever have to cook for me … we can just go out!" She took a large gulp of her wine. "Refill, please." She held out her glass as Asher dutifully refilled it.

"Noted," Asher replied calmly.

"I have an idea," she said suddenly.

"I'm all ears."

"What if I went with you to Europe? I could be your assistant, of sorts. See how well we travel together. Might even be a good experiment in … exclusivity." Her eyebrows lifted expectantly.

"You do understand that I'll be working, right?"

Chloe dropped her shoulders but would not be defeated. "Of course! That's why I said I'd assist you."

"And about the travel and lodging arrangements?" Asher asked.

"Well, I can stay with you … if you don't mind." She lowered her chin seductively.

"And your plane ticket?"

"Can't the magazine cover it?" Chloe sulked. To hear Chloe tell it, she's the brand ambassador and marketing representative for her father's perfume company, but aside from a few Instagram posts and TikTok videos, Asher was hard-pressed to understand exactly how she spent her workdays. Furthermore, for someone in the family business, she seemed to have no understanding about little things like "budgets" and "overtime."

"I'm afraid not."

She lifted her chin abruptly. "Asher, if I didn't know any better, I'd think you weren't that keen on me going with you."

"On the contrary," he protested. "I love the idea. I'm just a little apprehensive about the fact that you're only willing to explore exclusivity when it's wrapped in a trip to Europe."

"Well, that's just not fair." Chloe folded her arms and pouted. "I just thought it'd be romantic."

Asher softened, thinking on this a moment. "Okay, if you're that eager to come, let's go to England together."

"Yay!" She squealed, bounding from her seat and wrapping her arms around Asher's neck. He cautiously moved his wineglass out of the way lest she knock it to the carpet. "And don't worry about tickets. I know you can probably only afford economy anyway. I'll make sure Daddy gets us First Class."

The sentiment rubbed Asher the wrong way. But then, he'd never dated anyone quite her caliber before … No, that wasn't the right word. She may have come from a wealthier family than most, but he'd dated his fair share of sophisticated women—intelligent, talented, ambitious, and beautiful. Chloe was all of those things, but she lacked a certain … what was it? Empathy? Understanding of those less fortunate? Perhaps it was her reaction to his lack of wealth. *It's okay, Daddy can get it for us.* Did anyone over the age of eight still actually refer to their father as "Daddy"? Or was that a manipulation technique?

"Asher?" Chloe stood back. "Where did you go? Because your mind was clearly elsewhere."

"I'm sorry, Chloe." Asher tried to cover his tracks. "I was just imagining you and me in England and Paris."

She smiled approvingly, leaning in for a quick peck on Asher's lips before she did a little twirl in front of him, grabbing the wine bottle along the way and craftily emptying the rest of it into her glass.

"Asher, darling," she smiled coyly.

"Yes, Chloe?"

"If we're going to be a for-real item, you need to come up with a nickname for me instead of just calling me 'Chloe' all the time."

"What would you suggest?"

"Hmmm … well, I think I'm rather fond of 'darling' and 'my love.'"

"Okay, my lovely darling." Asher grinned. But something niggled in the back of his mind, a dark voice that told him, *This is never gonna work.*

CHAPTER SEVEN

FESTIVAL OF THE SKELETONS
SIBLEY—NOVEMBER

"Where are we supposed to meet this shaman again?" Asher asked in a voice that sounded vaguely critical.

"Shaman Theodore said we should meet in front of the community shrine off of Twelfth Avenue at 6 p.m. … Ah, here we are!"

There, on the corner, was a pink picket fence covered with handwritten, multicolored cards strung on it—a prayer, wish, or remembrance of someone who had passed. In front of the fence, a small table sat with pencils, markers, and crayons, along with blank cards with a hole punched through the top to lace the string that was to be tied to the shrine. There was also a painting and photos set on the table as a memorial to a villager who had passed over the last year. It was no one I had heard of, but from the looks of it, it was someone who was deeply missed.

I picked up a heart-shaped card and thought about my parents. I was a toddler when an unfortunate accident took them too soon, landing me in foster care. Sadly, I have very vague memories of them—so vague that I can't be sure which are real and which were told to me. Could you leave a note for two ancestors you never really knew? And could they read it?

"Miss Bloom," a gentle voice called. "You are Miss Bloom, are you not?"

I turned to see a bulky man, probably about a decade older than I, approaching in a Mexican charro outfit and sombrero, his belly spilling out over his waistline with a black shirt tucked in under a tight-fitting jacket to conceal it. He had an olive complexion with deep brown eyes, and a full dark beard and mustache giving him a bear-like quality.

"Guilty as charged," I joked, following up with a nervous chuckle. I'm not sure why I thought that saying was in any way funny or appropriate. "Nice to meet you, Shaman Theodore." I put out my hand by way of introduction. He took it gently and guided me toward him for a hug, wrapping his free arm around my back as he clenched my hand awkwardly on his chest.

"Please," he smiled softly. "We're all friends here."

"Hi, Theo." Asher held his camera off to one side and reached out a free hand. "Asher Starling—photojournalist."

"Shaman Theodore," the bear corrected, shaking Asher's hand after releasing mine. He didn't get a hug though. I guess Asher didn't make our "friend group."

"I love your outfit," Shaman Theodore looked down at me, standing a bit too close for comfort. If I didn't know any better, I'd say he was looking for cleavage. Sadly for him, I don't really have much to speak of. I took a small step backward and nearly fell off the curb before Asher craftily put a palm on my back to guide me upright.

"Thanks," I answered. It was meant for the shaman, not Asher, as I did my best to gloss over my near fall.

I was quite impressed with the Chiapaneco dress the journal let me rent from a high-end theater shop in town. Someone there was a makeup artist, and so I also sported a white sugar-skull face, complete with thick black eyeliner around my eyes and nose. My lips were bright red. The shaman was not wearing makeup, but many of the villagers, young and old, wandering through the streets were.

They were lovely, with colorful flower hair clips and face masks, flowing dresses, and several more people in charro suits wandering by with guitars in hand, some strumming as they strolled. The fronts of the art galleries were decorated with multicolored flags, candles, and skeleton folk art created by the gallery owners for this, their most popular festival of the year. In the distance, loud mariachi music blared from the shop of one of their resident artists.

I loved the Village of the Arts' take on *Día de los Muertos* (Day of the Dead), or as they call it, Festival of the Skeletons. Unlike Halloween, which feels gory and scary, *Día de los Muertos* is a way to honor ancestors or, in the case of the village, an artist or musician who has passed who influenced your work. Asher and I had a little time to meander in and out of a few galleries—some with shrines to Frida Kahlo, Salvador Dalí, David Bowie, Stevie Ray Vaughan, and one to Snooty, the longest-lived manatee who died in recent years, a symbol of Manatee County.

"You're not dressed." Shaman Theodore eyed Asher disapprovingly.

"What? Oh—" Asher realized he was pointing out his black jeans and T-shirt and distinct lack of costume. "No. Sibley is the star. I'm just here to capture her brilliance."

Asher's words took me aback for a moment. He didn't say it in a way that was comical or condescending. It felt rather sincere. The shaman must have thought so too, because he eyed Asher with a mixed expression of admiration (for the quality of his words) and competition.

Except, I didn't feel like anyone would or should compete over me. This was for a feature series, for goodness' sake. I was beginning to feel as if this were the start of a reality show where I was the bachelorette choosing between my suitors.

"I'm told you have a gallery near? Might we see it?" I asked brightly. Shaman Theodore wasn't exactly my idea of a blind date I would have chosen for myself, but isn't that what blind dates are for? Perhaps they are like when friends gift you an outfit you'd never think to wear otherwise, only to later discover that you love it and it becomes your favorite?

I tried to imagine who at *Positive Enlightenment* would have set us up …
Somehow, Phoebe came to mind. I made a mental note to ask her when
I was back in the office on Monday.

"I share a space with a local healing arts center, not a gallery per se.
But I think you might find it interesting." Shaman Theodore led the way,
stumbling along a crooked path where the asphalt road could have done
with a bit of patching, as tiny blades of grass and potholes marked the
entrance to the shared studio. The road was far removed from the festivi-
ties, growing quieter, and ever darker, as we progressed. "This way," he
said.

I didn't feel danger from the shaman, but I admit that having Asher
there as backup was a comfort.

We arrived at a somewhat tattered building that was artfully
refreshed with bright purple paint on the exterior, some sparkly Christ-
mas-inspired drip lights in the windows, and an odd neon sign that read,
Enlightenment is just a breath away.

Shaman Theodore fumbled with the lock, much harder to see in the
dark.

"Wanna light?" Asher offered, shining a small LED penlight that he
produced from his pocket.

Asher was nothing if not well prepared.

"Thanks," the shaman grumbled, finally unlocking the door. He
flipped the switch of the studio and ushered us inside.

It was small, with faux wooden floors and two windows at the back
facing what I think was a duck pond; but in the darkness, I couldn't be
sure. The dim lights were a purple and indigo hue, light enough to see
one another, but not with any clarity.

"So, how do you use the space, Shaman Theodore?" I asked. His eyes
seemed to light up a little every time I addressed him, so I continued to
do so.

"I'm so glad you asked," he answered, gleam in his eye. "I take
people on journeys here."

"Journeys? As in shamanic journeys?" I raised a curious brow.

"Exactly. You know your stuff. I'm impressed." Though no one asked, he suddenly produced a wind flute and began to play while Asher and I stood there awkwardly. Finally, the shaman paused and asked Asher, "Aren't you going to take a photo of me playing for this charming lady?"

"Oh, right." Asher nodded. He was so flummoxed by the action that the thought hadn't occurred to him.

"I look best at this angle," the shaman advised, motioning to the side angle of his body. "Here." He tugged at my arm. "You stand here."

Asher bit his lip. Exactly who is the photojournalist here? But in the interest of the story, he kept his mouth shut. After Asher lowered the camera, the shaman motioned for me to join him at a small table near the window. On it were two small, clay-colored cups.

"If you're willing, my dear, I thought I could interest you in trying a journey yourself, after we have a cup of tea."

"What kind of tea?" Asher piped up. "Surely not ayahuasca?"

"Uh, no." Shaman Theodore seemed annoyed. "While I happen to belong to an ayahuasca church, I would never offer that here. Just a simple reishi mushroom tea is what I had in mind … not hallucinogenic in any way."

"Well, that sounds lovely," I smiled, slipping into one of the chairs. The room felt unnaturally tense.

"I'll be back in just a moment." The shaman disappeared through a beaded curtain, where I could see a small efficiency kitchen partially obscured from view. Asher and I waited awkwardly until we heard the sound of a tea kettle. Our moods brightened as if to say, *Ah, he's coming back.*

Shaman Theodore poured me a cup. "Reishi mushroom has powerful healing properties," he assured me.

"Yes, like preventing infection, anti-inflammatory properties, great for regulating blood sugar, and—" Asher chimed in.

"Quite," Shaman Theodore interjected before pouring his own cup. He eyed Asher. "I don't suppose you would care for one too?"

"Me? No thanks. Still on the job." He clicked a close-up of Shaman Theodore holding up the tea kettle. Finally, the shaman sat across from me as we sipped our tea. I cupped it with both hands, creating a delightful warmth to my palms.

"I was hoping I could interest you in a short journeying meditation —perhaps to the Middle World? You can meet your spirit guides?" His eyes sparkled as he gazed at me. It was unsettling.

"Uh, sure. Why not?" I set my tea down, palms still wrapped around the cup. I found it oddly relaxing.

"Um . . ." Asher lowered his camera.

"What now?" Shaman Theodore set down his cup, his body twitching a little.

"Well," Asher fumbled with his words. "Obviously, you're the expert, and I could be completely mistaken. But I thought the Middle World was a bit more dangerous ... potentially negative entities and such hanging out. You can bring your spirit animal for protection, but if Sibley hasn't met any of hers yet, wouldn't a trip to the Lower World be safer?"

How surprising. For someone who seemed to thumb his nose at the metaphysical world, he seemed to know an awful lot about it.

"While I would always ensure Miss Bloom's safety, you do make a fair point," Shaman Theodore conceded. To me he asked, "How about a trip to the Lower World, then? It would take about twenty minutes."

"Uh, sure," I answered. "But what would I need to do? Meditate?"

"Yes, I'll provide a space for you to lay on the floor ... cushioned, of course, while I play drumming music and guide you."

"You'll stay too, won't you, Asher?" I eyed him nervously as he stood like a waiter at our table. I didn't like the idea of lying on the floor with my eyes closed, alone with a man I'd only known for less than an hour.

"Of course," he promised, holding up his camera. "I'll try not to disturb the experience, but I'll be sure to capture at least a few photos of the process."

"Em." Shaman Theodore shifted in his chair. It creaked noisily beneath his weight. "I don't suppose I could have a word with you, Miss Bloom—in private?"

"Uh, sure?" I shot Asher a confused look.

"Just for a moment," he promised.

"I could—" Asher pointed to the door. "Just step outside for a few minutes?"

"I would be much obliged," the shaman answered.

I forced a deep breath in and out and willed my shoulders to relax away from my ears. I haven't been in the room alone with a man since my husband and I were married. There were always other people around. I could feel my hands trembling, and so I held my cup a little tighter.

"You can relax, Miss Bloom," Shaman Theodore reassured me. "Your friend Phoebe told me about your recent divorce and the purpose of this meeting. I promise not to do anything untoward."

Phoebe! I knew it!

I let out a sigh. "I didn't mean to—"

"It's okay," the shaman answered. Oddly, his voice changed a bit. It was higher pitched, thinner, and less deep and robust. "But I feel I need to be straight with you," he confessed.

"How so?"

Shaman Theodore let out a sigh. "Your buddy there." He gestured toward the door Asher was presently on the other side of. "He doesn't trust me, and I can't say I blame him."

I felt my shoulders stiffening again as I sat upright in my chair.

"No, no, no." He waved a hand at me. "I'm not going to hurt you. What I mean is … while I do consider myself a shamanic practitioner, this whole Shaman Theodore act is really for the public. I'm good at what I do, don't get me wrong. I like to think I've helped lots of people through offering my services, but it's not my main gig."

"Well." I leaned in curiously. "What is your main gig?"

He leaned closer, quietly sharing his secret. "I'm in the insurance biz."

"Oh." I nodded, surprised. "Well, that's—"

"Utterly boring, I know." He leaned back, stretching a long leg out to the side.

"That's not true." I tried to defend his profession.

"Yes, it is. I know it is. But if we're going to go out again, I feel I should be honest with you."

My face flushed a little at the "go out again" statement. I hadn't given much thought to Shaman Theodore aside from this one blind date for this one article. But apparently, he had thought about us … a lot.

"Well, I appreciate your honesty. But you are able to lead me through a Lower World journey experience, yes?"

"Absolutely!" His eyes perked up. "I'm curious how the experience will go for you."

"Okay, let's do it, Shaman Theodore." I answered more enthusiastically than I had planned.

He put his hand over mine on the table and spoke softly. "Just call me Theo. Okay?"

"Okay." I smiled, gently relieving him of my hand, standing.

"And you'll keep my full-time gig out of the article, won't you?"

"Your secret is safe with me," I promised.

"Well, that's just fine." He walked over to the door. I noticed that his demeanor completely shifted as he puffed out his chest. He cleared his throat before opening the door. "You can come in now," he granted Asher access. His voice went back to a deep baritone. Shaman Theodore was back in character.

CHAPTER EIGHT

LOWER JOURNEY
SIBLEY

The "Journey," as it turned out, didn't involve going anywhere at all. I expected as much. While I may not have ever participated in one before, you can't work for *Positive Enlightenment* that long and not at least have an idea about it. Still, I was both comfortable and uncomfortable with Asher being off to the side. While I was certain my friend Theo wasn't going to try any funny business, that didn't mean that I one hundred percent trusted him, either. Particularly after Asher had pointed out a couple of flaws with regard to Middle World Journeys. Curious how Asher knew that. I made a mental note to ask him about it later.

"Comfortable?" Shaman Theodore asked after I'd settled on a Mexican blanket that was strewn over a yoga mat. He knelt beside me with a hand drum at his side. From the floor, where I lay looking at him, I was anything but at ease.

"Yes," I fibbed.

Asher remained in the shadows, doing his best not to make me feel any more awkward than necessary. I closed my eyes and laid the eye pillow that Theo had provided across them.

"Good," Theo answered. "Now, I'm going to start drumming slowly, and I want you to imagine that there's a small entryway to the Lower World on the floor. It doesn't matter how small. I want you to free your mind and allow yourself to fall into it, okay? Let it carry you to the garden we spoke about—a safe garden that's just for you."

I gave a slight nod. The fragrance of incense tickled my nostrils as Theo began to beat the drum rhythmically—like the sound of a heartbeat. I vaguely heard the sound of a camera shutter. If there was a flash, I didn't see it with the pillow over my eyelids.

Gradually, I began to relax, letting go of the tension in my jaw, then my shoulders, followed by the rest of my body. I felt drowsy, but not enough to sleep—just enough to be in what Theo described as the "theta zone"—a meditative state between the dream world and waking life. Occasionally, Shaman Theodore would offer a subtle prompt like "Notice the garden around you" or "Become aware if an animal comes forward as your spirit guide. If you're not sure if it's your guide, you can ask it."

I felt my body slowly melting, to the point that I could swear I was in line with the floor, and then beneath the floor, and then I began drifting downward … downward. The shaman's voice sounded muffled as he moved further and further away from me.

In my mind's eye, I observed the clear sky above me and the tops of tall trees surrounding me as I continued my descent. I swore I heard a waterfall in the distance. For a moment, a small iridescent bird flew by my head, as if he were following me downward.

Finally, my body landed gently on a thick bed of soft grass. I sat up effortlessly and eyed my surroundings. The blanket of grass was divided by a flattened but distinctive dirt trail. Behind me stood a tall oak tree, with hundreds more to follow on each side of it, along with a forest of sycamore and red cedars. I wasn't even sure they would naturally grow in the same habitat, but they seemed to in my new world.

I followed the winding trail on foot, and before long it sloped downward, revealing a large garden area ahead—presumably, the garden that Shaman Theodore said I should be looking for. It was pristine and well manicured, with rows of shrubs moving outward from a small fountain that stood in the center. Perhaps this was what I mistook for a waterfall earlier. There were rows of roses, lavender, and lilies, with hanging pots filled with a variety of orchids. I caught the scent of rosemary.

Somewhere in the back of my mind I thought, *I must be imagining all this.* But the thought that followed protested: *But you've never imagined something so precise, so vivid before.*

I spotted a wrought-iron bench. It appeared as if someone was sitting there. Hesitantly, I approached the shadow, watching as he came into focus.

"Asher?" I asked, surprised. "Why are you here?"

"Perhaps the better question is, why haven't you noticed that I'm here?"

"What?"

I watched as he transformed into a speckled, iridescent bird twittering happily as he flew away.

Suddenly, I felt myself being pulled rapidly up toward the sky. The sound of a fast-paced drumming grew loud in my ears. I awoke, startled.

"Take your time sitting up," Shaman Theodore cautioned, setting his drum down and helping me as I removed the eye pillow and rolled onto one bent arm to get up.

Asher set his camera on the tea table, and the two men flanked me, guiding me to my feet.

"Are you okay?" Asher asked. "You seem a little out of it."

I covered my mouth as I yawned. "Yes, I just feel a little funny in the head, but otherwise … surprisingly calm."

The shaman smiled. "The fog will lift soon and you'll end up feeling clearer minded in a few minutes. Would you like some water? Or more tea, perhaps?"

"No, I'm fine." I glanced at the shaman's hopeful eyes and realized, with a small amount of guilt, that this was the perfect excuse.

"But I would like to go home now, so I can record the experience while it's fresh in my mind."

"Certainly," Shaman Theodore understood. "Of course, you're also welcome to write here. I can leave you alone. I confess, it might be nice to witness a writer in action." His face grew hopeful.

I tried to let him down gently. "That's awfully kind of you, but I work best on my home computer, in my own space. You understand—"

"Of course," he agreed, somewhat woefully. "But before you dart off, dare I ask you what you experienced?"

"And ruin the suspense?" I smirked. "I'm afraid I'm sworn to secrecy until the article is published next month." He dropped his head, disappointed. "But I can tell you one thing."

"What's that?" The shaman's eyes perked up, hopefully.

"I found my own secret garden."

"Excellent," he smiled. "It was lovely meeting you, Miss Bloom. Thank you for the privilege of guiding you on your Journey, and I hope we will have the opportunity to meet again soon." He moved in for a bear hug. I patted him lightly on the back, noticing for the first time that he smelled of palo santo wood. When I pulled away, he pinched a card between his fingers, dangling it in front of my eyes. "Do give me a call when you'd like to talk again."

I graciously accepted the card while Asher escorted me to the door. "Thank you for this evening, Theo. It was truly memorable."

"The pleasure was all mine … though I confess, I'd like to see your lovely face without the—" He motioned around his face.

I had completely forgotten about the thick Day of the Dead makeup I was wearing. I'm not sure how, given how heavy it felt on my skin. I touched my face hesitantly, and the two of us shared a chuckle.

Outside, and once Asher and I were a good distance from the center, he turned to me and asked, "How did he become Theo all of a sudden? What happened to Shaman Theodore?"

"I guess we just left things on friendly terms." I pulled out my phone. "Think we can get an Uber on short notice during a festival?" As I spoke, the sounds from the Village grew louder as we once again approached the main strip.

"We have a car waiting for us just up the road," Asher explained.

"Really?" I stopped abruptly and looked at Asher. "For a struggling publication, Reed seems to be going all out."

"Not him," Asher confided, once we'd reached the corner where a black Cadillac awaited us. "His advertisers. Tourism is the biggest industry in Florida."

"Oh," I nodded as the driver opened the back passenger door for me.

Before he closed it, Asher leaned in and asked, "So, what exactly did you see on that magical little Journey of yours?"

"I'll give you the rundown later," I promised. "In the meantime, I can tell you one thing for sure … Apparently, you're my spirit animal!"

The next morning, Asher requested we make a stop at the Riverwalk in Bradenton.

"That depends," I answered flatly over the phone. "Do I have to be picture-perfect again? It took me nearly an hour to scrub my face clean from that Day of the Dead face paint. I won't even get into how hard it was to pry myself out of the dress—Vidalia had to help me!"

"I hope you didn't damage it. It was a rental—"

"The dress is fine!" I yelled into the phone before catching myself. "It's my ribcage that's not."

"Oh … well. Just wear whatever makes you comfortable, as long as you don't mind the photo ending up in the article."

"Have you seen my wardrobe?" I squinted, as if he could possibly see me through the phone. I heard him sigh loudly. "Okay, okay. I'll find a casual 'not trying too hard' outfit for a stroll along the Riverwalk. Will that work?"

"Perfect. Where do you live? I can pick you up."

"Pick me up?" I expected to meet him there.

"If we carpool it will preserve the environment. Besides, parking may be difficult that way. Makes more sense to go together."

"Well, okay. I'll text you my address. Give me, say, twenty minutes?"

"See you in twenty minutes."

I ended the call and stared at my cell phone, perplexed. This wasn't another date, was it? No, Asher would have told me if I were being set up. It's just two colleagues collecting a few more shots of the scenery for the sake of the chronicles. Why, then, was I so nervous?

A short while later, I met Asher in front of my apartment complex. Since it was the fall season in Florida, I settled on a pumpkin-colored blouse and bone-colored trousers. I went the extra mile and put on a thin coat of makeup and pinned one side of my hair up with combs.

Asher's eyes lit up when he saw me. I don't know what he was expecting, but it seems my wardrobe choice was acceptable.

I opened my arms out and glanced down at my outfit. "Good enough?" I asked.

"Most definitely," he answered, leaning over and clicking the passenger side open for me. "Hop in."

Parking was easier than expected. Perhaps Asher mispredicted how busy it would be. Before long, we were strolling the picturesque two-mile Riverwalk, complete with pedestrian traffic, bicyclists, and a few teens skirting around us on electric skateboards.

In my opinion, this would have made a better blind date with Theo —a stroll on the Riverwalk before heading back to the Village of the Arts for the festival. I also noted that it would have made far more sense had we spent more time perusing galleries and maybe stopping for food somewhere—even a food truck would have sufficed. It made me wonder if Theo was merely using the opportunity to pimp his services as a local spiritual guru.

"Look, look!" Asher leaned in and pointed as a large dolphin arced through the water below us.

"So I see," I laughed, feeling the warmth of him close to me. "But why is your camera hanging around your neck instead of you trying to get a photo?"

Asher blushed. "Aw, I just thought you'd appreciate it."

"I do," I laughed. "Maybe we can sit a moment and see if he or she comes back again?"

Behind us were two curved concrete chairs, which were surprisingly cool and not as uncomfortable as I would have thought. I sat, while Asher was now determined to catch a shot of the dolphin. I leaned back and closed my eyes, feeling the warmth of the sun on my skin, listening to the rush of the wind through the Mexican palm trees swaying overhead.

I heard a camera shutter click repeatedly. Shielding my eyes with one hand, I caught Asher photographing me.

"No fair!" I complained. "You should have warned me!"

"It's not natural if you know about it," he defended. "Besides, you'll get full control over what goes to print, okay?"

"Okay, but shouldn't you, as the photojournalist, be in at least one of those photos?"

"Me? No, I don't think so."

"Well, I do," I insisted. "There were a few swings back there." I gestured. "Let's grab one and see if we can take a decent selfie."

"But I didn't bring a tripod," he complained. "How can I set the timer to grab a shot?"

"Well then, indulge me in an amateur selfie for us to remember our work on this story, won't you?"

That made Asher's eyes light up. I suspect he was so used to being either behind the camera or exposing some hoax that he wasn't used to being included in things.

We found a large, unoccupied swing and sat, swaying back and forth as Asher conceded to take out his phone and lean in for a few shots. Afterward, he sat next to me, scrolling through them while I peered over his shoulder.

"You see!" I exclaimed. "These are fabulous."

"Kinda flies in the face of my expensive equipment though, doesn't it?"

"Asher?"

"Yes, Sibley?"

"Why don't we just enjoy the moment, shall we?"

CHAPTER NINE
VIDALIA'S MOVE
VIDALIA—OCTOBER

I walked the property that I'd shared with Tod for the past six months, saying goodbye to the land and sending a silent blessing to whomever might inhabit this home in the future. Oddly enough, I felt more attached to it than I did my soon-to-be ex-boyfriend. I hadn't told him I was leaving. My plan was to wait until he went on a weekend fishing trip with some of his buddies and pack what little I had there and leave.

Funny that I put most of my stuff in storage, as if I'd known this wasn't going to pan out after all. I could hear Tod's voice in my head: *You're like one of them self-fulfillin' prophecies and all that. You expected us to fail!* Somehow, I knew this would end up being my "fault," and I was willing to accept that.

What I couldn't accept was being with a man who took the bizarre death of his ex as an inconvenience, with no sympathy for the deceased. I shivered at the thought. I wondered what he would have done if it were me who had been discovered. And I wondered what he would do once he discovered I was gone.

Sibley had already agreed to let me rent the small extra bedroom at her place, God bless her. But I had to make her promise that, in no uncertain terms, was Tod to know where I'd gone. While I had little doubt that we'd run into each other at some point, I felt safer with him not knowing my new place of residence. Maybe I'd do him the service of meeting him in a public place to explain. I suppose he deserved that much—but not yet.

With my truck loaded up and ready to go, I waited while Skinny did his "business" so we could get on the road.

What was taking him so long? I watched as Skinny sniffed around the yard halfheartedly. Then something happened. His attention shifted. He'd caught the scent of something and began sniffing the ground incessantly, tracking the source with renewed focus and determination.

"Skinny," I called. "What are you doin', you goofy dog?"

He began digging his front paws around the base of a large oak tree that had been partially uprooted from the last hurricane. It was leaning to one side with chunks of dirt hanging off tangled limbs. Something felt off. Perhaps I had watched one too many murder mysteries on TV, but suddenly every hair on my arms stood at attention with an alertness like I had never felt before.

My stomach dropped as nausea overtook me. I shuddered, chills running the length of my body despite it being at least eighty-five degrees out and humid. I hugged myself as I approached the dog, who wagged his tail excitedly.

"Whatcha got there, Skinny?" I asked. There was a part of me that already knew.

Skinny's paw fumbled with a small white object that he'd unearthed at the foot of the tree. When I got closer, I saw what it was—a long, broken piece of bone. I couldn't say for sure, but it appeared to be the lower part of an arm …the ulna? Humerus? No, that wasn't right, but I wasn't terribly concerned about my anatomy knowledge at this very moment.

"Skinny! Leave it!" I yelled. He ignored me, tossing the bit of bone up in the air as if playing with it. I fought back being ill. "Skinny!" I yelled again. "You leave it this instant!"

Skinny paused momentarily, eyeing something behind me. I was about to turn and see what it was when—

"Why is your truck packed to the gills, Vidalia?" A calm voice startled me—Tod. I could suddenly feel the warmth of his body directly behind me. Chills ran through me once again. "You goin' somewhere?"

I swallowed hard as Skinny finally came charging toward us, his prize bone between his teeth.

Tod noticed it too. "Skinny," he asked. "What do you have there? Give it here!" Apparently, Skinny listened to Tod better than me, as he dropped the bone at Tod's feet. Tod kicked it with his boot but didn't pick it up. He eyed me slowly, as if making a decision about something. "The question remains," he tried again quietly. But I could feel the rage deep down inside him.

"I thought I might stay at a friend's house for a while, just until the investigation is done," I lied.

"Now, why in the hell would you do that?" Tod challenged. "You know damn well that dumb-ass detective fellow told us to stay put until they close the case. What's really going on here?"

I considered my words very carefully. "There's a human bone at your feet, Tod. Skinny dug it up from that tree over there." I pointed. "I'll be willing to bet it's related to Nadia's body on the roof, though I can't be certain how yet."

Tod didn't process information quickly, but I could see the whirring in his brain as he slowly put the pieces together and locked an idea into place. His face contorted. "And you think I had something to do with it, don't you," he spat angrily. "Jesus, Vidalia! Have I ever hurt you?"

"No," I confessed.

"Ever given you cause to think I might?"

I remained silent. I could see that Tod felt deeply wounded by my silence. "Really, sweet pea? You're afraid of me?"

"I'm just confused, is all." I tried to soften the blow. "You didn't seem very concerned about Nadia's death, even though you loved her once."

"That don't mean I had nothin' to do with that woman's death!" he defended.

"No, of course not." I felt myself shrinking, only to suddenly realize that I couldn't keep doing that—losing courage. I pulled my shoulders back and lifted my chest, summoning the courage to ask my next question.

"But why is there a human bone at your feet? And if Skinny were to dig further, what else would he find?"

Tod's eyes bore into mine, as if calculating his options.

Finally, he answered. "I have no idea."

"Well," I stammered, fighting with words despite a lump in my throat, "we need to call that detective fellow—Gerald … Gerard … Jameson, whatever his name is—and tell him what we found."

Tod dipped his head low, eyeing me sideways as if I were completely daft.

"Are you bonkers?" he challenged. "All that flatfoot would do is accuse us of something we had nothin' to do with. Do you want that?"

"No." I wrapped my arms around my shoulders and felt myself shrinking again. "Of course I don't want that, but—"

"But nothin'," Tod decided. "You go on in the house and git yourself unpacked, and I'll deal with whatever the hell it is that Skinny has dug up."

I paused for an inordinately long time.

"What?" he asked. "We're in this together. You can't very well up and leave me now. Just how selfish are you, woman?"

My mind whirled. What could I say to convince him that letting me leave was a good idea—his idea, even? Friend in trouble? No, I'd already confessed that I was afraid of him. That wouldn't work. Besides, he'd be determined to know which friend and where I went. Better if the two of us split up during the investigation? Make it seem like we'd naturally gone our separate ways? That way, it wouldn't appear as if we'd teamed up to murder a dead woman for her home and … what else? I wasn't entirely sure there weren't other factors at play. No, he'd think I was trying to pin the blame on him and somehow use it to my advantage— perhaps to assume squatter's rights on the house.

I shook my head, coming up with the only answer that Tod might actually accept …

I willed my eyes to fill with tears (thank you, third-grade theater lessons and my short stint as a child actor in commercials back in the day). My lips quivered. I hugged myself tighter, rocking side to side, my eyes darting frantically around as if searching for a place to run.

Tod took the bait. He leaned in, rested a hand on my shoulder. I jumped. "Aw, sweet pea. Are you on your period?"

I sniffled and forced myself to stay in one place as Tod gently massaged my shoulder. "I … think … so," I stammered.

"Want me to fix you a hot bath?" In the flash of an eye, he went from Tod the suspected sociopath to Tod the gentle-natured guy I met at the bar one night.

"No, that's alright." I lifted my arm and placed my hand over his. "But maybe I could call my mama and pay her a visit? That way, you don't have to deal with my complainin'."

He paused for an inordinately long time. "You know how much she loves you," I added. I watched the wheels turning once again.

"Good idea," he finally agreed. "Maybe she can talk some sense into you … "

I brushed back the tears and shrugged it off with a laugh.

"But don't you gotta work tonight?" he remembered.

I thought quickly. "I got someone to cover for me. Told 'em I wasn't feeling well."

"Hmm." He thought a moment. "You gonna unpack first?" He eyed me, squinting as if in a harsh light.

"Nah," I answered. "It'll be dark by the time I get there, so I best leave now. I'll be back tomorrow night." To Skinny, I called, "C'mon, boy! Wanna go visit Grandma?"

Skinny bolted toward me before Tod's hand shot out, as he bent down and grabbed Skinny by the collar.

"Why don't you jest leave Skinny with me while you're gone?" His menacing look told me that Skinny was insurance that I'd return.

"Okay," I agreed, sadly eyeing the pup that I had recently rescued. This time, I wanted to cry for real. I bent down and gave him lots of scritchins and a hug. He wasn't so fond of the hug but humored me by sitting there, confused. "See you tomorrow, boy," I told him.

"Aren't you forgettin' something, sweet pea?" Tod stood and pointed to his lips.

I dutifully moved toward him and left a light peck on his lips. As I backed away, he grabbed my wrist. "That's better," he leered at me. "And don't be tellin' your mama our business, neither."

"I … I won't," I promised.

Every hair on my body stood up. I could feel his eyes boring into mine as I walked toward my overstuffed dilapidated truck. For emphasis, I pulled out my cell phone and spoke loudly, "Hi, Mama, it's me … "

I knew I didn't have much time. I drove to the nearest gas station and parked in the corner, away from other cars. I pulled Detective Jameson's card from my back pocket, where I had it at the ready—just in case. My hands were shaking as I fumbled with dialing the number. Finally, after three tries, I got it right.

"Jameson," he answered on the third ring. Somehow, I expected a receptionist. I felt a cold chill go through me as I caught my breath, my nerves rattled. "Anyone there?"

"Yeah, sorry," I stammered. "This is Vidalia Oliveira … hurricane … dead body?" Words were failing me at that moment.

"Yes?" He answered with interest. "I remember. Do you have something you'd like to tell me?"

My mind was reeling—where to start?

Finally, I blurted out, "You have to get to the house now, before he gets rid of the bones. They're in the yard. Skinny found them. I had to leave!"

"Wait, slow down, Ms. Oliveira. Take a deep breath."

"There's no time!" I hadn't meant to yell into the phone. "Sorry, but you need to send men to the house now before my boyfriend … er, ex-boyfriend, Tod disposes of the bones. My dog, Skinny, found a human bone at the base of the oak tree out back—the one closest to the river. I think it has something to do with the dead woman found on the roof."

"Okay. Okay. Hang on!"

I waited while, through a muffled cell phone (he must have covered it with his hand), I could hear the detective barking orders. Something to the effect of *Send two men … Call for backup …*

"Okay, Ms. Oliveira," he finally said. "I've got men on the way. Where are you?"

At that moment, a large truck passed behind the car, drowning out my voice.

"What?" the detective asked.

"I'm at a gas station," I answered vaguely. "Trying to confirm my living arrangements and all." Detective Jameson paused momentarily. I was a flight risk and a person of interest. I knew that much. "I'm not leaving town, detective. But I don't want Tod to know where I am."

"You feel unsafe," he said. It was a statement, not a question.

"Yes," I whimpered. I hated feeling weak. "I have a friend I can stay with, but I wanted to warn you first … about the bones."

"I'm flattered," Detective Jameson chuckled at a pitiful attempt at a joke. When I didn't laugh, he continued: "If you tell me where you are, I can have someone escort you to wherever you want to go. But I am going to need a statement from you."

"Okay, but there's one more thing," I sniffed.

"What is it, Ms. Oliveira?"

"He's still got Skinny."

"The dog."

"Yes. Tod suspected I wasn't coming back, so he said he'd look after Skinny while I visited my mama. That's what I told him. Except my mama is on a Mediterranean cruise and can't be reached."

"I see." Detective Jameson thought a moment. "You have paperwork that proves Skinny is your dog?"

"Yes," I answered emphatically. "I have all his vet records too."

"Your dog friendly to strangers?" he asked.

"Give him a treat and he'll be your best friend for life." I smiled, feeling a sense of longing even though I'd only left Skinny about ten minutes ago.

"I tell you what. You let me know where you are, and I promise to bring your dog to you."

"How do you plan—"

"You let me worry about that, Ms. Oliveira."

I sucked in a breath. "I'm at the Circle K off of State Road 64, the one closest to the house." I darted quick glances around the parking lot. "I'm near the air pumps. I'm driving a small red truck that's seen better days. Not sure of the cross street—"

"That's okay, we'll find you. Just stay put, Ms. Oliveira."

I nodded. Then, realizing he couldn't possibly see me nod through the phone, I answered: "Okay—bye." After I hung up, I wished I'd asked how long they would be. I also wondered if I'd made the biggest mistake of my life, telling them where I was instead of just disappearing. But I'd seen one too many detective shows to know that they would eventually find me—or worse, Tod would. If only he hadn't come home when he did. Had I left even fifteen minutes sooner, Skinny and I would have been gone, with Tod left scratching that thick head of his. Well, at least they promised to get me Skinny. I hoped the detective was telling the truth.

"Hey, Mac?" Detective Jameson approached the officer's desk.

"Yes, Detective?" the young man answered.

"I told you before, Mac. Unless we're in the public eye, you can call me Gerard. No need for the formality."

"Yes, D—Gerard. What do you need … Gerard?"

Detective Jameson fought back a smirk. "Get a message to the boys to expect a dog on the property. We're gonna need to bring in this—" He pulled his notepad from his shirt pocket. "Tod Evans in for questioning … and collect the dog."

"Yes … Gerard." The officer leapt from his chair. He was new to the team and eager to please.

Just then, an oversized man with a thick double chin lumbered by. "Gerard, where are you goin'?"

"I'm going to meet the ex-girlfriend, Ms. Vidalia Oliveira, get her statement, and make sure she's safe."

"How do you know she isn't in on whatever the hell is going on over there?"

"She sounded afraid of him."

"Could be an act?" the large man offered, leaning his arm heavily on a nearby desk, his shoulder up to his ear as if struggling to balance against his weight. On the desk, a computer screen was lit, showing rows of small photos of the crime scene, several of which included Vidalia and Tod standing outside, watching the forensic scientist at work.

"Nah, my gut's telling me otherwise." Detective Jameson was convinced.

"She sure is pretty, that one," he motioned to the screen. "Sure you're thinking with your gut, and not something else," he chortled.

"Not funny, Jim." The detective's face turned red. "Nor appropriate."

Jim and a few surrounding men fought back snickers as Detective Jameson grabbed his car keys. He ignored them as he left the station.

CHAPTER TEN

GIVING THANKS

SIBLEY—TODAY

"Hey, hey!" Yolanda's voice chirped from the other end of the cell phone. "Just wanted to check in and see if you needed anything for your big Thanksgiving date with *Bodhi*?" She whispered his name for effect.

"They're calling it a 'Giving Thanks' fellowship, 'honoring all beings without exception'—whatever that means." I grumbled into the phone. After my unremarkable "date" with Shaman Theodore, I was wary about my next assignment.

After all, "Theo" had been messaging me every other day for the past few weeks with a roller coaster of emotional texts that ran the gamut of, *I can't stop thinking about you. Please call me,* to *You're not going to mention the insurance bit in your article, right?* And *I did a past life regression and saw that we were married once* to *I think it's rude that you don't answer my texts in a timely manner.*

"Right, well," Yolanda thought a moment. "At least there's a meal involved. And Cassadaga is supposed to be the spiritual capital of Florida. Make sure you get a psychic reading while you're there."

"Yeah, if it includes a turkey dinner with all the fixings and a large glass of wine, I'm certain I can manage. We'll see about the reading—"

"Em," Yolanda hesitated on the phone.

"What?"

"Did Phoebe not tell you about the dinner?"

"What about it?" I was still sore about Phoebe setting me up with the shaman. What has she gone and done now?

"Whoops, I'm in the car park and about to lose my phone signal. But I'll stop by and walk Skinny today, as promised. I know Vidalia won't be home until late. Bye!"

"What about the dinner?" I tried again, but Yolanda had already hung up the phone.

Just then, the doorbell rang. There stood Asher, wearing tan slacks and the ugliest green shirt with cartoon turkeys plastered all over it. He noticed my expression.

"What?" he defended. "I thought it would be a sense of occasion. You ready?"

"Yeah, but you could've just texted me. You didn't have to come up."

"Aww," Asher complained. "At least let me pretend I'm a gentleman."

Just then, another text came in. I let out an aggravated sigh.

"What's wrong?" he asked.

"Our buddy, the shaman. I made the mistake of taking one of his calls following our 'date,' and now he's accusing me of ghosting him since I no longer accept his calls and only respond to one in three of his ongoing texts."

"Wow," Asher shook his head. "Guess he has some pretty strong feelings for you."

"Maybe." I wasn't convinced. "Or he has pretty strong feelings for what me choosing him as my Valentine's date could do for his popularity. 'Professional American Shaman' could be a tough sell without the right endorsements."

"Professional, my ass," Asher grumbled, as I locked my door and we proceeded to the stairs.

"You would say that," I teased. "You think everyone is a two-bit hack."

"Well, that's just not true," Asher feigned insult. "I take pride in my research. And while there is a flourishing shamanic community in the area, with deeply spiritual practitioners who take their beliefs very seriously, I'm not convinced he's one of them."

"Hmmm," I answered. "Perhaps."

My phone buzzed again as we reached Asher's car.

"What? Are you driving?" I was surprised.

"Do you mind?" Asher asked. "It would give us a little more flexibility of when and where we go, and I can sort out my camera equipment the way I like without having to constantly change things up when we switch drivers."

"I don't mind," I answered, as he opened the passenger side for me. I think he was waiting for a 'thank you,' but I was too distracted by the current text from Theo.

Remember, you promised not to write about my other job.

I was about to text back something to the effect of, *I will keep my promise if you stop texting,* but was interrupted by an incoming call … Thomas.

"You're popular today," Asher said, as he pulled out of the parking lot for our three-hour drive to Cassadaga.

"That's one way to look at it," I mumbled. I answered the call, but clicked the speaker phone. "Hi, Thomas," I said pleasantly. "Just a heads-up. You're on speaker phone!" I said that a little louder than was technically necessary, but I didn't care.

"Oh," Thomas seemed perplexed. "Okay."

"It's just that Asher Starling and I—you remember Asher from the office, don't you?"

"Uh, I guess so?"

"Right, well, we're heading out on a big assignment … together. Can't chat long. What's up?"

"Well," Thomas was audibly uncomfortable. I felt a twinge of guilt, but it quickly passed.

"I'm sorry to interrupt … er … whatever that is. But I can't find my passport. You were much better at keeping things organized than I—"

"Heading somewhere, are we?" My cheeks grew red. Thomas never once took me anywhere requiring a passport, unless you count a four-day cruise early in our relationship.

"Well, it's just that Gemma … Uh, never mind. I'll keep looking." He was about to hang up.

"Hang on," I answered, before I covered the phone and explained to Asher, "Oh, don't worry about me, Asher, darling. Four star or five, I'll be happy with whatever you've chosen for us."

Asher pinched his lips together and wrinkled his nose. He shook his head slightly from side to side, and I couldn't tell if he was angry, indifferent, or amused. That was the thing with Asher. Sometimes, it was difficult for me to read him. He'd be a good study for Vidalia. While not a therapist, she was pretty darn adept at translating people's facial expressions and body language.

I could hear labored breathing on the other side of the phone. Thomas had let himself go, and as such, even the modest of movements disrupted his windpipes.

"Up the stairs and searching the attic, are we?" I asked, with grim satisfaction.

"How did you—"

"Because I know you, Thomas. I know how you think. We were married for fifteen years, after all." After a long pause, I finally saved him. "Check out—" I caught myself. "Check the walk-in closet … on the shelf above your collection of ties you'll never wear."

I waited as Thomas stopped mid-flight and made his way to what used to be our bedroom.

"Did you ask her?" I heard a woman's nasal voice ask ... Gemma.

"Shhh," I heard him say. I could feel him pointing at the phone. "One moment, Sibley." I listened for the slide of the closet door and a rustling as he fumbled through boxes. "Ah, here it is." I could hear the relief in his voice.

"Well, if there's nothing else—" I started to say.

"Wait a moment. It says it expires next month," Thomas complained. "What am I supposed to do with this?"

The old me was much more helpful. *Well, Thomas, you need to have it renewed ... probably need to submit a new photo and such, and an application. Try looking it up online.* The new me was beginning to feel a bit more disconnected.

"I don't know, Thomas. You'll have to just figure it out for yourself. I've got to go."

I hung up before he could reply. I was tired of Thomas calling me every other week or so—*I'm sorry to bug you, Sibley, but I can't find those lovely cufflinks you got me for Christmas that one year.* Or *How much detergent should I put into the washer? And which hole does it go in, for that matter?*

I was sick of ... all of it.

After hanging up the phone, I slunk back into the car seat.

"Everything okay?" Asher finally asked, about fifteen minutes later, when I'd failed to utter a word.

"Yeah," I replied with effort. "Sorry about that. The whole comment about the hotel ... and the speaker phone thingy. I'm just tired of Thomas calling me for every little thing as he gets on with his life with that whore ... sorry."

"No," Asher shook his head. "Let it out. That whore—" he motioned one hand for me to continue while he drove with the other.

"It's just become clear to me that I took care of his every need, and he's lost without me. I just wanted to let him know that I wasn't lost without him."

"I see."

"That sounds judgmental," I squinted at him.

He eyed me briefly before returning his attention to the off-ramp toward our destination.

"No judgment here, Sibley," he answered. "Not from me. Not ever."

We arrived at Cassadaga mid-morning. In front of the main building, where classes and metaphysical services are held, a swarm of people gathered around two folding tables, behind which attendants were checking people in.

Asher and I approached the table, and as if by magic, the sea of people departed and revealed a smiling woman wearing a lightweight white poncho with an enormous butterfly pattern across the front. Her dangling earrings displayed a series of sun, moon, and star charms, and she had at least three or four rings covering her fingers on each hand, each with different colored gemstones.

I hesitantly approached the table, Asher just behind me.

"Hi, I'm—"

"I know who you are, Sibley Bloom." Her smile grew wider, revealing a display of thick white teeth and dimples on her cheeks. "I'm such a fan of your writing!" She motioned to a display stand next to the last table, featuring three shelves of *Positive Enlightenment Journal.* "We all are."

"Oh." I was taken aback, flattered, and a little flustered at the attention. I wasn't sure I'd ever actually met a fan before—of the journal, yes, but not me specifically. "Thank you."

She leaned in as if sharing a secret. "We understand you have a Giving Thanks date with our Bodhi." She winked. "Such a nice boy."

The woman didn't look that much older than I, so I wondered about the age of the "nice boy" I was being set up with.

"I'm Carol, by the way." She stretched out a hand.

I took it tentatively and shook it. "Nice to meet you. Um, do you know where I am to meet him?"

"Ah, yes. Let's just get you checked in, and then I'll escort you myself to the Fairy Trail." She picked up different clipboards from the table, paused to ask another attendant a question, then nodded as if it had all been made clear. "I see you are on strawberry-picking duty with Bodhi."

"I'm sorry, what?" I was confused. "I thought I was here for the Giving Thanks meal."

Carol let out a chuckle. "Didn't Phoebe tell you?"

"Tell me what?" After Phoebe's last setup, I was beginning to question our friendship. What had she gotten me into now?

"It's a raw vegan celebration. All attendees have to source local foods, and we'll prepare the meal together."

A lump filled my throat. My belly grumbled as it realized that a traditional Thanksgiving turkey dinner was but a distant dream.

"Oh, I know that look, dear." She smiled kindly. "You're not used to raw vegan meals. Don't worry, we have certified chefs with us today doing the heavy lifting, and they'll guide the group through the recipes."

That wasn't at all what I was worried about. But I nodded and smiled weakly.

Asher puckered his lips in a way he always did when fighting back a laugh.

"Ah." Her expression changed as she eyed Asher. "You must be Asher Starling." She crinkled her nose.

Asher extended his hand. "That I am. It's nice to meet you."

Carol eyed it for a moment before tentatively taking it. She shook his hand briefly before pulling it back and wiping her palm on the side of her jeans, as if it were dirty.

"What brings you here today? Here to give your impression of our feast?" Her expression darkened, and I swear I could feel a cold chill sweep through the air. It was intense enough for a few bystanders to look up, alarmed.

"Not at all." Asher smiled brightly, as if unaware of her sudden change in demeanor. "I'm the photojournalist for today. I'm only here to support Sibley."

"Ah." She thought a moment. "Well, okay. But we'll have to make sure to get people's permission to photograph them. I'll make an announcement at the start."

"Excellent," Asher replied.

"Now, to the Fairy Trail." Carol drew her shoulders back as if on a mission.

Asher and I followed behind her.

The trail turned out to be a small forest loop, with tiny fairy houses, fairy castles, doors at the foot of trees, statues, and sparkly decorations hanging from tree branches.

We found Bodhi sitting on an oversized wooden chair with (you guessed it) fairy wings on the back, designed to make the people sitting on it look tinier than they actually were.

Bodhi was a young, thin man with sandy hair and brown eyes, and a thin goatee. His hair was tied back in a short ponytail. He wore a burlap sack—no, that's not fair. He had on a pair of brown linen trousers and a matching shirt, with a long row of rudraksha seeds around his neck and a similar mala bracelet on his wrist. In short, everything about him was just … brown. If he stood beside a tree, he might disappear.

"You must be Sibley," he stated gently, his legs crossed at the ankle and hands resting in his lap. He didn't stand.

"I am," I answered awkwardly. "It's nice to meet you."

"Please, sit." He motioned to the seat beside him on the oversized chair. It was barely large enough for two grown people, so we'd be getting cozy pretty fast.

I sat beside him as he eyed Asher, questioningly.

"He's here to photograph the feast for the magazine," Carol quickly explained. "Well, I'll leave you to it, then." Carol waved and made her way back to the spiritual center.

"Ah," Bodhi answered. "Namaste." He bowed his head lightly. Asher remained silent, which was odd for him. "Am I to assume you'll be following us around all day?" Bodhi's voice never rose to the decibel of human conversation, as if he were too weak to speak—or as if he'd just woken up.

"Unfortunately, yes," Asher replied with a smirk. "I'm afraid you're stuck with me for most of the day."

Bodhi eyed me as I sat beside him, shrugging my shoulders to give myself a little more space on the chair. "Pity," he said, his eyes boring into mine.

"Mind if I—" Asher raised the camera from around his neck and motioned to us.

"Of course—" Bodhi put his arm around me and squeezed me toward him, as if we'd known each other for years. My nose tickled. He smelled like Nag Champa.

After a few shots, I slid off the chair, creating some distance between Bodhi and me. It didn't last long before Bodhi took my hand gently in his and began walking, slowly. "I thought we might stroll the Fairy Trail before we board the bus."

"Bus?" I was confused.

"Phoebe didn't tell you?" He seemed surprised.

It seemed Phoebe neglected to tell me many things. Something I would have to address with my friend soon.

"Apparently not," I grumbled.

"Don't fret." He flashed a toothy smile at me. "It's not as bad as all that. We're on strawberry duty, so we'll be on the strawberry bus to go pick them for the feast. There's a blueberry bus, one that heads to a hydroponic farm for lettuce, etc."

"Oh, so we pick the food, cook it, and then eat at the end? What time do we eat?" I asked.

"Well, it's raw vegan, so there's nothing heated above a certain temperature. But I'd say … maybe around 3 p.m.?"

"Oh, wow," I commented. "That's a ways off." I suddenly regretted not eating a heartier breakfast.

Bodhi paused, dropping my hand momentarily. "We're not as time-based a society here, Sibley. It will be ready when it's ready." He picked up my hand again, and we continued walking.

Had this been anything other than a prearranged date for the chronicles I was writing, I might have had a thing or two to say about the early hand-holding.

As if reading my mind, Asher piped up.

"Why don't we get a photo of Sibley a few paces ahead of you, looking back and smiling? Create a little distance," he offered.

"Why would we do that?" Bodhi asked.

"Well, to build audience anticipation," Asher explained. "Her looking back shyly at you. You smiling warmly back, as if she's beckoning you to follow. Think of it as a 'meet cute' photo."

Bodhi thought a moment. "I like that." He grinned, eagerly following Asher's instructions and flashing me what I think was meant to be a seductive smile as I darted several paces ahead and turned my head to peer over my shoulder.

"You might try smiling, Sibley," Bodhi suggested helpfully. For a split second, an annoyed expression flashed across his face.

"Of course." I smiled.

But in the back of my mind, I was thinking: *I'm gonna kill Phoebe!*

The strawberry-picking experience was about as exciting as one might expect. The farm itself was a lovely slice of Florida. The heat and humidity? That was another story. I distinctly felt my hair matted to my head in an unflattering manner, and the heat burning into my brain. I wished

I had thought to bring a hat. But then, I wasn't prepared for a day spent outdoors under the intense sun.

I paused, basket in arm, to tug at my blouse in an effort to let some heat out and air in, followed by a meager attempt to fan myself with my hands. If I were seeking sympathy, I was aiming in the wrong direction.

"When one is attuned to nature," Bodhi commented, "temperature and environmental shifts don't affect us." He plucked a strawberry and added it to our basket. From what I gathered, once it was full, our job was done, and we could climb back onto the bus that—while hot— provided some respite from the blistering sun.

Asher shot a close-up of our basket. From his viewfinder, I could spot that he'd found the perfect berry to photograph. Afterward, he reached into the basket I was holding, plucked the perfect berry, and bit into it.

I shot him a death glare. He was hurting our basket-filling numbers.

Bodhi's disgust was different. Asher was quick to respond. "Don't worry. The journal is sponsoring this event—at least, our sponsors are sponsoring the event. You get what I mean. I'm not stealing a berry, if that's what you're worried about."

"It isn't," Bodhi answered in his quiet yet surprisingly condescending voice. "We don't typically eat without thanking and blessing the food first."

"Oh, I asked its permission first." Asher smiled, before quickly averting his attention to a bumblebee that needed its photo taken.

My face flushed. I confessed, "I think I might have heatstroke."

Bodhi responded by pulling a handkerchief from his pocket, dousing it with water from a reusable insulated bottle he had attached to his trousers, and dabbing the water-soaked cloth over my face—clumsily, not to mention parts of my chest.

I stood there like a human canvas, too astonished to speak.

"Better?" he asked.

"If I say yes, will you stop patting my chest?"

At that moment, Bodhi became distracted. A young blonde woman wearing a very short sundress plucked a strawberry in the next row over. If I didn't know any better, I'd say he was taking in her perfectly formed rump.

"Why don't we head back to the bus?" Asher suggested. "I'll ask the driver to crank up the air."

"Perfect," I answered, Asher taking the basket from me despite having a very uncomfortable and heavy camera around his neck. He looked a little more than sun-kissed himself, perspiration dappling his forehead.

Bodhi was busy chatting up the young woman, who giggled flirtatiously back.

It would be several minutes before he noticed me gone and reluctantly joined me, all the while eyeing her getting on the bus next to ours.

"You alright?" Asher asked, concerned.

"Yeah, fine," I answered. "Let's just hope the meal prep is indoors."

I could feel Bodhi's labored breathing beside me. Suddenly, his Nag Champa body smelled more like unpleasant sweat from a man who likely wore all-natural deodorant.

Finally, we arrived back at the camp, where meal prep ensued.

CHAPTER ELEVEN

THE FEAST
SIBLEY

Once back at camp, Bodhi seemed to remember that I was there —and that I was, in fact, there to write an article about the experience. Or maybe he had a reminder.

"Hello, everyone!" Carol called to us from the industrial-sized kitchen where we were presently set up at stations for our part of the meal prep. "We have a special guest for today's event. Please welcome Sibley Bloom from *Positive Enlightenment Journal*."

She pointed in my direction, and I waved and smiled, pressing my palms together and bowing my head slightly by way of a silent "thank you" from across the room.

"She's joined by her photographer friend, Asher Starling." Her face dropped, along with her voice, as if embarrassed to mention his name.

Asher gave a slight wave. The crowd murmured—some cheerful, others, well aware of his work as our resident skeptic, merely frowned.

"They are photographing this event, so if anyone does not want their picture taken, please let us know. Otherwise, there will be photo releases for you to sign on your way out."

From my count, exactly three people didn't want their mugs taken.

The team at the spiritual camp quietly relocated them to the back of the room and let Asher know the situation.

As for me, I was busy making some type of raw vegan strawberry cheesecake—except they were using a macadamia or cashew blend of nuts to make the cheese.

"Hey, man," someone called out to Asher. He had been standing behind me, almost as a silent guard, ensuring that I was physically okay after the heat exhaustion and possibly protecting me from Bodhi.

"Uh, yeah?" Asher lowered his camera.

I confess, the meal was beginning to come together in colorful fashion. The fruits and vegetables were vibrant, as teams created a blueberry soup; a "turkey" made from mushrooms, sage, and walnuts; side dishes that included green beans, cauliflower, and beets; and our strawberry creation.

"We're a chef down," they told Asher. "Any chance you know anything about meal prep? We could use an extra hand."

I swear, Asher's eyes lit up. Apparently, he had a hidden skill of which I was unaware.

"You okay here for a bit?" he asked.

"Yeah, fine," I told him.

Asher nodded, putting his hand on my shoulder momentarily before darting off. I could feel the heat of his hand for several moments after he left.

Honestly, I was starting to feel light-headed—heat exhaustion, dehydration, and hunger.

Fortunately, Carol came to my rescue with what seemed like a fizzy juice concoction.

"You look like you could use this, dear," she said, handing it to me. "Some electrolytes … natural ingredients." She patted my shoulder in a motherly fashion.

I drank the magic juice. It tasted like tangy tangerine sugary goodness. Within a few minutes, I could feel the difference.

At our table, we were finishing the touches on dessert—our contribution to the feast. Soon, we would finally get to eat.

We relocated to a large dining hall in the main room, which was, thankfully, air-conditioned to the point of near freezing.

I shivered for a moment as my body adjusted to the cooler temperatures.

"I believe we're over here." I could feel his warm breath on my neck as Bodhi spoke. He put his arm around me with a familiarity that he didn't deserve as he guided me to our seats.

The room was a family-style dining hall, our "seats" among others at an indoor picnic table.

However, as soon as we sat, we were served. I'm not certain who the servers were, but given their modest attire and tired expressions, I couldn't help but wonder what was going on behind the scenes of which I was unaware.

"Exquisite," Bodhi said as a very petite, young girl poured water into the cups on our table.

"Excuse me?" I asked.

"This entire day," he quickly answered. "And you, of course."

That seemed an afterthought.

"You don't need to say that, you know," I told him. "It's one prearranged blind date on one single day in a long history of days in this world."

He pondered my statement for a moment. "But I mean it," he finally explained. "You ... me ... us ... " He raised his water glass for a toast.

I clinked mine awkwardly, just as I caught a glimpse of Asher at the end of the hall, helping assemble and present the last of the meals laid out for our feast.

"Excuse me just a sec," I requested, leaving a bewildered Bodhi.

At the end of the hall stood Asher. Not sure where his camera was, but he looked far less imposing without the monstrosity around his neck. He was busy adding some type of brown vegan sauce to the top of a faux turkey, followed by a cranberry dressing.

I took out my cell phone and snapped a few shots, slipping back to my seat before he could notice—just as they were serving the first course: a blueberry soup.

I sipped it. "Well, this is quite lovely," I offered, surprised. I looked around the table.

"Agreed," Bodhi answered. "But what are you looking for?"

"A little salt," I answered. I could tell from his expression that somehow that was the wrong answer.

"You will find that most vegan dishes contain enough salt without requiring more. Besides, anything beyond the subtlest of spices detracts from the natural flavors given to us by nature."

The more time I spent with Bodhi, the less I liked him.

"Here you go." An older woman leaned over my shoulder, handing me a small grinder with Himalayan salt. "I always carry it with me to dinners," she confided with a wink.

I accepted it with gratitude, adding a twist to my soup before handing it back to her. She slipped it into the cloth bag she had hanging from her arm.

"Don't worry," she reassured me. "I'm just at the other table. Come round if you need it again."

"Thanks," I smiled. It was nice speaking with someone who wasn't judging my salt habits, my response to the heat, or overall discontent with my very being. I wondered what else Bodhi was going to find wrong with me next. Fortunately, it didn't take long.

"So, eh." Bodhi leaned in as if sharing a secret. "What's up with you and that Asher fellow?"

"Asher?" I was surprised. "Nothing. We're work colleagues. That's all."

"Hmm," he murmured. "Not sure he feels that way." He caught my defiant expression. "Oh, don't get me wrong, I've got no problem with open relationships. I've been part of a polycule for years. If you ever did decide to date him, that would be fine with me."

"While I'm happy for your approval, I'm more of a fan of monogamy," I confessed.

Bodhi sipped his blueberry soup thoughtfully. "Somehow, I thought working for a metaphysical magazine and all would have made you more open-minded."

I could feel a tinge of heat rising in my cheeks. "I've got no problem with how someone else chooses to love. I just know what I prefer for myself."

"Well, you're missing out," Bodhi declared. "You can't possibly understand the depth of human experience and connection that comes when we free ourselves from the possessiveness of 'you belong to me' and 'let's put a ring on it so everyone knows you're taken.'"

Servers came to remove our now-empty bowls. I leaned an elbow on the table and attempted to lighten the mood. "I imagine you've broken quite a few hearts, Bodhi," I joked.

Finally, a crack appeared at the side of his mouth—the beginnings of a smile.

"Perhaps," he agreed, as the next course arrived: a mixed lettuce salad with raw seeds, broccoli, and other colorful vegetables, topped with an avocado dressing. "But I'm always up front about—"

"Your lack of commitment?"

His face darkened. That joke didn't land well. I was beginning to realize—too late in life—that much of what sounds good in my head doesn't come out of my mouth the way it should.

"I'm fully committed to those I'm intimately involved with. Even if those commitments only last a year or two, I like to think I'm always there for people."

"Well, some of us prefer more than that." I argued, taking a bite of my salad.

"Well, some of us are obviously insecure," he retorted.

Only two more courses to go, and I'd be done with my date with Bodhi. There was something nagging at me—something that Vidalia said once.

"What?" Curiosity got the better of him. "What's on your mind?"

"I was just thinking back to a long-term study my friend Vidalia told me about, where they followed couples for decades to see, among those who stayed together, how many were happy."

"And?"

"Well, they could never seem to get data on polyamorous couples."

"Really?" Bodhi seemed interested. "Why was that?"

"Because they never stayed together long enough to be available for a follow-up."

"Hmph," Bodhi grumbled. "Well, they didn't talk to me, that's for sure."

Asher stopped by the table. "Hey, Sibley. I'm going to get a few shots of you two, the main course, and dessert, yeah? I was thinking we'd head back around four-ish. That work for you?"

Suddenly, the nonpossessive Bodhi chimed in. "Or," he offered, "I could take you back to your place. My scooter's just out front."

"Uh, thanks, but—" I had to think on my feet. "Not only do I have to get a draft over to the editor tonight, but we have a certain protocol."

"Protocol?" Bodhi seemed unconvinced.

Asher's face revealed that he knew I was up to something. He just wasn't sure what.

"Someone from the journal has to escort me to and from each date. And I have to give equal time to each person I meet so no one has an unfair advantage."

"Seems like a lot of restrictions around love," Bodhi observed.

"It's just for this article series. I don't make the rules," I shrugged. That was a lie—I had just created that rule two seconds ago. In my head, I justified it as a necessary boundary.

Fortunately, Asher jumped in. While he neither confirmed nor denied what I said, he followed with, "Okay, four p.m. it is."

Just then, the petite woman brought Asher a small plate of the vegan turkey. "Looked like you were doing double duty—taking photos and jumping in as chef." She smiled in a way that suggested innocence layered with flirtatiousness … flirtatious innocence.

I found it annoying. Asher didn't seem to mind.

He accepted the small plate and followed the woman to the end of one of the tables. "Back in a bit," he called over his shoulder to me.

"See?" Bodhi smirked.

"See what?"

"You're being jealous. Possessive. If you embrace the idea of nonattachment, you would celebrate that your boy there is interested in that young woman, independent of his interest in you. Both can exist without it diminishing his feelings for you."

"First," I explained, "he's not interested in me. Second, we're work colleagues. Nothing more."

"Yeah." Bodhi laughed, picking up a knife and fork and cutting a piece of turkey. "You keep telling yourself that."

CHAPTER TWELVE
ALLINGHOUSE
SIBLEY

We arrived at Allinghouse to a bit of a misunderstanding.

"I'm sorry," the man at reception explained, "but we have no reservations for either of you for two rooms in the main house. Perhaps I spelled your name wrong?"

"It would be under Starling, like the bird. Or Bloom, like what a flower does. No strange spellings," Asher explained tiredly.

"Well, this is very odd." He clicked the keyboard of his computer.

"What is?" Asher craned his neck to see over the counter.

"I have a reservation, but it's for 'Starling Bloom' in one of the private cottages."

"There must be some mistake," Asher explained. "Does it say who booked it?"

"Em … are you with *Positive Enlightenment Journal,* by chance?" he asked. "Looks like someone from the journal reserved it." He clicked a few more buttons. "Ah, here we go. There's a note on the reservation on behalf of Asher Starling and Sibley Bloom. Looks like they paid on the company credit card."

Asher shot me an apologetic look. "Er, any chance of swapping that for a couple of individual rooms?"

"I'm afraid not," he apologized. "We're fully booked on account of it being Thanksgiving weekend and all. But em"—he eyed us back and forth—"the cottage does have a loft, so there are separate sleeping quarters, if that helps?"

Asher eyed me for confirmation. I nodded, throwing my hands up in the air. I was tired from the travels, the long day, and a meal that technically managed to fill my belly but still left me feeling as if I were starving, for some reason.

"Okay, thanks." Asher finished signing in for us and procured the door code for our cottage.

I grabbed my travel bag from the car and followed Asher, whose camera equipment was packed up in a tidy fashion, though it appeared his overnight clothes and toiletries were dropped in two grocery store plastic bags that he slung haphazardly over his shoulder.

Along the way, we passed a family of four with their Thanksgiving spread on a picnic table outside their cottage. They smiled pleasantly as we passed. The smell of roasted turkey, ham, and savory stuffing filled my nostrils.

My stomach grumbled.

Our cottage, under different circumstances, would have been lovely. It was the kind of place I wished Thomas would have taken us for a weekend getaway, had he been the kind of husband who did that sort of thing—for his wife, I mean, not his mistress.

I eyed the fully equipped kitchen off to one corner, the bathroom in the other, and a king-sized bed smack in the middle, with a sectioned-off living room space with a couch and a small TV. A spiral staircase led to the loft.

"Not to worry." Asher set his equipment on the floor. "I'm good with the loft tonight."

"Yeah, well"—I eyed the loft—"be careful you don't break your neck if you have to get up to use the bathroom in the middle of the night."

"You're in a cheerful mood," he called, dropping his bags on one of the small single beds in the loft.

"Sorry." I dropped my bag on a bedside chair. "Think I'll be in a better mood once I get my notes written this evening and get a good night's sleep." I eyed the kitchen. "You think there are any places open today for a few groceries—for a late-night snack or fixings for a home-made breakfast?"

"Doubtful," he mumbled, oddly. "Didn't you bring your squirrel snacks with you?"

He knew me too well. I never went anywhere without some sort of trail mix, mixed nuts, or breakfast bars and bottled water. I supposed that would have to tide us over until morning.

I sniffed the air … an aroma of something.

"Asher?" I asked.

"Yes," he mumbled again.

"What are you eating up there?"

"Whatever do you mean?"

I heard the crinkle of paper. I bounded up the spiral steps, twisting with each step, in time to see him hiding what appeared to be a deli sub in one of his travel bags.

"You're hiding something … something delicious. Fess up!"

Asher reluctantly produced a turkey and gouda hoagie with lettuce, onions, oregano, and some type of fragrant oil and vinaigrette. A few bites had been taken out of it.

"Aaaah." I sucked in my breath, astonished. "Where did you get that?!"

"Mackenzie," he answered simply. I blinked at him, confused. "The young woman helping out at the Giving Thanks event."

"What about her?" I demanded. I felt the heat rise in my throat.

Asher's expression was one of confusion. He furrowed his brows in a quizzical way I'd never seen before.

"She tried to feed me, but I confessed I was there to cover the event, not really a raw vegan kinda guy."

"And?!"

"And she said that she was there at the behest of her aunt, but she wasn't much of a raw vegan kinda girl. So she ran back to her house— only a block away, by the way—and came back with a turkey sub she had been planning to eat later. She offered it to me."

"And you took the poor girl's sandwich?"

"She said she had more where that came from," he whined. "What are you, the turkey police?"

I paused momentarily, angry, but not entirely sure why. I glanced from the sandwich to him and back to the sandwich again.

"Want half?" he finally offered.

"What do you think?" I answered, grabbing the sandwich and running down the steps with glee as a somewhat befuddled Asher followed me.

When I got to the kitchen, I fumbled through the drawers until I found a knife suitable for cutting off a bit of the hoagie for myself.

"Here," I offered him. "I only took a small bit of it. The rest is yours."

"Well, gee. Thanks," he grumbled. "Nice of you to share my sand-wich with me!"

"If she had 'plenty more where that came from,' you might have thought of me," I complained.

"What? You were busy having dinner with the charming Bodhi." He paused when he saw my expression. "What?" He lowered his half of the sandwich before taking another bite. "Was he not-so-charming?"

"Didn't you hear him?" I asked.

"Not really," Asher confessed. "I catch a few video sound bites for social media, but most of it is comprised of pictures. What happened?"

"Maybe we should sit down." I pointed to the couch in the makeshift living room. "I can get us some water to go with our sandwiches."

Asher darted his eyes toward the loft.

"What? Did the darling Mackenzie supply beverages too?"

"No," Asher replied sullenly. "If you must know, I brought a bottle of sparkling wine to celebrate Thanksgiving and a successful event. I just didn't realize I'd be facing the inquisition this evening. What's with you?" He tilted his head to one side. Then, as if he'd figured something out, he let his guard down. "Maybe a little sparkling with our Thanksgiving … er … turkey hoagie?"

"Sounds like a plan," I grinned. I had no idea what was going on in Asher's brain, but maybe he understood, on some level, that my "date" with Bodhi had not been stellar. I mean, who wants to hear about a lovely young Mackenzie with her bright smile and positive attitude sneaking someone a sandwich while your day was filled with a man who disapproved of everything you were … affected by weather, a meat eater, a boring monogamist, and someone who didn't smile enough?

Not sure how long my mind wandered, but when I finally resurfaced, Asher was sitting on the couch near me, gnawing on his sandwich happily. He nodded toward two glasses of sparkling—in some ceramic cups from the cupboard of our cottage.

"Would you be offended if I changed into my pajamas first?" I asked. Back when I was dating Thomas, it was unheard of for a man to see you in your nightclothes unless you were actually a couple. "This outfit is scratchy and really uncomfortable."

"By all means, make yourself comfortable," Asher answered agreeably.

In the cottage, there was a three-panel divider set up between the bed and the bath. I snuck behind it and changed. Upon returning to the living room, I took the cup closest to me. "Thanks," I said, plopping down on the couch a few feet away from Asher.

Asher's face spoke volumes as he eyed my pajamas.

"What?!" I demanded, gazing down at my nightclothes. I had on my favorite green cotton pants with river otters printed all over them. My top was light green and had a cat on the pocket. He was wearing a kilt … I have no idea why.

"Nothing." Asher bit back a smile. "I just don't think I've ever seen that particular animal theme in nightwear before."

"Are you offended?" I snarked. Then I thought about the fact that I didn't have a bra on and considered that maybe I should have. I shrank into the sofa.

"Of course not," he defended. "Why would I be?"

"I dunno." I leaned forward and set my cup down, grabbing my half of the stolen turkey sub.

Asher eyed me curiously. "Wanna talk about today?"

"Would it be awful if I said 'no'?" I asked between bites. "Maybe we could watch a recap of the Macy's Thanksgiving Parade on YouTube, or some cheesy movie for a bit? Just to clear my head?"

Asher picked up the TV remote and clicked it on. "Cheesy is my middle name." He grinned.

"You are such a goofball. You know that, right?" I laughed, happily devouring the rest of my sandwich.

"Says the woman with otter pants, who literally sniffed out my turkey sandwich from across the room."

"You should have shared, anyway," I defended.

"Hmmm," he answered. "Perhaps."

CHAPTER THIRTEEN

CASSADAGA
SIBLEY

"Care to see more of the 'psychic capital of the world?'" Asher asked the next morning. He was surprisingly chipper. I guess the bed in the loft was comfortable. I smiled, thinking back to our parade-watching from the couch—a highlight of this trip, thus far.

At least once during the night, I woke myself up to the sounds of my own light snoring. I was worried Asher might hear, but it seems from the nasal sounds above me, he was a little congested as well. He sounded as if he were out cold. I've always admired power sleepers, and if he heard me, he was gentlemanly enough not to mention it.

"Yeah, just let me get changed." I was still wearing my otter pajamas and Scottish cat shirt. I grabbed a simple green sundress, tucking my bra and underwear discreetly beneath as I made my way to the bathroom for privacy.

"Okay, I'll get some coffee on," Asher offered. He was already dressed in black jeans and a baby blue *Life Is Good* shirt with an image of a sun silhouette over a body of water.

When I returned, we sat at the small kitchen table by the bed, sipping coffee and a couple of Biscoff crackers I had in my snack bag. "I suppose we could take in an early lunch in town before heading back?" I suggested.

"That works," Asher agreed. "Maybe a short historic walk to points of interest? I picked up a map from the Spiritualist Camp."

"As long as there's time to walk the labyrinth, hit the Haunted History Museum, and maybe visit a new age shop or two?"

"We have all the time in the world," Asher answered, sipping his coffee. "Besides, as you saw, the town is pretty small. The walking tour I'm thinking of will take less than an hour, including stops for photo ops."

"Oh, right," I remembered, looking down at my dress. "I didn't exactly plan for photos today. Do I need to change?"

"You look beautiful," Asher complimented as he stood, beginning to pack his camera bag. He didn't think anything of the comment. I suppose for him, it was the most natural thing in the world to say. But for me, I was flustered.

"I'll just add a bit more eyeliner then," I grabbed my makeup bag.

"You can if you want," he answered, eyeing my face like a painter looking for just the right light. "But I don't think you need it."

I didn't respond, merely nodding as we packed up and headed out. I sent a quick text to the caretaker, letting him know we'd checked out.

Cassadaga was quaint and quiet. You wouldn't have guessed there had been a huge event held in the center of town just yesterday. Asher captured a few candid photos of me in front of the Colby Memorial Temple, built in 1923 to honor Cassadaga's founder, George P. Colby, a medium from New York.

"You gotta give credit where credit is due," I observed. "Nowadays, you either believe in spiritualism and psychics, or you don't. But back in 1894? I'll bet it was risky."

"You're spot on," Asher agreed, as we opted to find the labyrinth trail next. "The National Spiritualist Association was founded in 1875 in Chicago to give Spiritualism structure and legitimize séances, healing arts, divination, and the like. Cassadaga brought these beliefs to the South, and is one of the longest continuously active spiritual communities in America. But they faced death threats and backlash from the Christian community and others."

I slowly began walking the labyrinth, and Asher fell silent. I was grateful to live in a time where I could peacefully explore various beliefs without fear—other than the fear of judgment, of course—but I was working on that. *Stop thinking,* I chastised myself. Finally, at the center of the labyrinth, my busy mind began to calm, and the path out, while slow and simple, was enough to quiet the mental chatter.

I smiled at Asher, who quickly snapped my photo. "Haunted Museum?"

The tiny museum at the end of Stephen Street was dimly lit and chock-full of memorabilia, historical photos, and even some animated "ghosts" and modern wizardry items from *Harry Potter* and other well-known movies and books. Too dark and cluttered for photo opportunities, Asher and I found ourselves enamored with a middle-aged couple and their medium-sized black-and-white dog as they wandered ahead of us. Apparently, the museum was pet friendly, and the pooch, who looked a bit like a border mix who had eaten a dachshund, kept sniffing and bumping into things with its long frame. One of the animatronic, life-sized dolls began talking, and the dog paused, paw in the air, deciding whether to growl or wag its tail while also seeming to attempt to size up if the doll was actually human or not. It settled on "moving away rather quickly with tail tucked." Poor puppy.

We seemed to have the same idea as the couple. After returning to the light of day, we made our way to the new age shop just next door. As we wandered up and down the narrow aisles of Florida water, sage, gemstones, and other trinkets, the couple was busy trying to get their dog to sit for an aura photo. "Green," the shopkeeper announced pleasantly, offering the excited dog a treat. "I just knew your dog was heart-centered. Full of love and healing from the heart chakra."

"Isn't that all dogs?" I whispered to Asher.

"Certainly all dogs who are given treats," he laughed. "Put a steak in front of me, and you'll see how my heart chakra shines."

"Noted," I laughed.

"Are you interested in a couple's tarot reading?" a thin young woman with exceptionally long braids asked enthusiastically.

"Oh. We're not a couple," I explained, pointing between the two of us.

"Hmmm." She tapped a long purple fingernail to her lip.

"But we are colleagues," Asher chimed in. "Do you offer readings for friends and co-workers on assignment?"

"Absolutely," she perked up. "We could do a thirty-minute reading, spending a little time focused on each of you and then on whatever this assignment is about."

For a skeptic, Asher seemed genuinely excited about the idea. "In the interest of research," he explained.

"You're a photographer?" the woman asked, guiding us to a small room and closing the door. We were back to a dimly lit, narrow space. Asher's and my knees knocked into one another a bit as I tucked my legs under my chair after we each sat. I found myself tapping the edge of the table nervously. She eyed Asher's camera.

"Yes," he answered simply. "What gave me away?"

"Well, you don't need psychic ability for that one." She turned to me. "And you're a creative—a writer, perhaps?"

I nodded.

"Again, no need to be psychic for that," the woman answered. "I'm Sarah, by the way. I noticed your fingernails were cut short, and the way you've begun drumming your fingertips on the table, I'd say you spend a lot of time at the computer."

"Sarah," Asher teased. "You're giving away your trade secrets."

She smiled as she began shuffling three separate tarot decks: one the traditional Rider-Waite, and two other colorful ones with mythical creatures, animals, and nature scenes. "Don't worry, I've got a few more up my sleeve," she joked back. I would wager she met a lot of skeptics, and I certainly didn't need to be psychic to know that.

"We'll start with you. Do you have questions for me, or would you like me to see what spirit has to say?" she asked me.

"The second part—" I twirled my finger to articulate, "the spirit thing—"

As Sarah shuffled one of the decks, cards began to pop into the air. She laid them out quickly. "Oh wow." She pursed her lips.

"What?" I sat up, concerned.

Before answering, she dropped a few more cards, lining them up so I could see them. "Okay, that's better," she sighed. She dropped a few more from the second deck. "Ah, nice!" She smiled. "Lovely."

"Okay," she began. "Seven of Swords and Five of Swords—you've got some dishonest people around you."

I looked at Asher.

"Not him," she motioned a purple nail at Asher. "Egos running high and people gaslighting you. Just be aware. Looks like you ended a relationship that needed to end … but look at this!" she exclaimed happily. "Three of Wands, Four of Wands, Ace of Cups, Queen of Cups, the Empress, and Nine of Cups." Sarah leaned forward excitedly. "Honey, you are going on an adventure!"

"I know," I sighed. "But I'm not sure I'm up for it."

"You most certainly are," she insisted. "This is all about romance and travel." She cupped her hands together and giggled dreamily. "This is soulmate kinda energy. Just use protection." She tapped the Empress card. "Unless you plan on getting preggers."

"I most certainly do not," I blushed. "Okay, enough about me. What about him?"

Sarah nodded, clearing the deck and resuming her shuffling, popping out cards from several decks and lining them up in front of

Asher. "Knight of Cups, Knight of Swords, the Lovers, Magician, Wheel of Fortune, and Two of Cups."

The young woman took her hands to literally toss her braids over her shoulder before leaning an elbow on the table. "Honey," she eyed Asher, tapping the Knight cards, "I don't know who wronged you, but you seem hell-bent on picking the wrong women so you don't have to commit."

"I beg your pardon," Asher scoffed. "I don't think I do that at all."

"Hmm." She eyed the cards. "You travel and keep yourself so busy with work, but you've got three major arcana cards here, and the Two of Cups. Whatever this journey is you two are on, it's destined. Maybe not romance between the two of you—"

"Definitely not," I answered. I could have sworn Asher sank back in his chair, disappointed. I don't think he's interested in me, per se. But I imagine it's got to be a blow getting shot down by someone you didn't even intend on dating in the first place. "We're work colleagues."

"Not sure how that matters," she muttered. "But this assignment that you're both on was meant to be, and both of you are likely to find a real meaningful spiritual connection by the time it's over. This is pure transformation, is what this is."

"Okay." Asher stood, and I followed suit. "Thank you for your insight." He smiled. I could tell his ego stung a little.

Sarah eyed us once more and smiled a wide smile that showcased all her teeth. "Have fun, you two." She winked.

CHAPTER FOURTEEN

NEW EVIDENCE

VIDALIA—OCTOBER

"Detective Jameson." I stood upright, touching my hair nervously with my hands as if to tidy my appearance. I had been alternating between leaning on my truck, arms folded, while tapping my foot nervously and pacing back and forth while passersby eyed me curiously. At least, I assumed they were curious, or thought I was crazy, or perhaps they didn't even care. "I … I didn't expect you to be the one to … to be here."

Why was I having trouble finding my words? I chalked it up to nerves—fear of Tod, fear of what might happen to Skinny, and fear over what the cops might do after finding bones on my property. I felt a knot in my chest and a hard lump in my throat as I struggled to swallow.

Detective Jameson approached me, his head tilted to one side while his hip seemed to slip to the other, giving him an odd swagger when he walked. He peered directly at me for a moment before asking, "Are you okay, Ms. Oliveira?"

The question surprised me. Up until that moment, I assumed he believed me to be a suspect, not a victim. Or was the jury still out on that one? Why would he care about my well-being?

"I think so," I answered. "I … I just left a message for my friend Sibley … asked if I could stay with her for a bit earlier than planned. I mean, I was planning on moving out soon but—"

"I'll need that address and how to get into contact with you and your friend," he stated, missing the fact that I was already planning my escape from Tod. I nodded, hugging myself and tucking my chin as if protecting myself in some way.

"Does your boyfriend know where this friend lives?"

"No," I answered. "And I think it's safe to say that Tod is no longer my boyfriend. Not after—" My voice trailed off.

"What did you discover, Ms. Oliveira?" he coaxed gently. "For the record."

Detective Jameson retrieved a pen and pad of paper from his shirt pocket.

I recapped the bones that Skinny found by the tree in our yard and my conversation with Tod, stopping to catch my breath every few seconds, as if winded from running.

Just then, Detective Jameson's cell phone rang. He held up a finger as if to say *just a minute* as he turned his head slightly to one side.

I observed him, cautious not to appear as if I were staring. He wasn't terribly tall, nor short either—maybe an inch taller than I am at 5'6". He also wasn't particularly thin nor heavy. Neither muscular-looking nor weak. His hair wasn't overly dark nor light, and wavy without qualifying as curly or straight. I couldn't quite see his eyes, but they definitely weren't a distinctive green, blue, or deep brown … hazel, maybe? He didn't have an imposing presence, nor did he fade into the shadows.

In other words, Detective Jameson appeared average in every possible way.

But he still made me nervous.

When he ended his call, he turned to me. "Once again, Ms. Oliveira, does your … does Tod"—he corrected himself—"know where your friend lives?"

"No, I don't think so," I answered. "He wasn't keen on my spending too much time with friends because he felt it detracted from time with him. So I often met my friends at the bar where I work and told Tod someone called out and I had to cover for them. If he ever questioned it and showed up, I could use the excuse that I was on break."

"Did that not strike you as odd?"

"Only now that I'm saying it out loud." I hugged myself harder. I'm supposed to be the one so interested in psychology. How did I miss the fact that I had been, most likely, dating a sociopath?

"Did you turn off your cell phone's location tracker?" he asked, concerned.

"I don't even know how to do that," I answered honestly. "And I don't see Tod as having the intellectual savvy to track me via phone anyway."

Detective Jameson's face dropped into a frown.

"Why? What's wrong?"

"It seems your boy—er, Tod—was not on the premises when we arrived."

"Oh," was all I could think to say.

"Any idea where he might have gone?"

"No," I answered simply. "He just returned from a fishing trip with some buddies of his. Maybe he went to one of their houses?"

"Do you have the contact info for any of these friends?"

It was now occurring to me just how little I knew of Tod. I'd heard of his friends but never met any of them. I snuck out with mine so that he wouldn't become jealous. Had I been living with a stranger all these months?

"I don't," I sighed. "Best I've got is his cell phone number, and I believe you have that already following the, uh—" I pointed upward, referring to the body found recently on our roof.

He nodded.

A thought struck me. "What about Skinny?" My heart began racing. "Did he run off with my dog?!"

Detective Jameson saw the urgency in my eyes, pausing carefully before responding.

"Your dog was found tied to the fence on the porch—"

My heart sank.

"He's fine." The detective reached out and touched my arm reassuringly. "One of my officers retrieved the friendly little fella. We'll get him to you later today. Only, we really need to know where you'll be staying. Got an address for this friend of yours?"

As if on cue, my cell phone rang. I looked at the name … Sibley.

"Hi, Sibley," I answered awkwardly.

"I got your message. Are you okay?" Sibley was concerned.

"Yeah, I'm alright. Got myself into a bit of a situation though." I eyed the detective oddly.

"Do you need me to come get you? Where are you?" Sibley offered.

"No, I can come to you if you don't mind sharing your address. Just giving a statement to the nice detective here," I motioned, which was silly because there was no way Sibley could see us. "I think I can come your way when we're done?" I eyed the detective questioningly.

"Just need to finish taking a statement, and then we can wrap things up here," he reassured.

"Is that okay?" I felt horrible. Sibley was a sweetheart, but between her crap ex-husband and my sociopath ex-boyfriend, I think our friendship had been more surface-level than either of us particularly wanted to admit. It was as if we both had our guard up all the time.

"Of course it's okay," Sibley replied on the other end of the line. "Been where you are not too long ago."

Not exactly where I am, I thought to myself. After all, Thomas might have been a philandering a-hole, but I'm pretty sure he wasn't a potential murderer.

Sibley rattled off her address as I typed it into a Notes app on my phone. I hung up moments later.

Detective Jameson let out a cough. "Eh, I will need that address, if you don't mind."

"Of course I don't mind," I joked. "After all, you're bringing Skinny to me." I showed him my phone so he could jot down the address.

"Just one more question before we wrap up here, Ms. Oliveira."

"Yes?"

"Does your ex have any violent tendencies?"

I thought back over the last six months and shook my head. "He would yell at times. Maybe throw an empty beer can across the room when he was angry." I thought some more. "I'll admit we got into some heated fights where I thought he might take a swing at me … but he never did. Always stormed off if it escalated that much."

Detective Jameson bit back a comment and made a note of it. "I may need you to come down to the station and give a written and video statement in the future, but this should suffice for now." He tucked his notepad and tiny pen back in his shirt pocket. "Now, let's get you to your friend's place. I'll follow along behind your car."

"Wow," I answered, surprised. "I would not have expected door-to-door service from a police detective."

"Just making sure you're safe. Which reminds me … your phone?"

I unlocked it and handed it to him, peering over his shoulder as he adjusted the privacy settings. "Just to ensure your ex can't track you that way. Unfortunately, that means the police can't either. So I'm taking you at your word that you won't skip town before this case is resolved."

"No plans to leave, Detective," I reassured him.

Sibley motioned through her window for us to come up. She was on a third-floor walk-up that had a service elevator if needed, but that felt like cheating. I huffed a little as I climbed the steps to her apartment. Florida is so flat that it's no wonder any of us living here have working quads anymore. Although, I suspect Detective Jameson would have bounded up the steps quickly if he hadn't been behind me.

When we reached the landing, Sibley was at the front door to greet us. She eyed Detective Jameson, confused.

"He escorted me here," I explained.

"Ah," she answered. "Where's your dog?" She looked around us as if Skinny would magically appear. It must have worked because a second police vehicle pulled alongside the detective's car. Moments later, a rotund female officer emerged with a very excited Skinny.

"You sure it's okay for him to be here?" I confirmed.

"Well, my rent may go up a bit when the landlord finds out, but we can figure that out. C'mon in."

Sibley's apartment was surprisingly neat, with a small living room to the left, a dining area to the right, and a tiny kitchen straight ahead. There was a hallway beside the kitchen, which I assumed led to the bedrooms and bath.

Skinny wasted no time sniffing around before jumping onto her lavender-colored couch and curling up into a ball.

"I'm sorry, he—" I was about to evict Skinny from the couch when Sibley intervened.

"No, it's fine," she laughed. "It's good he's comfortable. And lord knows Thomas was a mess. Your dog couldn't possibly be worse!"

I bit my lip. It wasn't Skinny I was concerned about. It was me. I worked so much that it wasn't uncommon for me to leave laundry, mail, and other household items in piles—including a full kitchen sink with a week's worth of dishes. I would have to do better … or at least ensure my messes stayed behind closed doors.

The officer came and went, but Detective Jameson remained.

"Interesting view," he observed.

Just over the couch where Skinny was presently napping (and

snoring too, I might add), a large window faced a bank building. On its balcony was a large twisted metal sculpture named *Serenity.* The sculpture was surrounded by raised earth boxes filled with assorted greenery.

"Yeah," Sibley commented. "I kinda lucked out that my window faces a pretty display that I don't have to take care of. Only downside is I can't exactly walk around naked in my apartment during the workweek. Don't think anyone could see in, but why risk it?"

"Indeed," the detective smirked.

I would have been too embarrassed to make a comment like that in front of a man I didn't know, but Sibley had no such filter.

After an awkward silence, Detective Jameson made his exit. "Just be careful," he cautioned me. "And let me know if Tod gets into contact with you."

November

It took about a month for Sibley and me to get used to being roommates. After the first week, we realized we'd need some ground rules. Otherwise, we were likely to irritate the other very quickly. Therefore, we actually sat at the table and made a list, including items such as the division of household chores—who took out the trash and recycling, who did the dusting and vacuuming, and how many days it was okay to leave dirty dishes in the sink (one, I learned; Sibley was neater than I, so waiting several days was not an option). She offered to take Skinny out for walks on the nights I was working, and I—in turn—was responsible for most of the grocery runs. We attempted to share a meal at least twice a week, sometimes prepared together or one person taking over if someone else was particularly busy that week.

We came to an agreement on when it was okay to blast loud music in the living room (that was me, and generally when Sibley was at work), who paid the bills (Sibley took care of that, and I paid her a modest amount for rent), and we took turns with TV picks if we both happened to be home at the same time. I agreed to keep my messes in my bedroom (excess mail, laundry, shoes lying around, etc.), but set the rule that she couldn't go in my room without asking (she might have been horrified).

We were like *The Odd Couple*: one neat, one messy; one who worked the day shift, the other night; one who played heavy metal and ate Cheetos for breakfast, and the other who listened to binaural beats and sprinkled bee pollen on her yogurt. Yes, *The Odd Couple,* with one exception—with a household agreement in place, we settled into our new routine with relative ease.

How funny, I thought. I tried something similar with Tod, and he either mocked me, said it wasn't necessary, or—when he finally agreed after one too many arguments—he would hold up his end of the bargain for all of a week before falling back into old patterns.

Which brings me to my last update … work. Without knowing if Tod was in any way responsible for the demise of Nadia Perdita, and knowing I also had to stay local until the case was settled, I asked my boss, a restaurateur with several gastropubs in the area, if he could relocate me from my current pub to somewhere closer to where I was now living but out of the way from any of Tod's known haunts. I was a skilled bartender and mixologist, and an amateur sommelier. He agreed. Sadly, that meant choosing one of his shabbiest and least exciting pubs … the Bar Fly.

CHAPTER FIFTEEN

LONDON CALLING
TODAY

Asher was very organized—possibly to a fault. Once again, he checked his passport, tickets, and a small amount of British pounds. Others might wait until they arrived in London to make the exchange, but he liked to be prepared for every eventuality. For example, what if he suddenly felt snacky when arriving at Heathrow, but for some reason, his credit card didn't work? How would he pay for crisps—and a taxi, for that matter?

He moved around his condo, humming to himself and smiling. Chloe was on her way over. This could be the start of something real, couldn't it? A whirlwind trip to England might be the romantic boost their relationship needed.

An image of Sibley wearing her ridiculous otter pants and shirt with a Scottish cat (in a kilt, no less) popped into his mind. *Where did that come from?* he wondered. Then he smiled again. He would never share with Sibley why her pajamas had been such a spectacle. No, not because they were gaudy yet comfy. Not because she looked bad in them, because, if Asher were being completely honest with himself, Sibley did look rather adorable.

It's just that … whenever Chloe stayed over on the weekend, she always wore these revealing, lacy little lingerie numbers that left very little to the imagination. Granted, Sibley and he were just work colleagues on assignment, and Sibley didn't anticipate sharing a cottage with him. Yet, he couldn't help wondering—when Sibley Bloom was in love, did she show up to her boyfriend's place with otter PJs and a green cotton shirt with a cat on it packed in her overnight bag?

Stupid thought, he chastised himself. Sibley married young and had little experience dating. Perhaps Thomas never had the joy of seeing her in sexy lingerie … He pushed it out of his mind as he finished packing.

A private driver, courtesy of the *Journal,* was picking up him and Sibley, respectively. He had a twinge of guilt about him and Chloe traveling first class while Sibley was stuck in economy. But that was because Chloe had money and connections. All Sibley had was a stipend from work.

Should he perform the gallant gesture of giving Sibley his seat? he thought to himself. No, Chloe would never forgive him. Not when she had a romantic getaway on the brain. He paused to look at his watch … 3:45 p.m. Chloe needed to be here by 4 p.m. at the latest if they were going to arrive at Tampa Airport in a timely manner.

Just then, the phone rang. A knot formed in Asher's stomach. Somehow, he knew …

"Hi, babes," Chloe greeted on the phone line. Except her voice didn't sound nonchalant—more crestfallen.

"Hi … honey," he practiced, remembering how Chloe preferred nicknames. "Everything okay? The driver should be here at any moment to take us to the airport."

"Yeah," Chloe began hesitantly. "About that, hon—"

"What's wrong?" Asher asked, a deepened anxiety growing in his chest.

"Okay, so don't kill me—" she began.

If Asher didn't know any better, he could swear he could *see* her remotely peering at her freshly polished red nails while conjuring up a regretful expression.

"What's happened?" he tried again. "Are you alright?"

"I am," she began hesitantly. "But I've had an epiphany."

"An epiphany?" Asher clarified.

"Yes." Chloe let out a deep sigh as if the victim of circumstance. "When I told Salvatore about our trip, well, let's just say he got a little jealous."

"Salvatore?" *Who the hell was Salvatore? And why couldn't she just say Sal?*

"Don't be angry," she continued in a sing-song voice. "After all, we were exploring exclusivity but hadn't made a firm decision on it yet."

Speak for yourself, Asher said internally. Call me old-fashioned, but if I'm sleeping with someone—no matter how infrequently—I consider it pretty exclusive. He knew she was dating other people, but now he realized he didn't have the heart to ask how serious those other dates were. *I'm an idiot,* he told himself.

"Are you still there?" she asked innocently.

"Yes, I'm here," Asher grumbled. "What is it exactly you're trying to tell me, *hon?*" He couldn't help but let a little venom drip on that last word.

"Salvatore heard about our little trip to England and booked us a three-week vacation to Italy and Spain. Can you imagine? Eeeh!" She let out a girlish squeal.

"I'm assuming by 'us' you mean him and you?"

"Of course, silly. Don't even pretend to be daft."

"Long story short," Asher began, "you're not coming with me to London. Is that it?"

"No," she pouted. "Salvatore and I are heading out on a red-eye flight tonight."

"Well, thanks for letting me down easy. Goodbye—"

"Hey, wait a second, mister!" Her pitch lifted an octave. "I don't want to close the door on us … maybe just put a pin in it? Revisit when I'm back."

"I'm sorry, Chloe." He shook his head. "I don't do … whatever the hell this is." He found himself motioning in the air, even though she couldn't see him.

Just then, his phone buzzed. The driver texted that he was downstairs.

"Asher! You're behaving like a child," Chloe chastised.

"Sorry to cut you off, darling, but the driver is here. Don't want to miss our flight."

"Hey, just a sec—" she called out.

"What?" Asher didn't know what to expect. An apology? A moment for her to reconsider?

"I talked to Daddy and your boss. We've upgraded your co-worker Sabine—"

"Sibley," he corrected.

"Whatever," she dismissed. "Anyhow, we've upgraded her ticket to first class so the two of you can travel together."

"What happens to her economy ticket?" Asher asked. Not particularly relevant, but he was curious. Did Chloe—er, Chloe's dad—merely change the name on Chloe's ticket, or was there now an unused extra economy or first-class ticket floating around?

"How the hell should I know?!" Chloe became impatient. Asher could actually hear her stamping her foot. She took a breath. "But I should tell you, it's only one way. I wasn't sure how long you and I— well, you and the old me—were going to stay in London and then France. So you might have to suck up economy, or whatever your work affords you, on the way back. Sorry, babes."

A horn buzzed from the parking lot outside.

"Listen, Chloe. I've got to go. Good luck with … your life."

"Well, you're welcome—" she snapped back, but by then, Asher had already hung up.

Outside, the driver helped load Asher's suitcase and carry-on into the trunk. Within about fifteen minutes, they arrived at Sibley's condo.

She was outside, along with a woman he didn't recognize and a mangy dog that looked like it needed a good meal or two.

Sibley gave the woman a hug. "Thanks for looking after the place while I'm gone," she offered.

"Of course!" Vidalia answered. "It's the least I can do after you lettin' Skinny and me stay with you. I'll be sure to bring in the mail, take the recyclables out, and keep an eye out for any bills."

Sibley scratched Skinny on the head before climbing in the back seat of the car, settling beside Asher.

As the driver closed the door behind her, she took one look at Asher's face and asked, "What's wrong?"

Neither Asher nor Sibley had ever traveled first class before. And while Asher was far more well-traveled than his colleague, his work had never afforded him more than Economy Plus.

When the two were directed to their seats—adjacent little sleep pods in the center aisle, with no other passengers except for one person on each side of the plane (each with their own private pod)—they were quite surprised.

"Would you like a glass of Prosecco?" a flight attendant asked Sibley as soon as she sank into her adjustable seat with ample legroom.

"Sure," Sibley answered eagerly. "Wait. How much is it?"

"It's complimentary," the attendant grinned, looking at her quizzically, as if Sibley didn't quite fit in first class. At least, that's what was going on in Sibley's mind.

"Okay, then!" Sibley accepted it. She set it on a small fold-down end table before she tucked her carry-on in a compartment at her feet.

What's this? she thought. A small welcome package was tucked at the edge of her seat. She opened it to find disposable slippers, earplugs, a bamboo toothbrush, a mini tube of toothpaste, and an eye mask.

She eyed Asher, who sat next to her, yet had his own little cocoon. He met her gaze and smiled like a kid in a candy store.

"Pretty nice, huh?" He smiled, momentarily forgetting that it was his noncommittal girlfriend who purchased said tickets.

"Your Scotch, sir." An attendant handed Asher his beverage. He eyed Sibley and wriggled his eyebrows excitedly.

"When in Rome." He held his glass up. I raised my small glass of Prosecco and clinked it against his.

"Too bad Rome isn't on our agenda, huh?" I joked.

Asher's face dropped, just a little. *Oh shit.* Sibley remembered too late. That was where Chloe's other boyfriend was taking her on vacation.

Moments later, an attendant offered both a dinner and breakfast menu. It wasn't the standard plane food she was used to, like a bag of peanuts and a microwaved chicken sandwich that tasted three years old. No, this was a full-course meal and dessert. She was to decide between the steak, the chicken Alfredo, salmon, or the vegetarian stir fry (vegan upon request).

"What are you getting?" Sibley asked. "I can't decide."

"Torn between the salmon and the veggie stir fry. What about you?"

"Same." Sibley furrowed her brow. "I don't think steak or Alfredo is the best for my stomach on a long flight," she confessed. Not that she really knew, mind you. Sibley was not well-traveled.

"How about if you get the stir fry and I'll get the salmon, and we'll go halfsies?" he suggested.

"Really?" She thought back to Thomas, who never shared his dinner plate with anyone. He felt that whatever you decided on is what you should commit to. End of story.

"Of course," he laughed.

Just then, a flight attendant circled back to get their order, plucking the menus with their selections checked off.

"Excuse me," he asked the attendant. "Any chance we could get a couple of extra small sharing plates?"

"Of course you can." The attendant's eyes sparkled as she eyed the two. Sibley could tell that she thought they were a couple. *Wonder what her thoughts are about that?* Sibley thought. She imagined that the woman thought Asher could do better, and what was he doing with a mousy woman like her? But that was just a guess …

"So, what are we going to do with our free day tomorrow in London?" Sibley asked, once they'd finished their meal and were preparing for sleep.

"Well," Asher answered. "I suggest we get as much rest as possible. We head to Stonehenge at 4 a.m. the next day."

"What?!" I didn't remember seeing details like that in the itinerary.

Asher didn't respond. He merely rolled to one side, sliding a blanket over his shoulders with a smug expression on his face.

CHAPTER SIXTEEN
STONEHENGE
SIBLEY

"Isn't this amaze-balls?" Yolanda squealed as she, Asher, and I squeezed into an overpacked bus heading toward Stonehenge from the Visitor Centre. "I'm so excited!"

Yolanda's arrival in London answered the question about the extra economy ticket. She texted me as soon as we landed, so Asher and I waited on the other side of Customs for her to finally shuffle through the gate. She looked weathered, confessing to getting only about an hour of sleep on the plane. I felt guilty, as our posh seating garnered me a few more. I fought back a yawn because I somehow didn't feel entitled to it.

With the plane ticket already purchased, Reed sanctioned her coming to assist. Yolanda had family in London, so all she really needed was tickets to the conference and for the Winter Solstice celebration at Stonehenge. It worked out for him as she could cover events at the conference that didn't include me.

"In all the time your family has lived here, you've never been to Stonehenge?" I yawned. We had most of the day to sleep and recover, but jet lag was no match for arriving at the sacred site while still dark in order to witness the sunrise.

"'Course I have. But during the rest of the year, visitors aren't allowed to touch the stones or walk through the inner circle. Only during summer and winter solstices can we do that … It's to preserve the stones."

I perked up a little. I'd read that Stonehenge was used for centuries as a ceremonial and burial site for farmers during the Neolithic period, and that many believed the area to be highly energetic, providing healing to those who were sick. Some even purported that the inside of the stone circle was the portal to other worlds.

"Do you believe that?" I asked Asher, groggily.

"Believe what?" Asher and Yolanda both eyed me curiously.

"Do you believe that Stonehenge has healing properties and can connect us to other dimensions?"

Asher paused. "Is this one of those times where you have a thought in your head and assume that you actually said it or that we're mind readers?"

"Oh," I blushed a little. "Sorry. Still fighting with jet lag."

"It's okay," Asher sympathized. "But better perk up soon. You're supposed to meet your Christmas date out here."

The bus came to a stop just as it began raining … a cold, miserable rain on a winter's morning. I pulled my hood over my head and tightened the straps under my chin to secure it in place.

Yolanda wrapped an arm around me after we'd exited the bus and began walking the short path to the stones. "Cheer up," she had a gleam in her eye. "I picked this date for you. Or at least, my mum did."

"You had your mom pick a date for me?" I was incredulous.

"Actually, I think she was secretly hoping I would leave my Bert. Thinks he's too dull. So it's a date for you, under pretense."

Asher did his best to shield his camera from the elements, but his face indicated he was not enthusiastic about being here either. Yet somehow, he expected me to be.

"For someone who has worked for a metaphysical magazine for so long, I would have thought this was a dream come true," he chastised.

"Criticism from the resident cynic," I answered flatly.

"I am far from cynical," Asher answered. "If I didn't have to contend with the weather and my equipment, I'd be ecstatic. I've got no problem with spirituality. It just happens to be my job to debunk the charlatans."

"And your thoughts on people who visit Stonehenge?" I challenged.

"I believe anyone willing to make an early-morning pilgrimage here, drumming, chanting, meditating, and walking through the circle, are devout in their beliefs. I'm appalled that you'd think otherwise." Asher answered loudly, smiling at a lovely redheaded maiden dressed in a flowing green gown, wearing a leaf crown, who shyly smiled back.

"Funny what you'll believe when a pretty woman is present," I murmured under my breath.

Once we'd reached the stone formation, Yolanda began scanning the crowd. "We're supposed to be looking for a rugged Scotsman, dark skin, wearing a brown tartan, hunter green hooded shirt, lambswool manket, and boots … oh, and he's carrying a wooden staff.

"Rugged, you say?" A man's deep voice spoke from behind us.

I felt a chill behind my neck.

We turned to face a broad-shouldered man with an ebony complexion and the brightest green eyes I have ever seen. They were mesmerizing.

"I'm Arran," he greeted. "If I'm not mistaken, you're Yolanda," he gestured. "Asher and … " He paused dramatically, before flashing a wide, pearly white smile at me. "You must be Sibley."

Jackpot, I thought to myself. Maybe I should let Yolanda's mum set up all my dates from now on.

Yolanda's jaw dropped before she recovered, closing it and letting out an uncomfortable cough.

"So," I giggled absurdly. "You're my date for solstice?"

"Aye, that I am. And what an honor. A beautiful woman from the States."

I stifled back another giggle. What was wrong with me? I realized at that moment, that mystical famous stones aside, I could just stare into those green eyes and listen to that accent until the end of time.

Just then, the rain stopped.

"How fortuitous," Arran grinned, raising his arms toward the heavens, holding his staff up. "Blessed be."

"Well, listen," Yolanda interjected. "I'll leave you two lovebirds to your date. I've got my own article to write for the journal." To me she whispered, "Meet you at the hotel later this afternoon to compare notes?" She eyed my date again. "Or, not," Yolanda wriggled her eyebrows suggestively. I slapped her arm and shushed her.

Arran lowered his arms, offering one to me. "Shall we? Probably a good time make our way through the center of the sacred circle. Given this crowd, it may take a bit."

"Sacred circle," Yolanda snickered to Asher. He merely shook his head.

Really, sometimes Yolanda behaved like a teenager.

Just then, my phone buzzed. I glanced briefly to see two text messages from Shaman Theodore, and to my surprise, one from Bodhi. There was also one missed call from Thomas.

I noticed Arran eyeing me, cautiously.

"Sorry," I felt I could read his mind—eerie. "I'll just silence my phone. Forgot I had it on."

"No apology necessary," Arran answered. "I was merely noticing we had the same phone. And, as I understand it, tonight is part work and part play," he smiled a devilish grin at me.

"Speaking of the work part," Asher fell into step beside us. "Try not to mind me. I'll keep my distance, for the most part. But I may need to orchestrate a few shots for our cover. You understand?"

"Of course, whatever you need, mate," Arran's deep voice answered with the warmth of a cozy weighted blanket on a cold day.

Come to think of it, I could have used one such blanket at this moment. I shivered.

I felt Arran resist the inclination to put his arm around me, as he and I knew it was far too early on for that kind of familiarity. Instead he observed. "You're cold. Let me give you my cape to keep you warm." He began to remove the manket around his neck.

"No, I'm alright," I hugged my arms around my wool jacket. "I'll just … stand a little closer." I inched over to him, his large frame blocking the wind. I could feel the heat from his body.

"Closer is always welcome," he grinned. "Here we are."

At first, I was distracted by the crowds. There was every variety of garb, some dressed like Arran, others wearing flowing gowns and flower crowns, or simply bundled in a swath of sweaters and hats. Several visitors balanced intricate headpieces across their shoulders, including one person wearing a giant sun mask that disguised their face.

We managed to secure a spot arm's reach from one of the tall sarsen stones. "After you," he encouraged.

It was only then that I noticed what felt like a light buzzing through my body, and I was overcome by a sense of calm. I liked to believe that my line of work made me more open-minded, but I always keep a sliver of "Asher energy"—that healthy skepticism that kept me firmly grounded in the present moment.

I caught Arran looking at me with a knowing smile.

"You feel it too, don't you?" He grinned. Honestly, I wasn't completely certain whether he was talking about the energy at Stonehenge or the energy between us.

"Yes," I answered (to both).

I felt compelled to rest my bare palms on the cool stone and touch my forehead to it. I glanced beside me, and noticed that Arran did the same.

The buzzing became stronger. The only way I could describe it is that floaty feeling when you awaken from a delightful nap on a lawn chair in spring. There's the briefest of moments when your mind is completely clear, but you've not yet remembered where you are and what day it is … just that feeling of pure bliss and a water-like energy rippling through you.

Except, this was less fleeting.

Suddenly, an odd thought came to me, *That's enough. Leave some energy for the next person.*

I stepped back just as Arran did.

Without words, Arran took my hand. "I recommend we touch the blue stones as well."

"Of course," I joked. "Wouldn't want them to feel left out." I blushed as soon as I'd said it, gazing at our intertwined hands.

Arran laughed, generously.

It was then that I heard the click of Asher's camera. As I glanced up at him, I could have sworn I caught a micro expression. It felt like judgment. I almost pulled my hand from Arran's, but then remembered the redhead Asher was so fond of, and gripped Arran's hand tighter.

He squeezed my palm back.

We paused at one of the flat blue stones, and I bent to touch my palms on it. Oddly, the energy felt different. The only way I could describe it was centered, grounded, this internal knowing that everything in my heart and mind was realigning. Arran did the same.

Just then, a large group of dancers, waving their arms and beating drums and singing, paraded by us. Arran nodded his head toward a clearing in the grass, and I followed. This time, he put an arm around my shoulders. I didn't mind.

Once we'd reached a clearing, he gazed upward. "About ten minutes or so until the official dawn. We can watch the sun stream through the stones. It'll be brilliant."

"I'm going to sit," I explained, plopping less-than-gracefully into the grass and crossing my legs in front of me. Funny, I wasn't feeling cold anymore … just peaceful.

Arran joined me.

"Did you notice a difference between the energy of the stones?" Arran asked.

I nodded, and explained how they felt to me. His eyes widened in surprise. "How interesting," he offered. "I felt the exact opposite … more of a grounding on the sarsen stones and more buzzing of the blue stones."

"Good thing there's no wrong way to experience Stonehenge at Winter Solstice," I laughed.

"You're right about that."

"So, what makes this event so special to you?" That sounded like an interview question, but I really was curious.

"Well, as a practicing modern Druid, I hold nature and spiritual places such as this one with deep reverence. It carries the energy of all the people who came before us. And, I like to think that I have been here in other lifetimes and other realms." Arran spoke with conviction, and unlike Shaman Theodore (who had this underlying showmanship or insecurity), Arran merely exhibited a confident humility.

I liked it.

I liked him.

"And what about you?" Arran asked. "What is it that you believe?"

"Well, Arran," I answered honestly. "You'd think after spending decades working for a new age journal I'd have it all figured out. But the truth is, I'm not entirely sure."

"I can respect that," Arran nodded. "But's it's beautiful that you are open to new experiences. Sometimes, the strongest spiritual practices come when we take the time to explore what's out there, ask questions, and eventually, decide for ourselves. There's no real time limit on it, is there?"

"Hmm, I hadn't thought of it that way," I confessed. "I'm always chastising myself for not having it all figured out yet."

Arran let out a booming laugh. "Well, in my profession, I can honestly tell you that the people who think they've got it all figured out are among the most lost because they're so resistant to change. Therefore, they often remain unhappy."

"Ah, and now the dreaded question," I joked. "What is it that you do for a living?"

"It's what I do as my life's purpose," he gently corrected. "I'm a social worker. It's not a high-paying job, but very fulfilling."

I had a flash of insight. "Oh, is that how Yolanda's mom came to refer you to me?"

Arran's smile widened. "Yes, her mum and I have worked on several programs supporting a youth center near East Kilbride. I was hesitant about this match-up, if I'm being honest. But, I'm always telling my clients to take more chances. I'd be a hypocrite if I didn't follow my own advice."

I resisted the urge to ask, "How is a handsome and charming man such as yourself not taken?" But I hated whenever I was asked similarly. So I let that thought settle.

"There," Arran raised his arm and pointed at the horizon. "It's time."

A hush fell over the crowd. It didn't last long, but we sat in silence for the next ten minutes or so.

Finally, I broke in with a few more questions about his life and work. We chatted for what seemed a very short time before Asher's voice broke into our conversation.

"Sorry to rush you two," Asher announced. "But our bus is loading up to head back to the Visitor Centre. I've already flagged Yolanda down and she's on her way to the drop-off location."

"Well," I turned to Arran, "I hate to end such a lovely occasion, but you're going to be at the London Holistic Conference later this week, yeah?"

"I am. May I leave you my number to make sure we can connect there?" he offered.

"Exactly my thinking," I pulled out my phone and handed it to Arran. "Since you have the same one, maybe program your number in for me?"

He tucked his staff under one arm so he could thumb his name and number into my contacts. Arran handed it back to me. "You have me at a disadvantage. I didn't want to be tempted to look at my phone, so I left it in my car. Perhaps you can phone me?" He paused before adding, "Anytime. You don't have to wait until the conference." He moved toward me. "Do you mind?" He handed his staff to Asher, who took it reluctantly, already having his hands full with camera equipment. Asher did his best to juggle everything while Arran brought me in for a big bear hug.

He smelled faintly like sandalwood.

He retrieved his staff and watched while Asher and I boarded the bus. I passed Yolanda, already seated inside.

"Well if you don't look like the cat that ate the canary," she grinned.

"Not yet," I smirked.

"Ooh, listen to you, girl!" She giggled. "I want details after I have myself a little nap. What say we meet around 4 p.m.-ish at the hotel? Reed can treat us to tea and crumpets."

"That sounds like fun," Asher chimed in.

"You're not invited," Yolanda's expression dropped. "Girl talk."

"I wasn't hinting," Asher assured her. "I'll be having a drink with a lovely lass I met today."

Asher and I slid into the seats behind Yolanda, who became distracted by her seat-mate, an American asking for directions to Bath.

"I don't get you," I hadn't meant to sound so abrupt, it just came across that way. "I thought Chloe was supposed to be joining you for a romantic getaway. You sure got over her fast."

"Thanks for the reminder," Asher's expression dropped. "I hadn't realized I needed to justify my actions to you. I'll be certain to check in first, next time."

I felt a knot in my stomach. This wasn't how I wanted to end an otherwise near-perfect date—even if it was with someone else.

"Sorry," I apologized. "I didn't mean to sound so judgey."

Asher sighed. "Believe me, I was all for trying an exclusive relationship with Chloe … but then came Salvatore." He emphasized his competitor's name.

"May I share a thought?" I asked. "A non-judgy one?"

Asher grinned as he nudged me with his shoulder. "Go ahead, then."

"If it hadn't been Salvatore, it would have been someone else."

"Still judgey, but not directed at me, thankfully." He smiled warmly, letting me know it was a gentle ribbing.

"Well, hear me out," I continued. "Based on what you've told me about her, which I'll admit, isn't much, I believe she likes a certain lifestyle … bright and shiny things. I believe she had some feelings for you, as much as she could afford to, anyway. You're kind. You're cultured, smart, and funny … all things she found attractive—" Asher tilted his head sideways, surprised, I think, that I saw him in that light. "But unless you can treat her to all the things in life as 'Daddy' can, you won't stand a chance in the long term."

"So, she'd inevitably leave me?"

"Worse," I replied. "She'd string you along to get to experience all that you are … all the while dating someone else … or maybe several someones. It's fine if you're okay with a surface-level relationship. But that's all it was ever going to be." I searched Asher's face for a response, fearful that I'd, once again, gone too far.

"I appreciate your candor, Sibley." He nodded, somewhat sorrowfully. "You really did pick up some ancient wisdom from those stones, huh?"

"It had to have been the stones," I joked. "Given my failed marriage and limited track record in the dating world, I'm not entirely sure where that came from."

"Speaking of which," Asher reached into his pocket. "I got you something from the Heritage Foundation gift shop on site."

He handed me a tiny box. Inside was a blue stone ring pendant hanging on a small silver chain.

"Well, that was very thoughtful of you!" I felt even worse about delivering the sour news I'd just offered.

"It's the same blue stone that we saw at Stonehenge ... so you could take a bit of the experience back home with you."

"Thank you." I was touched. "I read that the blue stones were supposed to be imbued with a magical, healing energy. I know I felt grounded when I touched one. I can certainly stand to be more grounded." I smiled up at him, just as the bus pulled up to the Visitor Centre. Not sure how he retrieved such a trinket, as I was certain the store was closed when we arrived. Asher must have pre-planned it. "Help me put it on before we drive back to the hotel?"

I turned my back toward him as he set his camera bag under his seat and fumbled with the necklace chain. His fingers touched my neck ever-so-slightly. I shivered. Must be the energy of Stonehenge, I decided.

I was groggy when I met up with Yolanda for high tea at the Queen's Gate Hotel back in London. I threw on a black-and-white striped sweater dress and black flats and hoped this would suffice.

At least Asher isn't here, so I don't have to worry about my picture—

Yolanda snapped a photo of me with her camera phone as soon as I walked in the room.

"Hey, hey!" She waved excitedly. "Get a look at these little finger sandwiches and scones," she squealed.

The room was lovely, with French-style white wooden shutters, a skylight, and high ceilings decorated with hanging plants. There were splashes of turquoise lounge chairs and strategically placed greenery, giving it a spacious, outdoor feel. Next to our table sat a wide array of pastries, clotted cream and jellies, and, as Yolanda mentioned, tiny, triangle-shaped miniature sandwiches.

"I ordered us some Darjeeling tea, but they've got others."

I pulled out a chair and sat across from Yolanda. I eyed the room, in awe. In the entire time I'd been married, Thomas never took me to places like this—or anywhere, really.

"I could get used to this," I murmured.

"That's right, baby." Yolanda snapped her fingers. "Nothing but the best for my favorite girl from now on."

The server delivered the tea to our table, pouring each of us a cup, leaving behind lemon wedges, cream, and a choice of brown or white sugar cubes.

Oddly, I noticed Yolanda put one each of the cubes in her tea.

"What?" she asked. "Why not?"

"Why not, indeed?" I agreed, putting one raw sugar cube and one white one in my own cup. "Cream?" I asked.

"Let's not get crazy now," Yolanda laughed.

I wasn't much of a "cream in my tea" person, either.

Just then, my phone buzzed again.

"This is getting ridiculous," I complained. "I feel as if I'm getting cyberstalked by Theo the neo-shaman, Bodhi the raw vegan Buddhist, and Thomas the 'couldn't keep it in his pants' ex-husband."

"Nothing from the Druid?" Yolanda wriggled her eyebrows.

"That's just it," I answered. "He didn't have his phone on him. I have to be the one to contact him."

"Oooh! That's perfect," Yolanda proclaimed. "You have all the power."

"I don't know the rules anymore. How long do I wait before I text him? Or, should I call?"

"Forget the 'rules.' You wanna text him, text him," Yolanda suggested, biting into a profiterole. "Hmmm, this is heavenly. You gotta try this."

"Soon," I picked a lemon macaron from the tray and devoured it. I was hungrier than I realized, and went for a salmon and brie galette next. "In the meantime," I asked between sips of tea and my tasty treats, "How do I get rid of the ones I've got?"

"Well, what made you give them your phone number in the first place?" Yolanda put her hand on her hip, then realized it prevented her from eating, so she reached out and snatched a cucumber sandwich next. "Thomas, I get. But why the other two?"

"They asked, and I thought it was the polite thing to do."

"Are you planning on choosing either as your Valentine's date at the Eiffel Tower?" Yolanda eyed me, knowingly.

"No."

"Then you could have said that you prefer not to, or get their number. Tell 'em it's contest rules, or something."

"I'm not great at lying."

"Well then," Yolanda reached beside her chair and pulled a small laptop out of a briefcase I hadn't noticed before. She cleared a space on the table and opened it up. "I'm adding it to the rules, right now … 'Contestants may not ask the love interest for her number. They, however, may choose to offer their number if asked.'"

"This sounds very mechanical," Sibley answered. "But, at least I don't have to see them anymore, right? And once Valentine's Day passes, and they read my article, they'll give up, right?"

"Um," Yolanda swallowed hard.

"What are you not telling me … this time?"

A server dressed in black was about to approach the table, heard me raise my voice slightly, and decided against it.

"Reed sort of decided to invite contestants to the conference … paid for their flights and hotels too … or at least, one of the sponsors did."

"What? Why didn't anyone tell me this?"

"I'm sorry, Sibley," Yolanda apologized. "I thought you were given the same briefing as I was. And Phoebe was supposed to fill you in on the Florida dates. I was to keep you up on those this side of the pond. I guess Reed figured it would be more interesting if you had a bit more time getting to know your fellas at the conference."

"Do you have said briefing in your notes?" I pointed to the laptop.

"Sure, I'll email it to you," she agreed. "But can we get back to Arran? He sounds like Mum chose well." She rested her chin on her upturned palm.

"She did," I blushed. "And, I think he liked me. Said he wanted to meet up before the conference at some point."

"And, I saw him holding your hand," Yolanda commented.

"How did you know that? I thought you were writing a story of your own?"

"I've been married to Bert for eons. I have to live vicariously through you."

"Well, I get that we had a connection. And I know that Theo was interested, but why on Earth would Bodhi even bother? He was visibly annoyed by me."

"Probably just after the re—" Yolanda caught herself.

"The what? Yolanda? What were you about to say?" I demanded.

"The $25,000 reward to the person who wins your heart," she squeaked out.

"Are you kidding me?" I was infuriated. "How is this, in any way, supposed to lead to 'real love'? Or has Reed just been gaslighting me the entire time?"

Yolanda pointed to the laptop. "It's in the brief. I promise. I think he just wanted to make sure each date gave you a chance?"

"And they wouldn't have, otherwise? As if an all-expense-paid trip to England for the London Holistic Conference wasn't enough?"

"I don't think this was all Reed's doing," Yolanda defended. "Look at your New Year's date. He's the main sponsor."

"A business tycoon?" My itinerary only included first names and a bit about each person … minimal at best. "I read that my next date was a big-time businessman. Never mentioned he runs a chain of resorts and spas across Europe, not to mention that he's the founder of the conference. Why on Earth would this Jack fellow want to go on a date with me?"

Yolanda eyed me, curiously. "We really need to do something about your self-esteem, girl. Why wouldn't he be interested? You're super smart, got a heart of gold, and now that you have help with your wardrobe, you clean up good, too." She joked.

I couldn't argue there. I peered down at my winter dress and flats, feeling the weight of the gold dangle earrings I was wearing. I had to admit, this was an upgrade from my usual attire. Still, I'm certain he could have his pick of women … so could Arran, for that matter. I was having trouble seeing me as a viable love interest.

"And that look right there is why you need to go on these dates. Even if they are duds, even if they are only in it to win it. You could benefit from some dating experiences. Have fun. You deserve it!"

I sighed. "Okay, one more scone and cup of tea, and then I'm heading back to my room to see what else Reed and Phoebe didn't tell me."

"I wouldn't go too hard on Phoebe," Yolanda confided.

"Why? What's wrong?"

"I dunno, but she seems distracted lately. I figured we'd plan a gals' night when we get back … sort it out."

I nodded. I also made a mental note to ask Asher how much of this he knew. But in the meantime, I had a high tea to finish.

I returned to my room. It was early, but I was still jet-lagged. My only plans for this evening were a long hot bath, to review this brief from top to bottom, and possibly binge-watch BritBox. I know it seemed silly to be in London and preferring to stay in for the evening, but I figured I had plenty of time to both see the sights and enjoy the conference. Everything in my marriage to Thomas had been a rush. There never seemed to be enough time for anything … certainly not time for me. That was going to change.

I looked at my stream of texts and sighed. Given that I would likely run into Theo and Bodhi at the conference, and now knowing they had a reason to court me, I texted a polite response back to each of them. "Went to Stonehenge today for Winter Solstice. It was as amazing (as expected). Still recovering from jet lag but look forward to seeing you at the conference next week." I thought to apologize for the delayed response, but then thought better of it. The new me was beginning to recognize that I didn't really owe these men anything. I was tired of getting guilted into doing things I didn't want to do.

Which brought me to Thomas. He texted, and phoned, asking if I knew where his favorite golf shirt was?

I began to reply, "They are where they always are—" but stopped myself. Instead I typed back, "I have no idea. Ask Gemma."

No further comment after that.

Before I put the phone down, I glanced at my contacts. I sucked in a breath, gathered my courage, and typed, *Hey Arran. It's Sibley. Still recovering from jet lag today, but if you have time, might be fun to meet up in London this week?*

Less than a minute later, he texted back. *So good to hear from you, Sibley. It was lovely welcoming in the Winter Solstice with you. I would be delighted to show you some of the sites. Care to text in the morning and we can plan something together?*

I texted back an affirmative, a warm glow settling in my chest.

Wonderful, he texted. *Get some rest, and I'll see you soon.*

CHAPTER SEVENTEEN

LONDON ADVENTURES
SIBLEY

Meet you on the corner of Elvaston and Queen's Gate? Arran texted the next morning, replying not five minutes after I reached out. I thought to call, but since he specifically asked for a text, I followed suit. Honestly, it felt strange calling a man up for a date … I mean, it was a date, wasn't it? I wasn't sure. I really had no idea what dating was like these days. And Reed's little experiment wasn't helping.

Though, I smiled to myself. It did lead me to Arran. And that was a good thing, wasn't it?

I'll be there, I replied, happily.

Great, he texted. *See you at 10 a.m. Lose the chaperone, though, yeah?* This was followed by a wink emoji.

I assume he meant Asher. And yes, that was going to be a problem. Asher was supposed to be photographing my every move for the story, but if I didn't know any better, I'd assume that he was also acting as my self-appointed bodyguard. Most times, I didn't mind—appreciated it, even. But no, today was different. And three was definitely a crowd.

I slipped out of my room and quietly closed the door behind me, knowing full well that Asher's hotel room was next to mine.

Once outside the hotel, I spotted a tall man wearing a wool jacket and a red scarf … Arran.

I sucked in a breath. *God, he was handsome.* Which led me to my second thought, *Why on earth would he choose me?*

"Stop it!" I heard Yolanda's voice in my head, chastising me. *"He'd be lucky to have you on his arm."*

Then I heard a second voice. It was my own, reminding me, there is a $25,000 prize for the man who wins your heart.

I hated that second voice.

"Good morning, Sibley," Arran greeted me with a warm smile. "Don't you look radiant this morning? Did you sleep well?"

"Yes," I lied. In truth, my stomach was in knots all night, but he didn't need to know that.

"Have you had breakfast yet?" he asked.

"Just tea in the room this morning, and a biscuit," I answered.

"Settling into London nicely, I see," he smiled.

My stomach gurgled. I was certain the whole world could hear it. I somehow realized I was smiling awkwardly at him, for a moment too long. *Stop being so weird!* I yelled at myself. *It's just like riding a bike …* That brought other images to mind. I pushed them aside.

"I wouldn't mind a bite," I confessed, hoping he couldn't hear my nervous belly betraying me.

"Well, I happen to know an excellent pastry shop up ahead. We can dine in or get a sausage roll, or whatever you like, to go."

"That sounds fun," I smiled. We paused at the shop, which, by this time, was bustling. "Perhaps to go," I suggested. "A pastry and maybe a bottle of water?"

Arran nodded, promptly ordering us two pastries and water for the road.

We walked as we tucked in to our breakfast, a bite here and a sip of water there.

"What would you like to see today, Sibley Bloom?" Arran asked, eyeing me with an uncomfortable level of intensity. "Or, if you're not sure, I can make some recommendations … Tower of London, Big Ben, Westminster Abbey?"

"Okay, this is going to sound really dorky," I confessed.

"Dorky is my middle name," Arran joked. "Whatcha got?"

"Well," I hesitated. "I realize I live in Florida—"

"Yes?" he encouraged.

"Well, we have our bogarted version of Hyde Park. And we've certainly got lots of water but—"

"Spill it, Sibley. I'm all ears," he laughed. Gosh, even his laugh is sexy.

"I wanna visit Hyde Park and maybe take one of those little paddle boats out on the water?" I blurted out. There, I said it. Me. The imagination of a four-year-old.

"Ah, yeah. Brilliant," Arran graciously cheered me on. "You mean those pedal boats people take out on the Serpentine?"

"Yes, that's it!"

"Well then, boating we shall go," Arran offered his arm. "You up for a walk first? About thirty minutes that way—" He pointed. "But, we'll get to wander through Hyde Park first."

"Why not?" I agreed, taking his arm. "It's a beautiful day. And, unlike Stonehenge, it's surprisingly warm today."

It was also unlike Florida, where the humidity smacks you in the face as soon as you walk out the front door in the morning. London weather was refreshing. Unpredictable at times, but I think that's part of its charm. I decided that I would enjoy even the foggiest and dreariest of London days. But then, part of my mood could have been the Scottish gent on my arm.

Perhaps others didn't share my enthusiasm for boating in winter. It was fairly secluded when we finally arrived at the Serpentine. Along the way, we passed a few young people playing soccer (or, football, as I am told), an older man throwing a ball that his dog eagerly fetched, and an older couple snuggled for warmth on a park bench.

It was nice to not be in a hurry. I didn't realize just how much of my time with Thomas was about rushing to work, rushing to get home and make dinner, rushing to clean the house—only to be criticized if I wanted a night out with the girls. *Well, that was old Sibley*, I thought to myself. Things are going to be different.

"Penny for your thoughts?" Arran asked, as he guided me into the little blue boat. I hung onto his arms, laughing as it swayed. The boat attendant did his best to steady it beneath me, but I was less than delicate as I plopped ever-so-gracefully (or not) into my bucket seat. "You still use that expression, yeah?" he asked.

"As a writer, I try to avoid all clichés … 'burger joints,' 'check it out,' 'penny for your thoughts,' but, yes." My face flushed. "Ooh, sorry, that came out wrong."

"It's fine … writing snob." Arran laughed.

I let out an unpleasant snort before grabbing my offending nose. "Well, I'm just embarrassing myself all over the place, aren't I?"

"Not at all," he settled in next to me. I could feel the heat kicking off of his body juxtaposed to the crisp morning air. "I find your authenticity refreshing," he said in this low voice, met with a steely gaze that made me look away.

"Well," I blushed. "There's plenty more of that authenticity …where … that comes from." I cupped the side of my head. "My God, am I this out of practice dating?" I whined.

"Hey," he grinned, paddling the boat away from the launch site. I decided it was best if I kept up my end, and began pedaling as well while he steered. "I'm not exactly an expert myself."

"I find that hard to believe," I muttered.

"And why is that?" He smirked, glancing away as if focussing on navigating … not that there was that much of it to be done on a small touristy boat such as this.

"Oh, c'mon," I scoffed, gently. "You've got everything going for you … looks, personality, not to mention work that points to someone who is an obvious humanitarian—lover of the people."

"You forgot intelligent," he added. "Joking! Just joking. But my head just got a bit bigger now, didn't it?"

"Anyway," I changed the conversation. "Since you asked earlier what I was thinking, I'll tell you."

"I'm all ears," he said. "Hah! There's another cliché for you. I'm afraid I'm full of them."

I rolled my eyes. "Anyway—" I continued. "I was thinking how the old me was always in such a rush … bogged down by obligations. I want to take the time to slow down and savor life more."

"Stop and smell the roses, yeah?" Arran smirked. I reached into the lake, scooped a handful of water and flicked it at him. "What was that for?" he laughed, in mock offense.

"You're just throwing those trite phrases around to wind me up, aren't you?" I accused.

"You know, 'wind me up' is one of 'em, right?" Arran drew his arms up in defense. "No! Don't splash me again! I'm all sugar. I might melt."

Just then, my phone buzzed. I had it tucked securely in my coat pocket. I fished it out … Asher.

"Uh oh," Arran read my expression. "That wouldn't be your chaperone checking in now, would it?"

"Asher?" I asked. "Yeah. But it's not like that. It's his job to capture photo footage, and some video, for this chronicle."

"Well," Arran answered, suspiciously. "I'd say he's doing his job exceptionally well."

"Do I detect a little sarcasm in that voice?" I asked, carefully.

"Maybe a little. Or, maybe I'm just jealous … "

"Why on earth would you be jealous?" I asked, surprised.

"Oh, come on now. It's pretty easy to see he fancies you," Arran answered.

"What makes you say that?"

"Let's just say that in the short time I've been around the guy, I've noticed he takes exceptional care in looking after you, is all."

"Well, could be my naïveté about the world … I am newly divorced and all. He's a colleague just trying to keep me safe, I think."

"Yeah," Arran nodded. "I remember hearing that … about the divorce. So, what's your chaperone got to say?" He motioned toward my phone.

"Em … " I looked at my phone. "He says, 'rise and shine! Care to see some of the sights today? We can grab a few establishing shots of the area?'"

"Well, he's a bit late, isn't he?" Arran chortled.

"What should I tell him?" I asked, concerned.

"What's the problem?" Arran was surprised. "Tell him you're out for the day, and you'll catch him up when you're back."

I sighed. "I just feel guilty out having fun when I'm supposed to be on assignment."

"Sibley, can I ask you a serious question?"

"Sure," I answered, nervously.

"Do you always play by the rules?" He picked up the speed on his pedals, and we were moving at a nice clip as we wound the Serpentine. If I didn't know any better, I'd say he was slightly annoyed. *No*, I thought. *I'm just reading too much into things.*

I made up my mind. I texted back, "Sorry to have missed you. Out for the day with Arran. I'll catch up with you later?"

All that came back was a thumbs-up emoji. Asher didn't communicate via emojis … He was disappointed.

"All good?" Arran asked.

"Yup," I answered. "I followed your suggestion."

Just then, the phone buzzed again. This time, it was Bodhi, asking if I cared to meet up for a vegan lunch the day before the conference. And, for that matter, did I think that my work would cover the expense?

It buzzed a third time …

"Oh, for Christ's sake!" I yelled at my phone. The last one was from Thomas, telling me how much he missed me. "That's it, I'm turning this thing off."

"Finally!" Arran laughed. "No offense, but I'll admit I don't like sharing you with the rest of the lot."

"Well," I smiled. "You're in luck. You've got my undivided attention for the rest of the day."

"Perfect," he grinned.

We eased our way back to the dock and climbed out of our tiny blue boat, not without a little struggle on my part. Arran put his arms out for support. *Ooh, strong,* I thought as I felt his muscles as he half-lifted me from the boat.

"Where to, next?" he asked.

"Dorky request number two?" I cringed.

"Go for it!" he encouraged.

"Perhaps the Natural History Museum? Only if you're interested. I kinda wanna see the first edition of Darwin's *On the Origin of Species* on display."

"Wow!" Arran was taken aback. "Brainy and beautiful." I blushed, tilting my head away, embarrassed. He tilted his head to meet my gaze. "Not good with compliments, eh?"

"Just not used to them," I admitted.

"Well, you'll get used to them with me," he nodded, confidently.

We meandered for a time, exiting the park and making the trek, on foot, toward the museum.

"Depending on how you feel after this excursion, we could visit the Victoria and Albert Museum too," Arran added. "They've got a brilliant Cast Court with plaster replicas of the world's most famous sculptures. It's massive, and impressive."

"Ooh, you're on!" I picked up the pace as a cool wind blew through us, sending a shiver down my spine.

"Good thinking on the pace," he acknowledged. "We might have rain on the way. Welcome to London, foggy in the morning, sunny five minutes later, followed by a random shower mid-afternoon. Never know what to expect."

Given the line outside the museum, I realized we were not going to be lucky against the rain. I pulled up the hood of my coat while Arran took his jacket off and held it like a shield over his head. By the time we'd reached the entranceway, we were a soggy mess.

"Be right back," I informed him, as I popped into the loo to find paper towels to dry my hair a bit. I caught a glimpse of myself in the mirror … ratty hair matted to my head, eye makeup streaming, and it appeared as if my blush became patchwork on my face. I cleaned up as best as I could. "Screw it," I finally told my reflection in the mirror. "He'll have to deal with me ugly."

I returned to join Arran as he marveled at the massive blue whale suspended from the ceiling. "Her name is 'Hope,'" he shared.

"Well, isn't she lovely," I admired, resisting the urge to snap a photo with my phone. In fact, I was vowing not to touch my phone for the rest of the day.

"C'mon," he gestured. "Let's go find Darwin's first edition … Can show you Audubon's *Birds of America*, too, if you like."

The remainder of the day was filled with the extensive Minerals Gallery, an impressive collection of gemstones, meteorites and minerals that would make my metaphysical friends swoon at their spiritual and holistic properties. We meandered through the dinosaur and mammals exhibits, where I was both in awe of, and slightly put off by, the collection of animals preserved through taxidermy.

"I know," Arran read my mind. "But the museum does its best to procure animals that have died from natural causes."

Somehow, I could hear Bodhi in my head saying, "Fat chance of that." I didn't want to hear Bodhi's imaginary two cents, so I put him out of my mind.

"Victoria and Albert Hall next?" Arran asked.

"Perfect," I answered.

We spent the next hour or so exploring the Cast Courts, the Medieval and Renaissance Galleries, and while not particularly a fan of religious stained-glass art, there was something moving about the art and artifacts on display. They left me feeling introspective, and filled with a sense of calm, not unlike those few moments during Solstice at Stonehenge. My heart was definitely telling me, *more of this, please.*

"I've lost you again," Arran commented as we exited the museum.

"Aww, sorry." I smiled, sheepishly. "I get lost in thought, sometimes."

"About me, I hope," he joked. "Sorry, that was self-serving."

"Well," I confessed. "There is one thing."

"Uh oh, here we go," he joked, before seeing my hesitation. "Wait," he continued. "I think I know."

"What? No. Stop," I laughed, punching him lightly in the arm. The mood threatened to get heavy all of a sudden.

"Correct me if I am wrong, Sibley Bloom," Arran paused for dramatic effect.

"Please tell me," I lowered my eyes and pursed my lips. "You're killing me."

"Not 100% sure what that expression means—" Arran gestured, "But, I suspect you're asking yourself, 'Is this guy for real, or is he only after the prize money?'"

"Admittedly, that thought had crossed my mind."

"Well then, let me enlighten you, Ms. Bloom," he circled his arm around my waist and pulled me toward him. Before I could panic or pull away, he gently kissed me … waited for my reaction (stunned), and then kissed me again. While I was recovering (After all, my only kisses in recent years were beer-laden ones from Thomas before he passed out on the couch.), he added, "There's a Third Sector charity I plan to donate the money to. It's a nonprofit that supports kids in foster care."

"Oh," was all I could think to say.

"And while I love the cause dearly, I like to think I have enough integrity not to use an innocent writer for my own personal aspirations."

The entire time, he never removed his hand from my waist, and we stood, belly to belly with me looking up at him, marveling.

"So." My brain struggled to connect the dots. "You like me?"

"Yes," He smiled that bright beautiful smile. "I most certainly do like you, Sibley Bloom."

He kissed me again. This time, I felt this weird fluttering in my belly. Can't recall the last time that happened.

When our lips finally parted, we walked hand-in-hand down the street.

"Time for one more adventure?" I asked.

"What did you have in mind?" He lifted a brow at me, quizzically.

"Never been to Harrods. Care to go?"

"Marvelous," Arran answered. "If your feet are up for a bit more walking, I can get us there."

"Lead the way," I answered. Though, I had to confess that my dogs were barking, and I'd need a good foot soak later.

Harrods proved to be everything that I am not … rich, pretentious, definitely out of my league.

"I've come to realize," I confessed to Arran as we hopped from floor to floor. "That the only things I can afford at Harrods are in the store's gift shop. Isn't that odd though? To have a gift shop in a department store that's all about buying gifts and such?"

"Aww, come now," Arran defended. "Look at this lovely fascinator." He walked over to a mannequin sporting a sequined dress and a bright red hat tilted to one side. He lifted the tag on the fascinator. "Only £2,900."

I nearly choked at the number. "And the dress?" I gasped.

He eyed the tag. "£4,400."

"Well, that's nearly $10,000 for one outfit. That still leaves $15,000 in prize money!"

"That's the spirit!" Arran laughed. "But seriously, you hungry? If so you have to see the Food Hall. We can grab a bite and find a quiet spot back at Hyde Park to eat."

I agreed, not thinking much of anything labeled "food hall"—until I witnessed it first hand. It was marvelous, filled with gourmet food stations complete with fresh meats, seafood, artisan cheeses, exotic ethnic dishes, and pastries. Imagine your local farmer's market, but replace it with decadent cuisine worthy of a king … Well, poor example, as I think everyone is worthy. But, you get my meaning—

We settled on two salmon cakes, fresh-baked bread, two sticky toffee treats and a Harrods-branded Pinot Grigio. Arran insisted on paying for all of it, and we took our spoils to the park. At our request, the salmon cakes were wrapped in foil, retaining their temperature. And, the wine counter was kind enough to provide two plastic, champagne-like flutes as takeaways.

"Here's to an amazing day with an amazing woman," Arran toasted, after pouring us each a fluteful of wine.

I toasted, cheerfully … sailing the Serpentine, a walk through Hyde Park, two museums, a trek through Harrods and a picnic dinner with the handsomest man I had ever had the fortune of dating … *jackpot*.

Arran walked me back to my hotel, and insisted on seeing me to my room. I suspect he was expecting an invitation inside, but that was a bit too bold a move for me, the new divorcee.

"Thank you, for an amazing day," I told him. This time, I leaned in to initiate a kiss. He accepted, wholeheartedly.

I was halfway into the kiss when I noticed Asher pausing at the end of the hallway. Apparently, he was arriving from … wherever the heck he went for the day. He would have had to either circumvent our public display of affection or wait.

It seems he chose to wait … oddly, at the end of the hall.

I broke free from Arran's kiss and embrace, thanking him, once again, for a lovely day. We agreed to meet again tomorrow. And that was that.

As Arran passed Asher in the hallway, he took a moment to nod in Asher's direction. "Hey, mate," he said. Asher nodded in return, but the exchange was … odd.

By the time Asher passed me, fumbling with the keycard to enter his room, I said, "Sorry about today. I would have let you know up front, but it was sorta last minute."

"Sibley," Asher turned to me (in what I perceived to be disappointment tinged with judgment), "You don't owe me any explanation. For the sake of the piece, it'd be nice to catch a few sights in London prior to the conference. Tomorrow, maybe?"

"Er," I stammered. "I sorta promised Arran we'd meet up again."

"Wow," Asher answered quietly. "Seems kinda serious."

"I don't know," I felt odd telling Asher this. I wasn't not sure why. "But he might be the one."

"Not just 'for the sake of the chronicle' but *the one*?" I felt disappointment from Asher. Or, the possibility that he didn't trust me, somehow.

"Obviously," I lightly kicked the bottom of the door of my room with the edge of my toe, nervously. "It's too soon to tell. But …maybe?" I bit my lip, unclear why Asher's opinion was one I held in such high regard.

"Well, okay." He answered simply. "The conference doesn't officially start for a few more days. I'm sure we can squeeze in a bit of time to capture a few iconic sights … Big Ben, St. Paul's Cathedral, etc."

"Absolutely," I promised with a yawn. "But I swear to you that I must have walked a good ten miles today, and if I don't rest my feet, there's going to be a rebellion."

"Okay," Asher put his hands up. "I get it. Go rest. I've got to get ready for a date tonight, anyway."

"A date?" I was surprised, though I should not have been. There was some lovely redhead he had been chatting up recently. "Never mind," I shook my head. "None of my business. Have fun."

"Oh, I intend to," Asher grinned as he opened the door to his hotel room. He paused when he saw my repulsed reaction. "Get your mind out of the gutter, Sibley. It's just a dinner."

"Whatever," I shrugged. "Good night."

I disappeared into my lovely hotel room, elated by my date with Arran, and deflated by the way things went down with Asher. Honestly, I'm not sure why it bothered me so much. I attributed it to a long day.

As I drew a bath, preparing my feet for a long soak, a message came in from Arran, "Loved seeing you today. Text me in the morning for another adventure?"

"Absolutely," I replied, adding in a heart emoji.

Finally, I thought. *My life is coming together.*

The next morning, I eagerly texted Arran … the same time as I did just yesterday.

And then … nothing.

No response.

Maybe he was sleeping in? I told myself. After all, it was quite a long day with lots of walking. And, maybe his work schedule was rigorous, and he's taking advantage of a few days off?

My stomach began to grumble. I summoned the courage to actually call his cell phone, holding my breath when the message was picked up … it went to voicemail. And not the voicemail that leaves a warm-fuzzy message for the caller. No, this one recited back the number and beeped. That was the kind of "out of office" message that told callers that they weren't interested in talking to you … in anyone, really. And that you should understand what an imposition it was, having to listen and return your call.

Or, perhaps I was overthinking it.

I decided to wander to the main dining room, where the hotel laid out a full spread buffet breakfast with everything you could imagine, including a few European favorites less common in the U.S.: blood pudding, Scottish smoked salmon, smoked herring, haggis and baked beans.

I settled on a small plate of eggs, salmon, roasted tomatoes and two slices of melon, coupled with a cup of Earl Grey tea, and sought a corner of the room where I could eat, and wallow, in peace.

"Hey! Hey!" I heard Yolanda's voice. A glance in her direction told me that she wasn't alone … she was having breakfast with Asher. "Come, join us, lady!"

Reluctantly, I sat across from them at a small table set for four.

Asher didn't waste any time.

"No Arran?" he asked.

"No."

Yolanda raised an eyebrow. "What am I missing?" She leaned over to whisper in my ear. "Did he stay over last night?"

"What? No!" I whispered back. "It's just that we were supposed to hang out today, but he's not answering his phone."

"Again," Asher noted for Yolanda's benefit. "They spent yesterday together, and he was meant to return today."

"Wow," Yolanda's eyes lit up. "See what I miss when I'm out for the day visiting family?"

My phone beeped. I pulled it from my purse, eagerly, before my shoulders dropped, deflated. Not Arran. Just Thomas asking if I'd consider giving him a second chance … followed by another from my phone service, reminding me that I was saving roaming fees thanks to my international plan. I put my phone away.

"Not him?" Yolanda asked, sympathetically, taking a bite of haggis. I tried my best not to cringe. I had sampled haggis once … never again.

"No," I sighed.

Asher took a sip of his coffee before perking up. "Well, you can always hang with us for the day. Yolanda knows her way around the city better than any of us, and I can get the shots I need for a full spread."

"Can't you just buy stock images of the major sights?" I blurted out. "Photoshop me in front of a couple of them. Look!" I held an arm up and pointed. "There's Winston Churchill's statue!"

Asher was visibly aghast. He was old-school. He avoided stock images as much as possible. Even his edits were minimalist in nature. I think that's why people resonated with the magazine and his work so much … his work was authentic and raw.

"It feels as if your anger is misplaced," Asher answered gently. "Spend the day with us, and I promise, if Arran calls, you can ditch us in a moment's notice."

Yolanda nodded in agreement.

So it was settled. Since we had plans to visit the London Eye with one of my final "dates," we avoided the Tower of London, St. Paul's Cathedral, and a few other spots, in favor of the Greater London Borough of Westminster: Westminster Abbey, Parliament Square, Big Ben and Buckingham Palace … and yes, I did get a photo with Churchill. And Asher nearly got himself run over, as a result, darting in and around traffic with wild abandon.

"You're going to get yourself killed!" Yolanda warned him.

"The dangers of being a hard-hitting photojournalist," Asher caught his breath after jogging over to us from his previous perch, mid-traffic.

"You're not a hard-hitting photojournalist, Asher," I reminded him. "You work for the third best-selling metaphysical journal in the country … and I'm not sure that's saying much."

Asher peered down at me, briefly. "You're not as much fun when you're cranky," he observed.

My face flushed. I knew I was being unfair, but this was a new feeling for me. Sure, I was used to Thomas betraying me, but never a date, not like this.

"Where to now?" I asked.

"Piccadilly Circus," Yolanda wiggled her eyes. "It'll be fun."

The West End was bustling, with tourists and locals alike flocking to the Eros statue like seagulls looking for a respite after stormy weather. We snuck in for a few shots of Yolanda and I pretending to be struck by Eros' arrow, before meandering through the streets of Soho.

Not surprising to any of us, it began to rain. Asher darted under the awning of a vape shop to protect his gear, packing it away in a water-resistant camera bag. Meanwhile, Yolanda and I walked arm in arm, faces toward the sky, smiling through the rain.

Yolanda had a way of brightening moments easily. Everything was joyful to her. *Note to self: Be more like Yolanda.*

Asher's face brightened when he saw us, but was wise enough to note my abrupt mood change with caution.

"Trafalgar?" he asked our tour guide for the day.

"Nah," Yolanda shook her head. "The square is filled with protestors. Best to steer clear."

"What are they protesting?" Asher asked.

"Not sure, if I'm honest," Yolanda answered. "Seemed a bit rowdy though."

Within minutes, the rain died down and the sun began to peek through the clouds. I shivered. Maybe a dance in the rain during the winter months was not the best idea?

"What's this?" Asher stumbled upon a sign. "Frameless."

"Ooh," Yolanda's eyes grew wide. "I've heard about this. It's an immersive art display with four different galleries. It's supposed to be fab. Wanna see if we can get tickets?"

"Got 'em," I announced, quickly pulling the website up on my phone. "Three flex tickets. Shall I buy them?"

"Why not?" Yolanda nodded. "Even if Reed doesn't reimburse us as a business expense, it'll still be fun."

We three entered the dimly lit hall, promptly being greeted by an attendant. I flashed my phone at him so he could scan us in.

"Which one?" I scanned the two exhibits on each side.

"Eenie, meenie, miney … this one!" Yolanda grabbed my arm and tugged me along after her. Asher followed suit.

As we entered the room, my eyes lit up. From ceiling to floor and wall to wall, we were greeted with Monet's Waterlily Pond … no, we were at the center of it. And as I stepped forward, I noticed something miraculous … the picture moved. I waved my hands in the air and watched as the fragments of the painting danced with me. I watched as others chased color up the walls.

After a time, the scene changed. This time, we were dancing along with Morisot at The Garden at Bougival. Asher, not wanting his camera to be a distraction, reached for his cell phone instead, covertly capturing a few pictures and one silly video (to be later discovered) of we two women joyously dancing around the room like children.

Later, back in my hotel room, I sent a video call to Vidalia, who picked up on the first ring.

"Hey, babes," she answered. I could hear a shuffling in the background. "Everything okay?"

"Oh, shit!" I somehow forgot about the time difference. "You're at work. Geez, I'm sorry."

"No worries. Give me just a sec," I heard her call out to someone, "Jill, can you cover for me for five minutes? I gotta take this!" It sounded as if the woman agreed and I heard the sound of a door opening and slamming behind her, followed by some unusually loud cicadas in the night. "Okay, I'm back."

"I need your dating advice … as a person who understands psychology."

"Okay, first of all, I'm shocked. Second, how can I help?"

"Abridged version? I went on what I thought was a fabulous date. We met at Stonehenge—"

"How romantic!" Vidalia interjected.

"I know, right? Well anyway, we decided to meet up again the next day to tour London … food, museums, boating in Hyde Park, etc."

"Sounds great so far." Vidalia was cautious.

"Yes! And he was affectionate, gave me compliments. We chatted lots, and at the end of the night, he gave me a kiss before dropping me at my hotel room."

"He walked you all the way up to your room?" Vidalia asked.

"Yeah, is that bad?"

"Well, not necessarily, but I suspect he didn't want the date to end there."

"Probably not, but we had plans to meet today and—"

"He ghosted you," Vidalia stated.

"How did you know that?" I demanded. "I texted and called him before Yolanda and Asher saved me from myself by dragging me to Soho for the day."

"Well," Vidalia was cautious. "While it is possible that he had some emergency come up, his behavior is suspect."

"Suspect how?" I felt deflated.

"Love bombing, making you feel like the most important person in the world and then ghosting you?"

I cringed as I whispered into the phone, "Do you think he dumped me because I didn't invite him in for the night?"

"No," Vidalia was adamant. "I promise you, this would have happened either way." On the other end, I could hear a crowd of loud and likely inebriated people cackling in the background. "Listen, I've got to get back, but I want you to remember one thing for me, okay?"

"Sure."

"The love-bombing ghosters often come back, floating in and out of your world at their convenience. Be careful."

"I will, thanks, Vidalia."

"Sure thing, babes."

I hung up the phone filled with a new resolve. If I saw Arran at the conference (and it was likely that I would), I would be polite, but not fall for any more of his advances.

Before settling in with a good book for the night, I sent Asher and Yolanda a group text. "Hey guys, thanks for looking out for me today—despite my crankiness. I appreciate you guys."

As I was silencing my phone for the evening, Yolanda sent through a bear-hugging-a-heart emoji. Asher sent a simple message, "We appreciate you too. Get some rest."

CHAPTER EIGHTEEN
SEEING THINGS
VIDALIA—DECEMBER

I t had now been two months since I heard from Tod, and the knee-jerk reactions began to subside—every time I thought I caught a glimpse of him in his stupid red baseball cap when visiting the Home Depot, or in the corner of my eye when I walked down to the lobby to collect the mail. Periodically, Detective Jameson phoned to check on me, which I appreciated. And, if I didn't know any better, those phone calls seemed to get a little longer each time—always a few extra minutes of banter that had nothing to do with the investigation.

More news had come to light. The remains discovered underneath the oak tree were a match to the corpse found on the roof—meaning they all added up to Nadia Perdita. "I shouldn't be telling you this," Jameson confessed on the phone, "because, well—"

"You haven't ruled me out as a suspect," I finished, climbing into Sibley's car. I sold my truck because it was too conspicuous and used the extra money on rent. Sibley was good enough to let me borrow her car while she was away. I fumbled with the car keys, my purse, and the cell phone pressed against my ear.

"Strictly speaking … no—" he confessed on the other end of the line.

"Are you at least allowed to tell me how the heck her body ended up on the roof?" I shivered at the thought.

"From what we can tell, the body was in a shallow grave. Along with hurricanes, we get the random tornado. It's my suspicion that the body got dragged onto the roof during the storm."

"Hence the noise I heard that night," I concurred. "I remember a scratching on the roof the night before she was found … or at least, when part of her was found."

"I know Tod's connection with his ex. But did you have any interactions with Ms. Perdita?" he asked cautiously.

"Me?" I answered. "None."

At that moment, I wasn't sure who would look more incriminating, Tod or me. "She was his ex-wife. You know that of course."

Detective Jameson cleared his throat. "Indeed. Uh … this may warrant an in-person conversation. Any chance you can stop by the station?"

"Now?" I grew anxious. Money was tight as it is; I couldn't afford to lose more, particularly not on one of my busiest nights. "I'm just about to head into work."

"At 4:44 p.m.?" Jameson caught himself. "That's right," he remembered. "You work a lot of night shifts."

"Exactly," I answered, starting up the car. "And to be honest, I can't afford to lose the time. Any chance you could meet me there? I promise I'll answer any questions you may have."

"Okay," he agreed. "Be there soon."

"Wait," I stopped him. "I didn't tell you where I work."

"The Bar Fly," he answered.

"How did you—" I was surprised.

"I'm really good at my job." I could feel him smirk across the phone line.

I arrived at work during the slowest part of the evening, but I knew it wouldn't stay that way for long. In hindsight, I probably should have given the detective some guidance about what time to stop in, but then I really didn't want to inconvenience him too much—not while it seemed he was still on my side. I knew I was innocent, but I could see how that might look fuzzy from an outside perspective.

To my surprise, someone else was waiting for me.

"Phoebe?" I could tell something was wrong. She generally approached life calmly, with a quietly fierce presence. Today her mascara was runny, and I could tell she had been crying. She was at a corner pub table nursing a beer. "What's going on? Are you okay?" I touched her shoulder.

"I'm not sure," she answered sadly.

"What happened?" I half sat on the stool opposite her. I still had a few minutes before my shift started.

"It's Amir!" She sobbed.

"Oh no!" My mind whirled. "Is he okay? Is he ill?" Then I saw the scowl across her face. "He didn't—"

"No," Phoebe shook her head. "I know what you're thinking. No, he has not been unfaithful and none of those 'affairs of the heart' I hear you talking about either."

"Then what is it?" I asked gently.

"It's just … the spark is fading," she cried.

"What? No! I saw you guys in here recently, role-playing. You appeared smitten with each other."

"Oh, not the sexual spark," she admitted. "That part is business as usual. It's just that we are bickering more and more. We've become very critical of one another. And the other night, I heard him complaining about me to his mother."

"No!" I gasped. I may not be the expert on relationships, given my own checkered past, but I knew enough to recognize that you don't take marital problems to the family (aside from abuse cases and all). You certainly don't talk smack about your wife to your mother.

"Yes," she nodded. "I got mad, then he got defensive. And somehow, everything that I have ever done to bother him over the past twenty years got thrown in my face."

"Oh no," I touched her arm. "That sounds awful. What will you do?"

"I don't know." Phoebe wiped her face with the back of her palm. "That's why I came to you!"

"You came to—" I was shocked. After years of friends reminding me that I was not a therapist and had no qualifications, this was the second friend to seek out my advice.

"Well," I answered softly. "One thing I do know is that it's best to keep the conversation between the two of you—unless you both agree to see a therapist or a relationship counselor of some kind."

"Tell that to Amir," she whined, just as her eyes grew wide.

"You can tell it to me yourself." Amir appeared, seemingly out of nowhere. His face seemed just as tear-stained. "But I already know it. I'm so sorry, my love."

Phoebe stood and the two embraced. Meanwhile, I could see the bar back tapping her watch, impatiently in a message that said, *I can't cover for you all night, you know.*

"Listen," I told them. "I've gotta go, but I have a book to recommend by John Gottman. I'll email it to you later. But for now, I have one suggestion for you."

"What's that?" Amir was curious.

"When working through the hard stuff, remember to spend some time focusing on the good. Try noticing when the other one does something right, not wrong. Call it out. Thank them for it. It'll help!" By then, I was yelling from across the bar.

Others might have gotten embarrassed, now that the bar was beginning to fill up. But not them. They were already holding hands and sitting, gazing into each other's eyes.

"They'll be okay," I whispered, but asked the bar back to drop off a beer for Amir, and some cocktail peanuts—on the house.

I smiled as I went to work. I could count on one hand how many times Phoebe and Amir were on the outs over the years, but they were committed to one another, and they always worked it out.

"You seem happy," a voice called. I looked up to see Detective Jameson at the bar.

That's when I saw him—a glimpse of Tod in one of the bar's security mirrors. I glanced around the room like a lost puppy, the panic in me rising.

"What is it?" Jameson was concerned.

"I thought I saw Tod," I gasped.

"Where?" He stood.

But then, nothing. He was nowhere.

"It must have been in my head," I confessed, embarrassed.

Jameson wasn't convinced. He slid off the pub chair. "Be right back."

"Can I get some help over here?" an annoyed young man called. "Sorry if I'm, ya know, making you do your job and all."

He looked to be about eighteen. Beside him were two of his buddies. Seemed they started their weekend early, as they all seemed a bit tipsy.

"You got some ID to go with that attitude?" I asked.

"You gotta be kidding me?" He was incredulous. "I'm old enough, you old hag."

That hurt. I thought I looked rather well—no, not for my age—just in general. I certainly took better care of myself than this pimple-faced patron seemed to.

"The lady asked for your ID." Detective Jameson returned to his stool. Behind him, I could see two officers scanning the premises. They were in uniform, while Jameson was dressed in jeans with a white dress shirt.

"What's it to you, old man?" he laughed.

"That your truck out front? The one with a broken taillight and expired tags?"

"No?" he asked, in a way that suggested it was damn well his truck and he damn well knew the tags were expired. "You a cop?" The patron stopped laughing.

"As a matter of fact—" Jameson pulled out his ID. "Now, I'm willing to let you go with a warning provided you apologize to the lady before you go."

"Sorry," he said under his breath. "Let's go, guys. This bar is a dump anyway."

"Well, he got that right," I laughed. "Get you something to drink?" I asked the detective.

"Club soda would be fine," Jameson answered.

"Oh, right," I understood. "'Cause you're on duty and all."

"Nah," he answered. "I just don't drink, generally."

I fetched him a club soda and offered a wedge of lime on the side. "Don't think I've ever had anyone defend my honor before," I grinned.

"Well, somebody had to set those punks straight," Jameson laughed.

"So, what'd you wanna ask me?" I asked. "Now's the best time before it gets too busy."

"All right," Jameson agreed. "I'll cut to the chase … Did you have any interaction with Nadia in the time approaching her death?"

"Well, first of all," I leaned my arms on the counter, meeting him eye-to-eye. "I don't know when she died—you didn't tell me. And second—no. She and Tod were over long before I came on the scene."

"Any reason you or he might benefit from her death?"

"Wow, Jameson," I answered. "You don't waste any time, do you?" I caught myself. "Sorry, Detective Jameson. I didn't mean to address you by your last name." My face flushed, and I grew increasingly flustered. I'm not prone to mistakes like that.

"No, I like it." His eyes lit up. "Call me Jameson from now on." He paused to sip his club soda. "But I have to ask … you understand."

"Yeah, I get it," I answered. "The only thing I can say for certain is that Tod and Nadia went halfsies on the house even before they got married. A good bit of my salary I gave to Tod in the hopes that we could buy her out of her half. That's why I'm so damn broke now."

"I see," he answered simply. "And just how long were you paying into the house before this happened?"

My face burned. "Five months," I confessed. "Plus, I gave Tod about $13,000 I had in savings."

"I wonder who stood to inherit if anything happened to her?" Jameson said aloud. I knew he wasn't directing it at me, but it certainly felt that way.

"You'd have to ask Tod that. For some stupid reason, I trusted him to put my money to good use. He kept saying, 'The house will be ours soon. Don't worry.'"

"Were you?" Jameson paused for dramatic effect.

"Were I, what?" I was confused.

"Worried?"

"Oh, hell no," I confessed. "I may not be the best judge of character when it comes to my personal life, but at least I like to think I wised up quick."

"How so?"

"It didn't take me long to figure out that Tod and I weren't going to work out in the long term. It just never occurred to me that I had something to fear in him."

"And now you do?" Jameson pressed.

"You can stop with the bullshit psychotherapy," I crabbed at him. Immediately, I regretted it. "Sorry, but when a dead body ends up on the roof, and a dug-up bone in the yard, it gives one cause to pause."

Just then, a uniformed officer approached Jameson. "No sign of him, sir," they confirmed.

"Guess it was just my imagination." I felt stupid.

"Just to be on the safe side, I'll stop back when your shift is over to escort you home," Jameson offered.

I was surprised. "With all due respect … er … Jameson, but my shift doesn't end until the last call. You could be waiting until around 2 a.m. I feel that someone of your importance would have better things to do with his time."

"I can't think of a single thing," he smiled, standing. "I'll be back at 1 a.m. to check in and make sure you get home safe."

He left before I could protest.

I stood aghast, thinking: *Well, aren't you just my knight in shining armor?*

Jameson waited just inside the door while I closed up. Some of our particularly clingy patrons lingered as long as they could. I gently reminded them that we'd open back up at 11 a.m. and ensured they each had an Uber or some other form of transportation that didn't involve them driving. It was nearly 1:20 a.m. before we were finally able to leave.

Jameson watched as I surveyed my surroundings, including peering under and around the car, as well as in the back seat, before climbing in.

"Sorry," I apologized. "I'm a bit paranoid."

"Nothing paranoid about it," Jameson replied. "I wish more people had that level of caution when out alone." He gestured over his shoulder with his thumb. "I'll, uh, follow behind in my vehicle."

I nodded, starting up the engine. Sibley's car was way more efficient than mine … in better shape too. Another reminder of what might have been had I not given everything I had to Tod. What was I thinking? We weren't even together that long, and somehow I bought into a dream that seems outright ludicrous now.

I pulled into the parking area of the complex Sibley and I lived. Jameson pulled in beside me.

"I'll just make sure you get in safe," he said, following me as I opted for the stairs to climb several flights to our floor.

"You okay with the stairs?" I asked. "Unless you prefer the elevator?"

"Stairs are fine." He huffed a little. "Could probably stand to climb them a bit more often, if I'm honest."

He seemed a little winded when we'd reached the apartment. "I can wait here while you look around to make sure everything is copacetic … unless you prefer me to go in first and look for you?"

"Nah," I shook my head. "That might be overkill … no pun intended. I'll give a quick sweep."

I appreciated his attention to my safety, and that he was considerate enough to wait outside. *That shows a healthy respect for boundaries*, I thought to myself.

"All clear," I told him. The only other presence was Skinny, who was jumping all over me as if I'd been gone for years, not hours. After I was fully slobbered upon, he turned his attention to Jameson.

"All right, well, just lock up behind me." He paused to laugh, leaning over with both hands to rub Skinny on his sides. Skinny was ecstatic, balancing on hind legs in an attempt to lick the detective's face. "And let me know if you see anything suspicious or hear from Tod again." He put his palm out, and Skinny actually settled.

Huh? I thought. *That damn dog never listens to me but seemed to respond to male authority.*

"Will do," I answered, turning my attention away from Skinny. "But, er, Jameson?"

"Yes?"

"You never did tell me when she died … or how, for that matter."

"Nadia?" Jameson scratched his head. I could almost see the wheels turning in his head as he weighed how much to tell me. Finally, he answered: "About three months ago."

My stomach began to turn, and I could feel the color draining from my face.

"Ms. Oliveira, are you okay?" Jameson put out a hand to steady me.

"So, she was near the house after I had moved in?" I gasped. "How did she … How did she—"

"Most we can tell is that she fell from a great height, causing internal organ damage and broken bones. She has a head injury, so she was either struck by something or hit her head during the fall."

I sucked in my breath. "But you don't really suspect me … or else you wouldn't go to such pains to ensure my safety." It was less a question and more a confirmation.

The pause was almost unbearable, but Jameson finally cracked. "No," he shook his head. "By all accounts you called the roofers because of storm damage with no apparent knowledge of a body being there. Then you alerted us to the remains under the tree. You've been cooperating fully in this inquiry and, save for your former address, there's nothing tying you to this."

"But Tod—"

"Let's just say, it fits his MO from past offenses. His disappearing act doesn't help."

"Past offenses?" I was aghast. "What past offenses?"

"Can't go into it with you, Ms. Oli—"

"Vidalia," I interjected. "You can call me Vidalia."

"Okay, Vidalia—"

A slight chill ran through me when he said my name. *Silly woman*, I chastised myself.

Jameson continued: "I've already shared more than I should have, and I'll kindly ask you to keep what I've told you to yourself. But the long and short of it is, I have no reason to suspect you of any crime … other than your questionable taste in men."

"Hey, now!" I chastised. "That was mean! It might be true, but still mean!"

"Sorry." He backed down, taking a long pause before adding, "Maybe next time, you'll make a better choice. Good evening, Vidalia."

My head was spinning when he left. *What other offenses?* It seemed I knew even less about Tod than I thought. And why was his ex-wife at the house? Why didn't he tell me?

I knelt on the couch, drawing back the curtains to peer at the street below. I watched as Jameson's vehicle pulled out into the street and gazed as he slowly faded into the distance. Something in the distance caught my eye. It was coming from the bank building. There, on the balcony, I could have sworn I saw movement … possibly someone all dressed in black. For a moment, I thought they were looking back at me, but now they were gone.

I shuddered, let the curtain fall back, shielding the room from prying eyes.

CHAPTER NINETEEN

THE INTERNATIONAL HOLISTIC CONFERENCE (DAY ONE)

SIBLEY

"No need to panic," Yolanda assured me when we arrived at the International Holistic Conference the first day. Today was primarily about registration, with only a handful of scheduled events planned for this first afternoon to welcome everyone and kick things off. It was to be followed by an optional mixer that evening. "You're under no obligation to spend any more time with each of your fellas aside from those initial dates. However, if you choose to sign up for some of the same breakout sessions and get to know each other better, well, that's up to you."

"That's not what I'm worried about," I explained. "Is it weird to be wigged out about randomly running into not one but three past dates—not to mention this Jack fellow, who I haven't met yet?"

At that moment, I caught a glimpse of someone talking to a group of men in the corner of the reception room … laughing. It was Arran. For a moment, I thought he spotted me, but then he followed them into the large auditorium adjacent to the reception.

"No." Yolanda placed a supportive hand on my shoulder. "It's not weird at all. And I can understand why this might make you uncomfortable. But relax, this place is huge. What are the chances of you accidentally running into—"

"Sibley," a quiet voice called from behind me. I jumped.

"Sorry," Shaman Theodore said. "I didn't mean to startle you."

I almost didn't recognize him outside of his Día de los Muertos garb. Today he wore an unusual black jacket with floral embroidery and a turquoise bolo tie, black jeans, and leather cowboy boots.

"It's okay, nice to see you again," I offered, before adding, "and this is my friend and colleague from *Positive Enlightenment Journal,* Yolanda Jennings."

"Oh, nice to meet you." He put a hand out and shook hers awkwardly before pulling her in for an uncomfortable bro hug—half hug, half slap on the back.

"Likewise." She shot a grin in my direction.

He then moved on to me, offering a bearlike embrace reminiscent of old friends … except we weren't. Today he smelled like sandalwood mixed with some sort of fabric freshener. It tickled my nose. When I finally pulled away, he asked, "Could we talk—" he glanced at Yolanda —"privately, for a moment?"

Yolanda shot me a *sure you're okay with this?* look.

"Of course," I answered. To Yolanda, I said, "I'll join you in the auditorium in a few minutes."

"Right." Yolanda nodded, disappearing faster than the Green Flash across a Gulf Coast sunset.

Shaman Theodore motioned toward the front door. "Perhaps we can chat outside. There's a nice park bench just out front."

I followed him outdoors, filled with a mix of curiosity and concern. We sat on a bench—me with my knees tucked and ankles crossed. Meanwhile, he sat, his right knee bobbing up and down nervously.

"First," he said, "I wanted to apologize for the overabundance of text messages. I admit I can get a bit carried away when I am enamored with someone. And you, Ms. Bloom, are very charming."

I blushed a little. "Well, thanks for that." I could feel myself pursing my lips and rotating them around in an unattractive fashion, but I couldn't help it. I wanted to hide my face but couldn't. "I didn't mind so much," I fibbed a little. "I just couldn't respond as much as I'm on assignment … and I have to give consideration to all of my blind dates."

He held his hands up. "I totally get that. I also felt so stupid for asking you not to mention I was … er, am … an insurance rep. Like it would kill the façade or something of me being some great shaman. That was my ego."

While I wasn't initially particularly fond of Theo, I found his honesty refreshing. Maybe I hadn't given him enough of a chance? "Well, for what it's worth, I had a great shamanic experience with you, and wrote as much."

"Oh, I read it." He reached into his jacket and pulled out two pieces of paper and unfolded them. "I printed it out. I loved when you wrote —" He eyed the crumpled paper that presumably contained a copy of my article. "'Shamanic journeying taught me ways to tap into my subconscious mind and explore the possibility of animal spirits and guidance from other realms. I will always be grateful to Shaman Theodore for introducing the Lower World Journey to me.'"

He folded it back up and tucked it into a pocket on the inside of his jacket.

"I appreciate the feedback. If we had more time, we could have tried an Upper World journey too." I laughed. He was fawning over me in a way that was flattering but uncomfortable. Somehow, when Arran complimented me, it didn't feel … creepy. Or maybe I was being too critical.

"More time." Theo jumped on those words in particular. "That's exactly what I was thinking. We need more time to get to know one another better." He reached back into his outer pockets and frowned, tapping them as if he'd lost something, before he remembered and reached back into his jacket pocket, this time choosing the one on the opposite side. Theo produced a small piece of paper. "I've made a list of seminars and workshops we could attend together: a Reiki Healing Circle, a Food Is Medicine kitchari class, there's a lecture on the spiritual shift happening in the world today, and—"

"Wow." I glanced over his shoulder. "You've got a lot picked out for us."

"Well, you can pick some too. What are you attending? Maybe we can sync our schedules."

Alarm bells were beginning to sound in my head.

"I tell you what," I answered cautiously. "I haven't even had a chance to review the agenda for this event yet. When's the kitchari class?"

"Eh … tomorrow morning at 8:30 a.m.," he answered.

"Okay, well, let's commit to that one, and I'll review all the breakout sessions and whatnot tonight to see what else I'll be attending. I have to check in with my colleagues as well—"

"Of course, of course." He touched my knee. "I'm open to whatever you're doing. Just let me know."

"Shaman Theodore—" I began.

"Theo," he encouraged.

"Theo," I tried again. "As I mentioned—"

"I know, I know … sorry." He slid a foot away from me on the bench. "I'll give you some space. I know you have other things to do and people to see."

"But it was good seeing you again." I tried to soften the blow. "And this Food as Medicine class looks fun!"

His eyes brightened a little as we returned to the convention center. It was nearing the official welcome message from the host of this event, luxury spa franchisor and business owner Jack Vex.

Yolanda and Asher flagged me down as soon as I entered the room. As I headed down the aisle to meet them at their seats, Theo thought to follow me … and then thought better of it, motioning that he'd sit across the aisle. We were in some VIP section near the front of the stage.

"Everything okay?" Yolanda asked, as I took my seat.

"To be determined," I answered. Before she could question me, another voice crept over my shoulder, startling me for the second time today.

"Ya know, it's usually considered polite when someone sends you a text message, that you message them back." I spun around to see Bodhi, my Giving Thanks date, sitting right behind me. I could swear he was wearing the same earthy burlap-sack of a shirt and pants, a mala bead necklace, and to make today more formal (I guess?), he had a yin-yang beard clip clasped to his goatee like a ponytail for men. His eyes darkened in anger for a split second before his expression broke, replaced by that same smug smile I remembered from Thanksgiving. "I'm just funnin'." He waved a hand at me and chuckled. Then he added, "But seriously, did you get my texts?"

"I did," I confessed. "I thought I responded?"

"You did, to a couple of them … not all," He accused me.

"Must be our international phone plan," Asher chimed in. "I know I've been missing a bunch of texts, and then they all flood in a week later, all at once."

I eyed Asher, gratefully. "Well, in either case, I'm sorry if I missed some." Inside I was thinking, *Is there a specific rule about text messages … or any message, for that matter? There seem to be a lot of expectations and obligations around this annoying little facet of dating.* "Been working too, so it's been hard keeping up."

"No worries." Bodhi leaned his arms on the back of my chair and spoke over my shoulder—a little too close for comfort. "I forgive you." Then he dropped back in his chair, stretching his legs out in front of him like a rebellious child who has just been told he had a detention. A moment later, he was back in my ear. "You going to the mixer later? They've got vegan hors d'oeuvres and raw kombucha. I already checked."

I couldn't recall any moment in my life where I'd think to ask if kombucha was on the menu before agreeing to attend. "I'm not sure, honestly," I answered. "Depends on what the team is doing." I eyed Asher and Yolanda.

Yolanda picked up on my cue. "Nah, Sibley. You promised to have dinner at my mum's tonight. She's dying to meet you."

"Oh, yes. That's right." I nodded.

"Whatever." Bodhi shrugged. "I'm goin' anyway. Why wouldn't I? It's free, right?"

"Greetings, everyone!" A loud voice chimed over the speakers.

A tall woman with perfectly straightened blonde hair and equally perfect white teeth stood on the stage, her slender frame seeming to disappear every time she turned her torso. She wore a lavender suit with a bold pink shirt. On her earlobes, one simple studded pearl each. Her fingernails were long, pink with white tips.

See? I thought to myself. *That's exactly the kind of woman I would have expected Reed to have picked for this little assignment. Polished, professional, and ridiculously pretty.*

"We are so honored that you've decided to join us for the 4th annual International Holistic Conference!" Her smile beamed. A round of applause ensued. "Yeah, that's what I'm talking about. Woo!" She threw her arm up like a cheerleader and the applause grew louder.

As I glanced around the room, I saw him … Arran. He appeared to be sitting with a group of men in the far corner. Apparently, he saw me too. As he caught my eye, I quickly turned my attention back to the woman on the stage.

I must have missed a few things the pretty woman said, because the next thing I heard was, "Please give it up for the man of the hour, the only person with the charisma, energy, and vision to bring this event together for us, and the reason we're all here … Jack Vex!"

The crowd stood as he sauntered on stage, so we followed suit. After the cheers and applause died down, he spoke.

"Thank you for joining me on such a special occasion. I should be applauding you! Your dedication to holistic—or as I like to say, wholistic

—living is helping create a new paradigm for how the world views science and spirituality, Eastern and Western medicine, pushing the boundaries of what we think we know about personal transformation and the universe's answers to all of life's questions."

As I surveyed the room, people were nodding eagerly. Jack had their undivided attention—even Bodhi, who could be heard saying, "Here, here," and whistling behind me. Jack was an imposing figure, tall with dark brown wavy hair, not a one out of place, teeth as white as the lady who spoke before him, chiseled jaw, and broad shoulders that spoke of time at the gym that Reed would envy. His energy was a mix of pumped-up motivational speaker blended with wellness guru and a sprinkle of something else … shrewd businessman?

More like ruthless. Not sure where that thought came from, so I silenced it. There was something else that was bothering me, but I couldn't quite figure it out. I flipped through the syllabus for today's event—something I realized, in hindsight, I should have done last night, had I not been busy feeling brokenhearted. I read Jack Vex's bio … he franchised more than a dozen luxury spas all over Europe with his take on "wholistic wellbeing" and made a fortune from it. I suspect he was a large sponsor for my foray into dating. Otherwise, why would all my dates be meeting here for the conference? No doubt Krystal and Bertram hit up some of the other sponsors listed on the back of my agenda.

He pressed on. "When I opened my first spa in Milan nearly twenty years ago, I never dreamed how successful it would become. Before then, I was working as a personal trainer, earning little more than £34,000 a year and living in a dingy studio apartment on the edge of Croydon. But now—" Jack Vex paused for applause. He threw his arms out as if imitating Jesus on the cross and tipped his head as if bowing … or sacrificing himself for the audience? I didn't get the gesture. When the noise died down, he continued. "Now I oversee a four-billion-dollar operation!" He turned his palms upward and his face toward heaven.

I turned to whisper to Asher, "Are we supposed to be impressed that he has lots of money?"

Asher whispered back, "Just wait for it … Wait for the … 'I did this all for you' part."

"But it's not about me running an empire." He clutched the microphone tightly to his chest before raising it to his lips. "It's about how I got there," he continued. "It was by cutting through self-sabotaging thoughts that told me, 'This is impossible,' and harnessing my inner power to manifest the best possible reality."

"Here it comes—" Asher whispered.

"I did it for you." Jack wiped a tear from the corner of his eye. "I learned the secret to co-creating my dreams with the universe, so that I could bring this knowledge to you."

He paused again for the never-ending applause.

Where have I heard this before? I wondered.

I eyed Yolanda, furrowing my brows and pointing toward the stage, mouthing the words, *familiar, right?*

Yolanda whipped out her phone and typed into the keypad. Moments later, my cell phone buzzed with the message, "Five years ago. LIA. Remember?"

I shrugged for a moment before it sank in. *Oh! Yes.* I nodded to Yolanda, remembering. Silly me. It was *my* article. I had interviewed some spiritual guru who said his new earthly name was "Love in Action." He used almost the exact same words about co-creating dreams with the universe. A second aha hit me. I replayed his earlier mention about "pushing the boundaries of what we think we know about creation …"

Holy hell, I thought to myself. *He's quoting me!*

That was a separate article I wrote some twelve years ago on the merging of scientific thought with religion … that both could be right, and it didn't need to be either-or. And it was relatively odd news back when I wrote it. So why was he repurposing my words now?

A final applause erupted as he concluded his speech … something about his inspiration behind the holistic fair. I felt bad admitting this, even to myself (given that this is my line of work), but all of it felt a little … orchestrated.

Ah well, I thought. After this weekend, I could write my article, choose someone as my Valentine's date, and—with any luck—end it quietly, with a mutual understanding. Sadly, with Arran out of the running, that left Bodhi, Theo, and—

"Hi!"

I jumped, not expecting the pretty blonde woman who had just been on stage to be right in front of me, with her face a bit too close for comfort. I inched my head back slightly. She didn't seem to notice.

"I'm Harper," she beamed, eyeing the three of us. "You must be Sibley!"

"Sibley," Yolanda intervened. "Harper is the one instrumental in getting the International Holistic Conference to sponsor our feature series. Without her, it might never have been a go."

Aha, I thought. *So it's her I need to blame!*

I offered my hand, cordially, but she steamrolled past me. I quickly withdrew it.

"We are super excited you decided to hold your little event here!" She gushed. "It's like a gender reveal … er … except with dating!"

I failed to see the connection.

"Anyway, we're hoping you'll give us lots of coverage!"

I assumed she was talking about my chronicles.

Without waiting for a response, she continued. "So, you'll meet up with Jack tomorrow, late afternoon at the London Eye, after you sneak out of the Love Languages workshop." Harper winked at me.

I eyed Yolanda for confirmation, but she merely shrugged.

Harper caught the glance. "Oh, don't worry. We cleared it with Reed." She winked again. I was beginning to think something was caught in her eye.

"Then Sunday, fingers crossed—" she literally crossed her fingers, followed by making the sign of the cross, "you'll pick Jack as your Valentine's Day date."

"But I haven't even met him yet," I protested.

"Oh." She patted my hand. "I knooow. But just look at him!"

Harper motioned to Jack Vex, busy chatting up several older women who were asking for selfies.

"Wait." I sucked in a breath. "Jack Vex is my New Year's date?" Somehow, even after reading the itinerary, I didn't put two and two together.

"Well, of course he is." She was obviously taken aback. "Did no one tell you?"

I eyed Yolanda and Asher again, but both seemed about as lost as I was. It was as if Reed gave each of us little breadcrumbs of information —just to get us to do what he wanted, but never clearly outlined the entire assignment in a cohesive way. Do we need to compare itineraries and information to put the puzzle together? And does it even matter at this point?

Then I remembered something Asher told me from the outset: Krystal suggested keeping the "contestants" on a first-name basis so I wasn't tempted to internet stalk them before the event.

I sighed and resigned myself to the recognition that I was a pawn in whatever it was Reed had in mind when giving me this assignment. I could leave now, but I would be forfeiting what might actually turn out to be a pretty cool conference. More importantly, I could be out of a job if I didn't comply.

Harper got into a brief conversation with Asher and Yolanda, leaving me alone with my thoughts—

"Well, that sucks." Bodhi's voice was, once again, over my shoulder.

Once again, I jumped. "You really need to stop doing that," I chastised.

Bodhi merely leaned his arms on the back of Yolanda's chair, as she was standing at this point, laughing and exchanging pleasantries with Harper.

"I'll split it with you," he said simply.

"What are you talking about?" I demanded.

"The prize money, of course." He grinned. "Bet none of those other chumps would cut you in. Certainly not that guy." He gestured toward Jack Vex, still chatting up a group of women in the distance. "The rich get richer by not sharing."

"Hmm, for someone who claims to be so open-minded, that seemed quite opinionated."

"I just know people," Bodhi grumbled, sounding less and less like a peace-loving Buddhist the more I got to know him.

"I prefer to give people a chance," I answered simply, realizing that possibly came out sounding a bit more holier-than-thou than I had intended.

"Suit yourself," he answered, standing. "I just thought you were smarter than that," he whispered right in my ear. I could feel his breath on my neck. Part of his chest actually pressed up against the back of my shoulders and head. His closeness was not welcome.

I felt a strange shift in my very being. I've always been a people pleaser, and generally avoided confrontation like the plague. I'd be the one cracking jokes and making excuses for people ... until now.

"Stay away from me, Bodhi," I stated calmly.

I didn't have to turn around again to know that he was taken aback.

"Fine." He spoke calmly, but there was ire in his voice. He recovered quickly, returning to his smooth tone. "Let me know if you change your mind."

CHAPTER TWENTY

THE IVY

SIBLEY

"Thank you for giving me a chance to explain." Arran eyed me with a mild apprehensiveness that I hadn't seen in him before.

I paused while the waiter poured water into our glasses.

"Well, this ought to be good." The words leapt out of my mouth before I could stop them. Arran had cornered me at the entrance to the conference, earlier, begging for an audience so he could explain his abrupt disappearance.

Arran paused, mid–water sip, tipping his head to one side. "Suppose I deserved that," he answered.

The waiter presented us with menus. "Care for anything other than water?" he offered. "Our wine list, or something from the bar, perhaps?"

The bar was set behind us—or, from the outside looking in, we sat to the left of it. It was the original Ivy's centerpiece, making a long arc that divided the room into two sections. We sat at a table for two, Arran's back to the bar in an upright chair. I was in a long booth with couples on each side of me, with only a small gap between us. The room was noisy, yet still somehow intimate. It had the vibe of an upscale bistro from the 1920s, and it is rumored to cater to the upper crust and celebrities.

And yet, here we were. *Arran must be feeling really guilty*, I thought. This seemed a bit pricey for dinner on a social worker's salary. But what did I know?

"The wine list would be great," Arran answered, before checking with me, "unless you prefer something else?"

"Wine would be lovely." I flashed my most sincere smile toward our server.

The list appeared almost instantaneously. Either our server read us very well, or he was that efficient with the libations. He handed the list to Arran, who promptly handed it to me. "Would you like to choose a bottle for us to share?" he asked sincerely. "I'm good with whatever you pick."

That was a first—at least on a date. Not that I had been on many recently. Even in my younger years, before alcoholic beverages were an option, my dates always seemed to "know" what to order for me, and in Thomas's case, it was usually a low-fat something to not-so-subtly address the few extra pounds I'd put on since we'd been married.

I ignored my "jerk" response, which would have been to order the most ridiculously priced bottle on the menu. Instead, I settled on something I knew I could afford, should the date go south and I was stuck footing the bill.

"So, what was it—" I began.

"What looks good to you, on the menu?" he interjected.

Perhaps he was ensuring that I'd stay throughout the dinner if he secured wine and food first.

"I was thinking of trying this miso aubergine vegan dish," I answered.

"Really?" Arran was surprised, given the sausage rolls we ate together earlier in the week. "You're suddenly vegan now?"

"No," I answered. "But I was thinking about the experience sourcing and preparing a vegan meal during the Giving Thanks event I covered. I like the idea of eating healthier, leaving a lighter environmental footprint, and the humanity of it. Not saying I'm converting tomorrow, but I thought I'd give this one a try."

Arran nodded. "Very noble," he acknowledged.

The waiter returned with our French Bordeaux, and as he cut the seal from the bottle, he asked, "Do you have any questions on the menu, or are you ready to order?"

"I'll have the shepherd's pie," Arran answered without hesitation. "Supposed to be one of the dishes they are famous for."

Gee, that sounds good. No, I must stick to my resolve. "The vegan miso aubergine, thanks," I answered.

Once the wine was poured and the server gone, Arran raised his glass. "By way of apology, and explanation," he said. I clinked my glass to his and took a sip of wine but said nothing. Finally, he spoke. "I ran into a bit of a legal hiccup with one of my cases," he confessed. "Not me, personally, of course. While I can't get into details, it involved a family with young children and signs of abuse. The police and child services had to be involved."

"Oh, my God." My eyes grew wide. "That sounds terrible. Are the kids safe?"

"They are now, thankfully." He placed a finger to his collared shirt, giving it a nervous tug. "But I was so embroiled in the situation that I had to take the first flight back to Scotland the morning we were supposed to meet. I would have texted, but the flight's Wi-Fi was out. By the time I touched down, it was nonstop madness. Then, back on a plane twenty-four hours later to make it to the conference in time."

"The plane's Wi-Fi was out ... both to and from Scotland?" I remained unconvinced.

"You don't believe me?" Arran was astonished. "Not certain on the way back, if I'm honest. As I said, my mind was a little preoccupied. Surely you can understand that?"

I wiped the metaphorical froth from my teeth and settled down. "Yes," I answered. "I'm sorry. I can see how, in a rush, you would have forgotten to call or message me."

"No." He put his hand over mine on the table. "Never forgotten. I just … lost track of time. That's all." His deep green eyes pierced through mine, his expression soulful. "Forgive me?"

I caved. "Of course." I slid out of my seat. He stood for an awkward embrace while people circled around us in the small space. He planted a gentle kiss on my lips, and once again, Arran was all I could see.

When the meals arrived, I sampled mine … fabulous. Yet I could smell the tender meat from the shepherd's pie. "Sure you wouldn't like a taste?" Arran offered.

I wrinkled my nose. "Maybe a little one?"

My willpower was obviously weak this evening, both in my resolve to eat healthier and avoid men who love-bomb and then ghost me.

The rest of the conversation began to flow naturally, just as it had at Stonehenge and during our day in Hyde Park and London. He shared what he was permitted (given the confidentiality of some of his cases), and I opened up about my assignment—possibly letting him in on more than I should have. I recounted my interactions with Bodhi at the Giving Thanks event and at the conference earlier today.

"Tosser." Arran shook his head on my behalf.

I then filled him in on lovelorn Shaman Theodore.

"Sounds smitten," Arran agreed. "Should I be worried?"

"Not at all," I reassured him. "After the kitchari class tomorrow, I'll have to find a way to let him down gently."

"Poor sod," Arran answered. "Just out of curiosity, is *shaman* his official job? How does one go around … shaman-ing?"

"Well, no," I confessed. "He has another job, but I'm sworn to secrecy."

"Even from me?" Arran leaned in, one arm on the table.

"A promise is a promise." I sipped my wine. "But I will say that, according to Asher, who has some knowledge of the shamanic world … he even spent time with a shaman in the Amazon jungle in Peru—" I stopped mid-sentence. Arran had pursed his lips, so much so that as thick as they were (explaining to me why I found him to be a remarkably good kisser), they nearly disappeared in his mouth. "What is it?" I asked.

"I confess, I'd love to have one conversation that didn't include a reference to Asher Starling."

"Are you … jealous?" I never considered myself the type that brought out jealousy in any man. Yet—

"Maybe a little," he confessed. "Never mind him. Tell me about my last competitor to be your Valentine's date … assuming that I'm still in the running, of course."

"Of course you are," I reassured. "In the lead." I took a few bites of my eggplant before continuing. "I'm supposed to meet with Jack tomorrow, but our official date isn't until Friday afternoon—"

"Wait? Jack! You don't mean Jack Vex, by chance, do you?" Arran's eyes widened.

"Yes. Didn't even know it was him since the itinerary only says 'Jack' with no last name."

"Well, how am I to compete with a multimillionaire?"

"Oh, don't be silly," I told him. "Not only am I not interested in him, but do you really think this is more than just a publicity stunt? No, even if I did choose him … and I wouldn't … he would drop me as soon as the photo shoot ended. Too many Harpers of the world to deal with the likes of me."

"We need to talk about your self-esteem," he said.

"Now you sound like Yolanda." I wrinkled my nose at him. "And you're one to talk … checking out the competition."

"Touché." He sat back in his chair, laying his cloth napkin next to his plate.

"Guess we both need work in this area." I stared at him.

"What?" he asked. "What is that look for?"

"Just that … well, look at you. You're handsome, cultured, kind, and downright soulful—"

"Soulful, huh?" He wiggled his eyebrows at me.

"Yes, soulful. Frankly, I don't know how it is that some woman hasn't snatched you up already."

Arran placed a finger under his collar again, as if stretching out his shirt for air. His gaze fell momentarily toward the floor.

"How was everything?" the server interrupted us. "Can I get you anything else? Some dessert—"

"Just the check," Arran and I said in unison, before sharing a wicked smile.

After we'd settled the bill (Arran insisted on paying), we walked outside into the brisk air. The West End was bustling. Arran wrapped an arm around me. "Shall we get a cab?" he suggested.

"Good idea," I answered. "So, where are you staying?"

"At your place." He grinned seductively.

"Cheeky," I answered.

"Is that a yes?" His grin widened.

"It's a definite maybe." I answered with a confidence I in no way felt.

After all, Thomas was my first, and only, intimate partner. Nothing else ever got past a bit of grunting and groping. I feared my lack of experience, being exposed that way to someone I barely knew, getting hurt again, and above all … what would happen if I turned him down a second time?

"I'll take it," Arran answered, oblivious to my inner turmoil as he hailed a cab.

Fortunately, Asher was nowhere to be seen as I crept through the hallway with a very tall, very rugged, ebony-skinned Scotsman. It's not so much that I thought he'd judge me (though he might) as much as I felt like a teen sneaking out of her parents' house to meet up with a boy for the first time.

Arran wrapped his hand around my waist and kissed my neck as I fumbled with the room's key card.

Once inside, Arran wasted no time in dragging me onto the bed, lying beside me as he stroked my hair and then traced his fingers up and down my arm while we each lay on our sides, facing one another. He didn't immediately attempt to climb on top of me—that would have been a Thomas move. This, on the other hand, was some type of foreplay … or so I assumed.

He began kissing me—gently at first, then deeper. I could feel his tongue beginning to tease mine.

It was then that I noticed that the curtains in the room were open. I broke away. "I should probably close those." I blushed.

"Who cares?" Arran murmured as he began fumbling with the buttons on my blouse, undoing the first two and then, ever so accidentally, brushing his hands against my breast.

"I care." I laughed nervously. "The whole world doesn't need to see me in my underwear."

"I can't believe you'd deny the world such beauty."

He rolled on top of me, pressing his hips against me and placing one hand behind my head as he kissed me, while he ran his other hand up and down the side of my body before returning to the task of unbuttoning my blouse.

If I had any doubt that he truly wanted me, or found me attractive, they were quelled. His not-so-subtle hip maneuvers revealed a certain eagerness to get even closer.

I moaned a little, wrapping my arms around him, reveling in the kind of attention from a man that I hadn't experienced in a very long time.

And then … I panicked a little. "I'm sorry." I broke away. "But I have to do something about those blinds."

Arran groaned. "All right," he agreed. "I've got to run to the loo anyway. And I have been up since 5 a.m. and must be pretty ripe. I'm going to quickly jump in the shower, yeah?" He kissed me lightly on the lips. "But when I get back, you'd better be naked," he teased, tapping his index finger on my nose.

I lowered my eyes, embarrassed. I pulled away, rolling off the bed and rushing to close the offending curtains.

I waited until after he closed the bathroom door before climbing under the covers. I undid two more buttons on my blouse, got embarrassed, and buttoned them up again. I wasn't sure I was ready for this. In fact, I was almost certain I wasn't ready. I could feel a wave of panic wash over me. *How late is too late to say, Yeah, this seemed like a good idea at the time, but now I'd like a rain check for about a month or two until we see where this thing goes? After all, you live in Scotland and I live in the States and—*

The phone buzzed, interrupting my thoughts. I thought I had shut it off, but maybe not.

Phoebe popped up on my caller ID. Phoebe could help me. She'd tell me what to do. But what was she doing calling at this hour? It must be around 3 a.m. in her time zone.

"Hi, Phoebe," I answered, my voice shaking. "Everything okay?"

"Who the hell is this?!" a woman with a deep voice and a Scottish accent demanded.

"You should know, you called my phone," I answered. Then a second wave of panic, followed by a chill, washed over me as I glanced at the nightstand ... where my phone sat. He and I had the same model phone. Damn it!

"Put Arran on!" she ordered.

I glanced at the bathroom door. I could hear the shower running behind it. So, putting him on was going to prove difficult.

"Erm." I thought quickly. "I'm so sorry. I must have picked up his phone by mistake at the conference. I have the same model, apparently.

Let me see if I can track him down to return it. Arran, you say? Do you have a last name?" I was less trying to cover for him as much as I was trying to cover for me, and not get involved any more than I already was.

"I don't know who yew think yew are," the woman cantered, her accent getting thicker the angrier she got. "But I wasn't born yesterday. Yew get that sod on the phone right now or I'll come down there in person and scratch yer eyes out!"

She was yelling so loud in my ear that I hadn't heard the shower stop. The bathroom door swung open and Arran stepped out wearing nothing but a white towel around his waist, his abs glistening in a way that I wished I didn't find attractive. His face dropped as soon as he saw my expression. He glanced at me, at the phone in my hand, and then at my phone on the nightstand.

He sighed.

I handed him the phone.

I could hear Phoebe resume her yelling.

Arran glanced at me before lowering his eyes and tilting his head as he turned away. "Phoebe, calm down," he pleaded. "You're acting ridiculous. My colleague picked up my phone. Honest mistake." The yelling continued. Arran's face grew red, a combination of anger, frustration, and embarrassment. "Look, look, look." He tried to get a word or two sandwiched in between her accusations. "The boys are fine. I dropped them off at Nana's—"

He caught my facial expression.

He has children?

After a pause, his facial features shifted to disbelief. "You had me followed? You're nuts, you know that?"

I glanced around for a place to hide, but then remembered it was my room. So unless I wanted to hide in the bathroom, he was going to have to take his phone call out into the hallway. Before I gathered the nerve to open the door to escort him out, he abruptly ended the call.

"I'm sorry about that." He put his phone down next to mine. "If you hadn't picked up the wrong phone, you might have been spared my wife's ire."

"You have a wife, and children," I stated.

"Yes, but we're nearly separated," he defended.

"Nearly separated?" I was incredulous. "What does that even mean?"

"Sibley." He moved toward me as if to embrace me. I backed away. He held his hands up in surrender. "We've been on the outs for years now. I should have come clean, but I didn't want to scare you away. What you and I have … that's real. I can't talk to her like I can talk to you."

"The sudden trip back home. The ghosting? Was it really an emergency case?" I asked.

He became defensive. "God. Now you sound like her. Of course it was. Did you think I was making that up?" He put his finger up to his neck, just like he did at the restaurant, but without a collar to tug on, he was left scratching awkwardly behind his ear.

I gazed at his hand. He lowered it.

"You're a shitty liar," I told him.

"I was—"

"I don't need to know where you were."

"Sibley, come on," he moved toward me. "Don't let's ruin this beautiful thing we have between us."

For the second time in twenty-four hours, I felt a surge of courage. "Get your clothes, and get out." I motioned toward the door.

He removed his towel and slowly dropped it on a lounge chair by the window, pausing as if the sight of him would suddenly make me rip off my clothes and forget everything.

I moved toward the door and placed my hand on the knob.

"Okay, okay—" He rapidly threw his clothes on. "I'm going."

As he crossed the threshold of my hotel room and made his way down the hall, I couldn't help but wonder, *Is it considered a 'walk of shame' if the predator got nothing and it was, technically, the same night and not the next?*

Unfortunately, this was the same moment that Asher appeared from the elevator down the hall. The two passed each other, nodding a slight acknowledgment.

Once Asher passed me, he paused, not entirely sure how to react. He fumbled with the key card to his room before asking under his breath, "Are you okay?"

He never made eye contact with me.

"Yeah," I answered. "I think so."

He nodded, entering his room and closing the door behind him.

I was beginning to learn how Asher Starling exhibited disappointment. It was through "thumbs up" emojis and lack of eye contact. He promised once that he would never judge me. But at this very moment? I felt pretty darn judged.

CHAPTER TWENTY-ONE

THE CONFERENCE (DAY TWO)
SIBLEY

As promised, I met Shaman Theodore at the kitchari workshop at 8 a.m. the next morning. I did my best to appear enthusiastic, but in truth, I was sad, sleep-deprived, and over all of it. A part of me felt guilty, ungrateful even. Here I was on a trip of a lifetime. After all, I'd never made it much past the Southern U.S., let alone overseas. Now, in a short time, I'd gotten to see London, Stonehenge, and soon, Paris, staying in a luxury hotel and eating rather well. Yet, when I saw Theo's hopeful eyes widen when I walked in the room, I felt like a fake. I wasn't trying to lead him on, but given that last night I had my sights set on a much different man, this whole thing began to feel quite sleazy to me.

"Here," Theo said softly, "I've saved us two spots." The room featured a kitchen table at the front, covered with ingredients such as mung beans, basmati rice, and an assortment of fresh herbs, vibrantly colored vegetables, and spices. I caught the aroma of cumin and ginger, both of which oddly lifted my spirits. Behind it was a stovetop, oven, refrigerator, and sink. Surrounding the table was a U-shaped countertop and a series of wooden stools. I slid into the one Theo offered. At our space, there was a cardboard box that seemed to house the same ingredients as those displayed on the kitchen counter. Glancing around the room, it appeared that most people were in pairs—either friends or couples arriving together, or singles joining with another unmatched person for the purpose of the class. Interesting to me was the placement of extra prep stations behind us with mini stovetops and small stainless-steel sinks.

"Don't be shy," a woman called. Presumably our instructor, she stood regally at the front of the room. She was tall and had enviable long, thick, luxurious locks of black hair tied back with a bright red bandana. Her clothes were colorful and flowy, and she wore a large beaded necklace with stones on it the size of golf balls. She was one of those people who clearly had their own sense of style. I am not one of those people. I envied her. I sometimes wish I were. "Pick a spot anywhere. The kitchari stations are set for two people to work together, so if you're alone or have an odd number in your group, please get to know one of your neighbors. They'll be your partner for this class."

She waited a few moments while everyone found a spot. Sadly, there was one young woman, slightly larger in frame with a less-than-flattering visage, who silently took the last space at the end. Seems like someone was missing and she was working alone. Her sour expression and hunched shoulders gave the impression that this is exactly what was to be expected from her life.

"Hey," Theo whispered as everyone settled in. "Take a look at this." He produced a small printed image of a colorful little house with a purple picket fence.

"What am I looking at?" I asked.

"It's a house on the market in Village of the Arts," he beamed. "It might be perfect for us. It even has an extra bedroom, either for entertaining or . . ." He paused for dramatic effect. "A future baby. The prize money could help us with the down payment—"

My face turned pale.

"I'm being too pushy, I'm sorry." Shaman Theodore backed down, crestfallen.

"Let's just take one step at a time, okay?" I answered quietly. But in my mind, I was rehearsing my gentle "letdown" speech. After all, Theo had an entire life planned for us based on very little interaction. He'd created a fantasy version of me that I knew I was never going to live up to—nor did I want to. Perhaps he loved the fantasy me, but it felt very odd to me how quickly I seemed to become his lifeline ... his everything. And I didn't get the impression that it had anything to do with the reward of winning me over. I'd seen that look many times—not in men that I knew, mind you, but I'd witnessed many over the years falling for the likes of Vidalia and Yolanda.

"Okay," he agreed.

"Ah, just in time," the instructor greeted the latecomer.

The homely girl's eyes lit up as her partner joined her at the table. It was none other than Jack Vex. There were murmurs in the room, as if we had just been joined by—insert the name of your favorite celebrity. I'll admit it, he was quite handsome, and very sure of himself. Just then, he looked up and caught my gaze, his eyes seeming to pierce my very soul.

I averted my gaze, feeling the flush in my cheeks. A moment later, I turned to Theo. "This will be fun, yeah?" I smiled.

"Every moment with you is fun," he answered, seriously.

My stomach sank. He was laying it on a bit thick. I needed a plan to end this before he fell deeper in "love" with me. Perhaps I'd go on my last "match"—my date with Jack—and tell him I had a change of heart. And honestly, with Arran out of the way, and Bodhi not in the running, the self-assured businessman in the cooking demonstration was turning out to be my best option.

Jack caught my eye again, flashing me a bright, knowing smile. This time, I smiled back, just before Theo waved a tiny bowl filled with coriander under my nose, unsuspectingly.

"So earthy and fragrant, isn't it?" he offered.

It tickled my nose, and I had to quickly turn around and sneeze into my arm. I preferred a certain distance between me and my spices—namely, not up my nose.

"Uh-huh," I sniffed.

I glanced up to notice Jack let out a light chuckle. I shrugged in his direction and laughed. Fortunately, Theo did not notice. The woman partnered with Jack grabbed his arm in an effort to get—and keep—his attention.

Just as I was beginning to wonder what happened to Asher (after all, he was supposed to capture shots at all of the events I attended), he popped through a set of glass doors behind where Jack stood. When Jack saw him, he nodded approvingly. Since everyone at the conference had pre-signed waivers, understanding that photos may be taken and used for promotional purposes, no one really gave him too much thought. He didn't stay long (also a surprise), maybe ten minutes, tops, before making his exit. I hated to be paranoid, but a part of me wondered if he was angry with me at my poor choice to give Arran a second chance—and for all he knew, something happened last night. It didn't, of course, but there was no way for him to know that.

The class went on as planned. I was surprisingly delighted with our rice and vegetable dish. There was something very comforting about it—perhaps more so because we made it ourselves. While I didn't quite "get it" during the Giving Thanks celebration, I was beginning to catch on now—the joy of planting and growing crops, tending to your garden, and cooking a wholesome meal from scratch instead of throwing together a dish of microwave veggies and whatever frozen protein you happened to have in your freezer. I'm not saying I'd be turning into Martha Stewart overnight or anything, but I was definitely vibing off the healthy eating and connecting to the earth in a more meaningful way.

Jack Vex somehow managed to slip out of the class just minutes before it ended. He whispered something to his cooking partner and then the instructor, who merely nodded. He made one final glance in my direction before disappearing through a set of glass doors behind him.

Somewhere, in the back of my mind, a little nagging voice echoed: *This is all a setup.*

I was ambushed the moment I left the kitchari class. Harper conveniently cornered Shaman Theodore and engaged him in conversation. The only bit I could hear was something along the lines of, "We're delighted you've agreed to be here as one of Sibley Bloom's love matches. How are you finding London?" She led him, reluctantly, away from me as Yolanda grabbed me by the elbow, steering me into the conference's main lobby. The last I could hear from Theo was his resonant voice explaining calmly, "London is fine. The real delight is getting to spend more time with Sibley."

I felt a tiny pang in my heart—no, not that kind. I had no doubt that Shaman Theodore was a good man, and maybe he had fibbed and hadn't actually met the shaman of the Amazon jungle (as Asher suggested), but despite the façade, deep down, I believe he meant well. And he was probably lonely. I wanted the best for him and sent a silent wish that he would find love … but it wouldn't be with me.

"Sibley," Yolanda explained. "Harper asked me to make formal introductions between you and Jack Vex. And—"

"And?" I raised an eyebrow.

"I'm sorry this seems so sordid and planned out, but they'd like you to attend the Love Languages workshop at 11 a.m." Her lips pressed together, forming a jagged line. "About fifteen minutes before it ends, Asher is supposed to signal you to leave. That's when you go and meet Jack at the London Eye late afternoon. Asher's built in some time for photo ops."

"So, you and Asher knew the plan all along?" It came out before my internal filter kicked in.

"No," Yolanda answered curtly. "Truth be told, Asher had a one-on-one call with Reed yesterday, on your behalf. He said it wasn't fair to you—or the team—for us to be flying blind with half-baked plans."

"He said that?" I caught my breath. Asher seems the supportive sort, but I hadn't expected him to go out on a line for me.

"Yeah, Sibley." Yolanda lifted a shoulder toward her ear, tilting her head to one side. "He's a good egg. And finally, we have a bit more clarity."

"Enlighten me."

"The expectation"—Yolanda threw her hands up—"and I say expectation, not obligation, is that you would naturally pick Jack as the winner. He's the mystery sponsor who turns out to be bankrolling the *Chronicles*—"

"Wait," I clarified. "The *only* sponsor?"

"Unclear," Yolanda confessed. "But the cards were stacked in his favor, for sure … well, in a way. I guess Reed anticipated that you'd be as captivated by fame and money as much as he is. Guess Arran was a bit of a wild card, wasn't he?" She winked. "How did it—"

"Don't ask."

"Okay." Yolanda looked away, as if she were embarrassed for even inquiring. "I guess Mum got that one wrong."

"Yeah," I admitted. "But I don't blame her. He's skilled at manipulation and spinning a good yarn."

Yolanda paused for a long moment before answering. "After this is all over, you and I need to have a sit-down, yeah? I'm sorry I got involved in setting you up with him in the first place."

"It's okay." I touched her arm affectionately. "I escaped unscathed and came out a bit wiser." The eyebrow went up again. "Don't ask," I repeated.

"Sibley Bloom," a deep voice greeted me.

My breath caught in my chest as Jack Vex, despite his tall and commanding presence, seemed to appear from nowhere, suddenly in front of me with minimal space between us.

Yolanda stood on her tiptoes to glance over his shoulder. "Uh, yeah," she stammered, equally surprised. "Jack, this is Sibley Bloom. She's the feature writer for—"

"I know who you are," Jack answered in a deep voice. He placed a hand on my shoulder. "Did you enjoy the kitchari class?"

"Yes." My breath caught again, this time in my throat. "Very nice … the whole 'food is medicine' concept."

"Indeed," he smiled. "I'm heading over to the Love Languages lecture soon. I hope you'll join me?"

There was something intimidating about his presence. He was tall, good-looking, confident, successful … and I felt like a shrinking violet. After what felt like an excruciating silence, Yolanda saved me.

"Yes," she nodded fervently. "She'll be there!"

"Excellent." Jack rubbed his hand on my shoulder before removing it. I could still feel the heat of his touch on my arm.

I nodded, dumbly. God, I am terrible at this whole dating thing.

Love Languages, as suggested by minister, author, and relationship counselor Gary Chapman, are ways we prefer to be shown love: words of affirmation, acts of service, physical touch, receiving gifts, and quality time. For those unfamiliar with their "language," a ten-minute pretest was included in the lecture.

"Physical touch is my love language," Jack whispered in my ear as he sat next to me, emphasized by the way he lightly touched my back as he sat. He eyed the room to see who noticed, in a way that suggested he was trying to be subtle and obvious at the same time.

His presence made me nervous. I couldn't tell whether it was a negative vibe about him or whether I just found him attractive and out of my league … probably both. There was this "bad boy turned billionaire" energy that probably worked well for steamy romance novels, but I wasn't entirely sure how this worked in real life. In my mind, I wondered, *Do bad boys ever really change? I know they do in romantic movies after they've found "the one," and possibly (as in the case of my friend Tanya) after someone "accidentally" becomes pregnant and it's "a sign from God."*

But really? If left to their own devices, how many "bad boys" change from personal growth and a shift in values and perspective?

Perhaps I was being unfair. After all, what little I knew of Jack Vex was from the news and social media … and how accurate was that? Our lives curated as a "best hits" album for all to hear? Maybe it was all a façade and he was actually looking for love? But then, why go about it in such a convoluted way? *Unless*, I thought. *His spas were struggling and this is a marketing attempt?* If that's the case, then I'd be helping out by going along with this charade.

No, you're being silly, I chastised myself. Even if that were true, I'm certain that Bodhi, Theo, and Arran could do with a cash injection. Should I pick based on need?

My head hurt—

"And you?" Jack coaxed, bringing me back into the moment.

"Oh." I jumped, reviewing my Love Languages results. "Not sure, actually."

"What do you mean?" Jack leaned an elbow on the counter, eyeing me with an intense gaze.

I shivered a little.

"Well," I answered. "It's inconclusive. Look at my scores. It seems my preferences are spread out, almost evenly, among all the—er —languages."

"A woman who wants it all." He flashed a wide smile at me, not unlike the one Arran had. *Oh God, we need to put Arran out of our mind, shall we?* "Nothing wrong with that." He touched my shoulder, briefly, before he quickly pulled away.

It was almost as if he was pretending affection ... pulling away just as observers caught a glimpse. *No,* I told myself. *Sibley, you need to work on your self-worth. Your lack of self-regard is making you paranoid.*

I smiled back. "Perhaps," I answered simply.

The lecture continued, in a conference hall that had room for roughly 150 people. To my chagrin, I spotted Bodhi at the center of the room, surrounded by what appeared to be a harem of admirers—mostly those several years his junior; Theo, in one corner, eyeing me oddly while crossing his arms in what I could only determine was a sense of disappointment; and Arran—who I was most surprised to see—sitting at the furthest edge of the room with his chair oddly positioned inches away from everyone else, nearest the exit. Just before the presenter officially began discussing the importance of knowing how we prefer to demonstrate and receive loving gestures, the plain woman from the kitchari class stumbled in at the last minute, tripping slightly over what I could only assume was an uneven thread on the carpet. Theo rushed to her aid, catching her by the arms before she fell into the laps of several attendees.

She smiled gratefully. Theo offered her a seat beside him, which she accepted ... *and there it was.* Shaman Theodore, once again, had that lovesick puppy look on his face—only, this time, it wasn't for me. A light at the end of the tunnel.

The lecture itself, while interesting, wasn't one I could 100 percent get behind. I made a mental note to get Vidalia's thoughts on such things the next time we spoke. I mean, I could appreciate that people demonstrate love in different ways, but it felt oversimplified and lacking context. I fumbled with the little blue stone ring necklace that Asher gave me after our visit to Stonehenge as I mulled this over.

I thought back to my marriage to Thomas and my own acts of service—cooking, cleaning, working to bring home money for our dual-income household, not to mention other marital "acts of service" which were not always welcome nor appreciated. Did I get it wrong? Maybe I didn't understand my ex's love language and that's why he looked elsewhere. Maybe his was physical touch, and he felt he just wasn't getting enough of that from me. And more to the point, what good are love languages if you don't trust the person you are with? Case in point, when Thomas's infidelity was at its height, he was more prone to buy me gifts and shower me with compliments. Now, those two "love languages" are going to be harder for me to accept unless I change the context.

Jack stood, pulling me out of my reverie. He touched me lightly on the hand before slipping out the side door. Five minutes later, Asher peeked his head inside, signaling it was my turn next. Unfortunately, that meant darting past Arran, sitting just beside the door. He followed us.

"Might have known," he said in a low voice, just loud enough for Asher and me to hear.

"Known what?" Asher was guarded. He knew something happened between Arran and me last night, but not what—and he was too polite to ask.

"The whole thing's a scam," Arran accused. "You two are in it together."

"I don't follow," Asher answered, before turning to me. "Do you mind meeting me by the front doors? I'll be there in a minute?"

I nodded. I didn't know what was going on, and what exactly we were "in on together," but I didn't want to be around Arran any longer than necessary and was happy that Asher stepped in.

I wandered into the lobby, awkwardly. In my mind, I was playing out visions of *Bridget Jones's Diary*. But that was silly. No grown man was going to get in a fistfight over me—nor would I want them to. Furthermore, Asher wasn't Darcy and Arran wasn't—well, Daniel Cleaver. I mean, Arran was a philanderer for sure, but the truth was, he put me in the position of the "other woman" from the "American Office," and I really didn't appreciate being the "other woman."

Before I could go further down this rabbit hole, Asher joined me. "Ready to go?" he asked.

"Yeah," I answered. "But what was that all about?"

"The guy's got some mixed-up ideas about things, is all," Asher said simply.

"Oh," was all I thought to say.

CHAPTER TWENTY-TWO
THE CRIME SCENE
DECEMBER

"What can you tell us, Estelle?" Detective Jameson asked the forensics expert assigned to the case. Estelle was a large woman with a deep olive complexion, brown eyes, and black curly hair tied back in a fierce bun for work.

"Gerard, I gotta tell ya," she said, shifting her hip to one side, balancing a camera on it while securing it with one hand. "This is some weird shit."

Jameson pinched his lips together and shook his head. "I'm gonna need clarification on 'weird shit.'"

They stood outside the Evans residence—the one that Nadia and Tod once shared as husband and wife before they divorced, amicably, if you were to believe friends and relatives. Then Vidalia moved in … and then out. Now the grass was overgrown, and the state of the house, in a very short time, appeared in disarray.

"From what we can tell," she continued, "Nadia Perdita fell from the roof and cracked her head on one of the stones lining the driveway." Estelle pointed to a dried bit of blood that had seeped into the stone.

"Then, her body was dragged to that tree over there," Estelle pointed, "where she was hastily buried."

"Was she pushed?" Jameson asked, peering up at the roof.

"Not sure," Estelle confessed. "Based on the weather conditions we suspect were happening that day, she might have been pushed, lost her balance, or the wind took her out during a hurricane."

"And how did parts of her end up underground and the other parts on top of the roof?" Jameson rubbed his head, tiredly.

"From what we can tell, whoever witnessed this dragged her body to the tree to bury it. Only, I guess they didn't expect the weather to kick up winds so fierce that she'd end up back on the roof!"

"Anything tying her death to Tod Evans or—" her name caught in Gerard Jameson's throat "—Vidalia Oliveira?"

"That's where I come in," Officer Mac chimed in. Before that moment, Detective Jameson hadn't even noticed his arrival. He popped in like a ghost. Mac was all too eager to share his findings. "Seems Tod Evans has a history of domestic abuse. Can't say if he actually harmed the deceased, but his DNA was found on a shovel in the garage, along with some dried blood from Nadia Perdita."

"Footprints and similar evidence around the tree have long since washed away," Estelle said. "But based on Mac's findings, and my own, I'm gonna guess that Tod Evans buried his ex in the backyard and then took a runner."

"Except he didn't take a runner," Estelle added. "At least not right away."

"What do you mean?" Detective Jameson asked.

"Given the state of decomposition, I'd say she had been dead for at least three months."

"And he only ran when the dog dug up a bone," Jameson clarified.

"If you ask me, the alleged perpetrator was damn stupid," Mac said. "That grave was shallow. I'm surprised she wasn't discovered sooner. All you'd need is one good tropical storm."

"While I trust both of your instincts implicitly, this doesn't seem like much to go on," Jameson admitted.

"No," Mac answered, "except that I talked with several of Nadia's family members. Seems she had thyroid cancer and, despite their reservations, planned to leave her half of the house to Tod after she passed."

"Any chance of family interference?" Jameson asked.

"Doubt it," Mac replied, shifting his feet from side to side as if preparing for a track sprint. "They were more focused on her healing. Turns out, she didn't die, as expected. She was cured."

Jameson sighed. "Only to die a short time later—"

"In the oddest way possible," Estelle finished. "Somehow, she fell from the roof, then was buried, and then ended up back on the roof following a tornado. The only remaining questions are, did someone push her to her death, and if so, then who, and why?"

Jameson hated to ask the next question, but he knew he had to. "Could you find any evidence that there were two people involved? Not just one."

Estelle grinned, knowingly. "Someone has his sights on the suspect's ex-girlfriend, now doesn't he?" She twisted from side to side like a small child who was extremely proud of herself.

"Estelle," Detective Jameson chastised, "kindly wipe that smug grin off your face and tell me: one, was there evidence of anyone else on the roof when she died? And two, is there anything to suggest that there was more than one person involved?"

Estelle tilted her head and neck to one side in disapproval. "No, and no," she answered simply.

"Was that so hard?" Jameson asked.

Estelle's expression revealed that she was stifling an inappropriate joke that she decided to keep to herself.

The bottom line was this: Nadia was supposed to die from cancer—but she didn't. According to relatives interviewed, she was supposed to leave her half of the house to her ex-husband—but she didn't. But why on earth had she returned to their old home? And, furthermore, what was she doing up on the roof in the first place?

CHAPTER TWENTY-THREE

LONDON EYE

SIBLEY

"Are you sure we're heading in the right direction?" I huffed. Asher and I had begun our trek from the Tube at Tower Hill, crossed the Tower Bridge, hiked past the Borough Market, and were now on Queen's Walk. While not entirely terrible, this trip was definitely proving more difficult than traipsing through Florida, where the terrain is largely flat. According to my Oura fitness ring, I was averaging 8.8 miles a day.

"I'm certain," Asher reassured, shrugging his shoulder in order to relocate his camera bag to a spot that didn't involve bouncing off his hip with each step. "Be glad you're not carrying camera equipment."

"With all the funding going into this series, couldn't we have just taken the Tube?" I complained. "Or a cab?"

"What?" Asher protested. "And miss all of this? Look, there's the Tower of London! And the Shard? It's just over there. And there's the Walkie-Talkie—"

"I get it," I lamented. "There's lots to see. I just wish I had picked better shoes, is all." I glanced at my unfortunate footwear. I had on chunky shoes that were supposed to indicate "sophisticated but understated." Instead, they screamed, "Tourist who should have worn sensible shoes."

"Well," Asher protested, "I did suggest you wear sneakers and bring a pair of dress shoes to swap out for the photo shoot at the Eye. What were you thinking?"

"I didn't want to look silly wearing sneakers with a fancy dress," I whined. "In a foreign country, no less." I was rather proud of my little blue floral dress and matching cardigan. And, if I say so myself, I didn't look half bad in it.

"Hmm," Asher smiled, glancing at my feet. He slowed his pace ever so slightly so that I could keep up.

"What?!"

"In all the time I've known you, I've never witnessed you caring all that much about your 'fashion statement.'" Asher bit his lip in what I assumed was him trying hard not to laugh at me. "Why now?"

"I dunno," I sulked. "Maybe 'cuz it's for our story? It's different when I'm the center of a photo spread instead of working behind the scenes."

"You didn't seem to mind so much in Bradenton or Cassadaga, or even in Stone—"

He caught himself before he mentioned Stonehenge. That was a sore spot.

"Maybe my last adventure left me feeling less than … spectacular," I confessed.

"But I'm not photographing you now, am I?" Asher explained. "Except from the waist up—shots of you taking in the scenery, establishing shots and such." My face grew red. I picked up the pace, passing a few food trucks and street performers along the way. I resisted the urge to stop at the book fair … another time, I thought.

"Oh, I get it," Asher snapped his fingers proudly. "You don't want Jack to catch you not looking your best, do you? So you'd rather be in pain than actually wear shoes that won't hurt your feet when you walk."

"No!" I protested. "I just didn't know we'd be walking this far. I was

… misinformed!" I raised my chin proudly. Except I didn't feel proud. I felt stupid.

I wasn't entirely certain I was all that keen on Jack, so what was this? It almost felt like, during our brief interactions, he was being condescending, but in a subtle way that somehow made me want to prove that I was clever enough, talented enough, or … I don't know, worthy of being on camera with him? He was the CEO of a multimillion-dollar company while my biggest claim to fame was … well, this little photo spread.

"Sibley," Asher leaned his head toward me and asked, "is it that you might actually like the man or that you're intimidated by him?" He paused a moment before adding softly, "Or are you still feeling a bit raw about Arran?"

"I—I—don't feel comfortable having this discussion with you!" I continued my pace, which would have made a statement had I not suddenly tripped on the sidewalk.

Asher caught me before I landed on the concrete, grabbing my arm with one hand and wrapping his other hand around my waist. It gave me the chills. Other than Thomas, and recently, Arran, no man ever touched my waist before—not even innocently or when posing for a photo. My face felt flushed.

"Okay, sorry." He pulled his hands away once he'd realized I had regained my balance. He walked for a few more paces in silence. "It's just that—"

I sighed. "Okay, here we go—"

"'Here we go, nothing,'" he protested. "It's just that if you're intimidated by him because he gives you the creeps, you have to let me know that."

"You're not my bodyguard," I reminded him.

"I'm well aware of that … this way—" he pointed to the left as we turned the corner. "But I like to think that I'm your friend."

I felt a warmth at the center of my chest, followed by an odd mix of emotions. I was touched that he'd considered me a friend, but also a little … disappointed? Was that it? It wasn't that I had an intention of dating the man, but somehow, being "friend-zoned" didn't feel quite right, either.

"It's not that," I finally answered as the London Eye came into view. I slowed my pace as we passed the restrooms—or, as they called it here, the "loo" or the "toilets." "He's big and important and I'm just—"

"Just what?" Asher eyed me, confused. "We can have a longer discussion about your self-worth later. But for the time being, I'd like you to remember one important detail."

"Yeah, what's that?"

"He agreed to this shoot for a reason. Obviously, his company can benefit from the publicity and your story."

"True," I nodded. "Hey, give me a sec to hit the girls' room before my ride, okay?"

"Okay," Asher called after me. "Might I remind you that it would have been a great place to change your shoes."

Crap. I remembered. "Hey, you got a pound? The bathrooms cost money here."

"It costs one pound sterling to use the restroom around here? Geez!" Asher fished into his pocket. "Here, take two. In case you need one for later."

"Thanks! Be right back!" Me and my weak bladder—but I wasn't about to get stuck at the top of the Eye with no facilities.

I left Asher to fiddle with his camera lens and equipment while I was gone. When I returned, he was standing there—with Jack at his side. Apparently, Jack had changed garb for the occasion. He was now dressed all in black … black shoes, black jeans, and a button-down black shirt. He was a walking shadow.

"Jack," I blushed. "Nice to—uh—see you again." What is one supposed to say in these situations?

He took my hand and kissed it. "Charmed, as always," he

murmured. I could feel Asher rolling his eyes. Jack smelled of heavy cologne. Not unpleasant … just a lot. Something I didn't notice in the lecture, which meant this must have been newly applied. "Let's go, shall we?" He took me lightly by the elbow and guided me toward a private entrance to the London Eye, bypassing the lines of tourists chattering noisily as they waited for their turn. He waved some sort of badge at one of the attendants, who nodded.

"Just one moment," they said. "Your capsule will be ready in a moment."

"Got us the Royal capsule," Jack whispered. "Dedicated to our dear late queen."

"Oh," I nodded. "That sounds nice … Er … I mean, not that she's dead, just . . ."

Jack merely smiled that cool, suave smile of his. I wasn't sure how tall he was, but he definitely had at least seven or eight inches on me. His torso loomed largely over me, all but blocking out the light from the sun on the horizon behind us, casting a shadow over his imposing form.

"Not happening, Jack," the attendant apologized. Apparently, Jack was a frequent visitor to the Eye.

"Sorry?" Jack was visibly annoyed.

"That was a special offering we had to close down on account of vandals. But don't you worry. We've got a private one for you, just like you requested."

Jack merely grunted, his face flushed.

"It's okay," I said in the sweet voice I used on Thomas when he lost his temper over the littlest of things.

"No, it's not!" He barked at me. I leaned back, nervously. He calmed once he saw my expression. "I just wanted this to be special … for you and your first visit to London."

"It will be," I answered calmly. "I'm certain of it." That seemed to satisfy Jack, though he continued to tap his foot impatiently. I guess Jack Vex wasn't accustomed to waiting on anything.

Finally, our capsule arrived. "After you, love," he motioned. Unlike the other capsules, which were filled with at least two dozen guests, ours was reserved for two. Well, three, if you counted Asher.

Suddenly, Jack's palm flew out, stopping Asher in his tracks. It landed at the center of Asher's chest.

"What's the problem, man?" Asher complained, backing up.

"No problem … mate," Jack grinned. "Just that three's a crowd, is all."

"But I'm supposed to be photographing the experience," he protested.

"We'll be sure to pause for photos when we're back."

"But—"

"Don't worry," Jack reassured. "I've got my cell phone. I'll catch a few selfies while we're up there."

Before Asher could respond, the attendant shut the door behind us. "You can wait over there," he gestured to Asher. "They'll be back in thirty minutes."

"But—"

"Move along, please . . ."

Inside the pod, there was an oblong bench in the center. I sat, just as the door was closed with Asher on the outside and Jack and me on the inside. I got chills, momentarily, not expecting to be sealed inside with my date.

Next to where I sat, there was a metal ice bucket on a stand with a champagne bottle tucked inside. Attached to the stand were two stemmed flute glasses.

Moments later, the London Eye began to move.

"Wait until you see this view," Jack promised. "It'll knock your socks off."

I nodded. What happens if I want to leave early? Well, at least the ride was only thirty minutes. How bad could it be?

Jack took no time in plucking the two flutes from their holders and handing me one. He quickly poured a bit of pink champagne into each, careful not to pour too quickly and cause a bubbly spill.

"Come," he ordered gently. "Stand next to me over here. We can take in the sights together."

I stood hesitantly, realizing that the pod was moving so slowly that moving about the capsule was easy. I brought my glass over to where Jack stood, admiring a sunset view of the Thames and the London skyline. I'll admit, the romantic in me was impressed. Maybe I was just gun-shy about my dating experience thus far. Or perhaps my first few dates were just a warm-up. Maybe I should give the smooth-talking Jack a chance.

I took the metal rail that ran along the pod in one hand, with my drink in the other. I sipped and raised my glass to Jack in a tentative smile. He smiled back.

"That's more like it," he grinned a toothy grin … or maybe that's just because he seemed to have an unusually large mouth with really big teeth. Anyway, I'm not sure what he meant by the comment, but I kept smiling.

I turned back to the Thames. "You're not kidding about the view," I admitted.

"Yes, it is lovely," he whispered. I didn't have to look in his direction to know that he was staring at me. I knew he expected me to turn and share his glance … so I didn't.

Instead, he moved closer. I could feel the warmth of his presence over my shoulder just before he placed his right hand on my waist. In his left, he sipped champagne and somehow had this unique ability to straddle the stem of the flute between two fingers while resting his hand on the metal bar for balance. His cologne tickled my nose.

If I didn't know any better, I'd think he'd been here before … many times … with many different women.

As the pod ascended, he descended—that is, I suddenly felt his lips on the side of my neck as he bent over me for a kiss. I'm not gonna lie.

For the faintest of moments I thought, *This is nice,* but then I remembered who was doing the kissing, and I immediately pulled away.

"I'm sorry, Jack," I apologized, though I wasn't entirely sure why I was apologizing. "But I'm not ready for any kisses just yet."

He chuckled. I don't know why. This was followed by a long pause, where he stared deeply into my eyes as if trying to figure me out. He answered, "Why not? Are you afraid of love?"

"Um, no." I wiggled my way out of his grasp and retreated to the back of the pod. "I just think I need more than twenty-four hours to make that assessment."

"I see," he answered, obviously disappointed. He lowered his hands slightly, as if in prayer.

He was good enough to stay on the opposite side of the capsule, raising his voice ever so slightly so I could hear him. "Do you know how many women would love to be where you are at this moment … with me?"

"Just how many women do you love?" I ignored the arrogance that suggested being manhandled by him was a privilege.

He let out a boisterous laugh. "I run the hottest yoga retreats all over Europe—Greece, Italy, France, Germany, Spain … even Turkey. I don't mean to brag, but you are the first woman I have met who exhibited such resistance to my advances. You do like men, don't you?"

My cheeks grew red. I knew this, even if I couldn't see them. It was pretty obvious when I was embarrassed or—like now—irate.

"I happen to like men very much," I found myself explaining, even though I shouldn't have needed to. "But if it eases your ego, you may choose to believe whatever you like. Though, I promise you, Jack, I won't be the last woman who rejects your well-meaning advances after only having met the evening before. I have faith that some of us actually seek depth in their relationships—not just a pretty or wealthy side piece to enhance one's lifestyle."

"Hah-hah!" He laughed so hard, I thought the pod shook.

For a moment, I got a glimpse of the capsule as it reached the pinnacle view of the skyline and began to descend. *Pretty*, I thought. *A shame it was ruined by this megalomaniac. Would have been nice to experience it with someone who'd actually appreciate it … Asher, for example.*

"What's so funny?" I asked.

"You." He sucked down his champagne, and then proceeded to down what was left in the bottle—a lot, since we'd only shared a single glass each. "I agreed to meet with you to help save your little magazine. Reed's a good friend of mine. He pleaded with me to help a poor spinster renew her confidence."

For a moment, he even moved and sounded like my boss.

"By molesting me?"

His eyes grew dark. "Would you like me to?"

"Certainly not." I edged nearer the door. It was about as far as I could get from the man.

"Your boss is going to hear about this. I'm pulling all of my advertising … at once."

"Well, this will make my article very interesting, indeed." I clucked. I wasn't normally this confident, but I was angry as hell.

"You don't understand, little girl," he snarled. "The conference … the contest … the sponsors. Hate to break it to you, Sunshine, but that was all me!"

"Well, the *Positive Enlightenment Journal* appreciates your support. However, I am a writer, and have not—nor will I ever be—a prostitute."

"I've got lawyers," he gritted his teeth at me. "I'll bury you."

I'm not certain how much time had passed, but I spent it glued to the entrance of the pod, just waiting with bated breath until it reached the bottom of the Eye, from where we'd launched.

As soon as the attendant opened the door, I bolted.

"How was—" He started, then turned to watch me in surprise.

Asher was just a stone's throw away, at the bottom of the exit ramp. His face dropped as he saw mine.

"Are you okay?" He was alarmed.

"Let's just go, shall we?" I answered, walking at a brisk clip.

I could see Asher glance behind us. If Jack were near us, he didn't let on.

"Shall I get us a taxi?" Asher's voice went up in pitch.

"That would be lovely," I said, just as I spotted one in the lineup just down the block. "Hey," I waved my hand back and forth. "Are you available?"

The driver sat upright. "Yes, ma'am," he motioned for us to get in.

As we climbed in the back, Asher struggling briefly with his camera, I proclaimed, "You know that clause in the itinerary-slash-contract that says I can end a date any time I choose?"

"Yes?" Asher's eyes grew wide.

"I'm calling this particular date done!"

CHAPTER TWENTY-FOUR

THE FALLOUT
SIBLEY

Asher could see I was rattled after my interaction with Jack and calmed my nerves in the best way possible—with a Quattro Formaggi pizza complete with brie, gorgonzola, mozzarella, and parmesan from Cacciari's. We split both the pizza and a half carafe of Sangiovese, settling at a small café table for two outside—where I could both vent and people-watch.

At the next table sat a bicyclist, still in his cycle gear, with his racing bike sandwiched between him and the restaurant's window and his helmet occupying the opposite chair. He had a cigarette in one hand and an espresso in the other. There were two other espresso cups on the table for just a moment before a server came to remove them. The man nodded, picking up his cell phone with the same hand as the cigarette. His eyes never left the screen while he sipped his beverage. On the one hand, I was impressed at how coordinated he was. Had it been me, the espresso or the cigarette ash (probably both) would have ended up in my lap. On the other, the cigarette smoke was offensive to my nose and not a pleasant addition to my pizza.

I secretly willed him to leave. It must have worked, because moments later he tossed some cash on the table, hopped on his bike, secured his helmet, and was off. Another surprise: how could a smoker be that athletic? No judgment, just a curiosity. I bit into my cheesy pizza, fully recognizing that I, myself, was far from the healthiest.

"Thank goodness," Asher commented. "I thought we were going to have to relocate inside to escape the smoke."

I nodded, watching as a young mother expertly maneuvered a two-seater red stroller across the sidewalk with toddler twins in tow, shifting quickly to avoid a young man sporting an electric skateboard and not paying too close attention to others sharing the sidewalk. She didn't blink, and she didn't get upset. She just pivoted … that's patience.

I took a sip of wine, celebrating the unusually warm temperatures this time of year in London. It was probably the nicest day so far, despite my unfortunate hiccup with Jack Vex. I watched as a few dark clouds began to gather overhead. "We might have to anyway," I said, pointing to the clouds.

"One thing I have learned on this little adventure," Asher shared, "is how to adapt."

"Like that young mother with the two babies. Did you see?" Asher nodded, smiling. A tiny bit of cheese was caught on his chin. "You've got a little—" I pointed. Asher wiped his chin. I let out a light chuckle. "You've been hanging around me for too long," I joked. "Pretty soon, you'll start wearing your food as well."

"Well, if that's the byproduct of hanging out with you," Asher answered, "I'll take it. I quite enjoy your company."

I smiled but said nothing. It was moments like that when I couldn't be 100 percent sure if he was hinting at something more than friendship. Had I been a little braver, I might have asked. Instead, I did the safest thing—I changed the subject.

"So, what happens now?" I asked. "That last date was a disaster. Do we pretend it never happened, and I choose my Valentine's date at the end of the conference, as planned?"

"I don't know," Asher confessed. "I'll give Reed a call when we get back. He keeps odd night-owl hours and may be up for a chat."

I rested my elbow on the edge of the table, chin in palm, and sighed. "There is—literally—no one from my dating options that I'd want to go on a Valentine's Day adventure with. Perhaps I'll pick Shaman Theodore. He was the least annoying of the bunch."

As if his ears were burning, my cell phone buzzed. It was a text from Theo. I read it aloud for Asher to hear: "Dearest Sibley, it's been my honor getting to know you. But I must confess that my heart has been lured away by another. I just want to be honest with you because you are a lovely woman. So, if you want to go through with the Valentine's date, I'm willing. We can split the prize money. But, I'm afraid that's as far as our romance can go."

"What romance?" Asher raised an eyebrow.

"The one in his mind," I answered flatly. "And he's the second one to suggest that if I choose them, we could split the prize money."

"Who was the other?" Asher asked, surprised.

"Bodhi."

"Gee," Asher confessed. "I all but forgot about him."

"He's kind of forgettable," I agreed.

Asher cleared his throat, uncomfortably. "Dare I ask about Arran?"

"Married."

"You're joking?" Asher's jaw dropped.

"Not even a little. I accidentally answered his phone by mistake, and his wife gave me a what-for."

Asher looked crestfallen.

"Don't look at me like that. Nothing happened ... Okay, nothing much happened. But certainly not what you're thinking, based on that look on your face. Why do you care so much, anyway?"

"I don't," Asher coughed again. "I just don't want to see you get hurt. Did he offer to split the winnings with you?"

"No, he claims he's giving it all to charity."

"I'm gonna go out on a limb and call bullshit on that one," Asher said, biting into a side of pizza crust.

Once again, as if on cue, a barrage of text messages came in. I read them all to Asher.

From Bodhi: "No doubt you've made your choice with the rich boy. But my offer to split the winnings with you still stands. I don't trust that dude to stick around for long, anyway."

"Gee," I replied. "Pot calling kettle."

From Arran: "Don't let your contempt for me sway your decision about the contest. Remember, it's for the children."

Asher rolled his eyes.

"And then there were none," I said, as one final text popped up. It was from Thomas. I read it, and quickly deleted it.

"Hey," Asher pointed to himself. "What am I, chopped liver?"

"Of course not!" I defended. "But you weren't one of my suitors. I'd much rather hang out with you than the lot of them!"

"I think there's a compliment in there," Asher grinned. "But I might be mistaken."

Just then, Asher glanced at his phone. "Geez, I had mine on silent. Seems Reed has tried to call five times. I've got a flurry of texts from Reed, Harper, Phoebe, Krystal, and Bernard."

"Wow, good news travels fast. I'm guessing Jack expressed his displeasure to Reed?"

"Most likely," he said, putting his phone away. "Hey, I hate to end our dinner, but we should probably head back so I can deal with the fallout."

"It shouldn't fall all to you," I protested. "Let me help."

"Nah, you've been in the spotlight this entire time. Why don't you go back to your room and unwind a bit. I promise to fill you in as soon as I have more details."

Fortunately, neither the wine nor pizza went to waste, as we finished our last bites and settled the bill.

Halfway through our walk back to the hotel, the wind and rain decided to let loose. Had we learned anything on this trip, it should have been to bring an umbrella at all times—apparently we were not quick studies. We were soon drenched. As we reached the corner and merely had to cross the street to our hotel, a taxi rounded the corner, sending a spray of dirty street water over us. We did the only thing we could do— we turned to each other and laughed.

Once back to our rooms, we both saw a notice slid halfway under each of our doors. We were supposed to be there for three more nights. But instead, we received a note for our early checkout in the morning, with a bill for each of us that should have been covered ahead of time.

"Don't worry," Asher reassured me. "We'll work it out."

I nodded, emotional fatigue setting in. "I'm going to have a quick bath, but text me when you wanna fill me in?"

There was a slight pause from Asher before he answered, "Yeah, of course."

I closed the door behind me. *Well,* I thought, eyeing the room. *Guess I'm packing tonight. Too bad. It's such a lovely room.*

"What the hell did Sibley do?!" Reed barked into the phone. He was out of breath, and Asher could hear the hum of a treadmill and the sound of Reed's sneakers clunking as he walked. This was a far cry from Reed's usual calm demeanor.

"Don't blame Sibley," Asher defended, now back in his room. "Jack Vex is an asshole."

"Well, yeah. I know that," Reed said, stopping the treadmill to catch his breath. "Total narcissist. That's why I dumped him years ago."

"Wait, what?" Asher was taken aback. "You set Sibley up with one of your ex-boyfriends?"

"Oh, don't worry. He's bisexual. I'm sure he found her attractive … not that he's picky."

Asher let the "not that he's picky" part go, though anger surged through him. "Obviously he liked her—too much. He was a little too handsy."

"So, why didn't she tell him to stop?" Reed answered simply, as if the solution were obvious.

"One, she tried; two, she shouldn't have to!" Asher was all but yelling into the phone.

"All right, let's both just calm down and think," Reed answered. "We've already dealt with the fallout on this end. Jack is threatening to cancel the entire event and send all the contestants home."

Asher sighed. "That's the problem, Reed. They weren't supposed to be contestants. They were supposed to be dates. It was meant to be a romantic, healing, and spiritual journey Sibley was chronicling. Why did you have to add prize money into it and sully the entire thing?"

"What? I was helping," Reed sounded offended. "I wanted Sibley to have a fighting chance. How sad would it have been for her if no one liked her? At least now, she has—or, until today, had—four men vying for her attention."

"But for all the wrong reasons," Asher complained. There was a long pause on the phone line as both men considered their options. "So, what happens now? How do we fix this? We're supposed to be here for the rest of the conference. I'm supposed to get New Year's Eve footage and photos at the Eye, and then fly to France for the Valentine's Day finale. But we just got notice that the hotel is evicting us in the morning."

"Drama queen," Reed answered. "Not you, Asher. I'm talking about Jack. He never could handle not getting his own way. Let me think—"

The treadmill started up again, and Asher waited for several minutes, pacing the floor. The treadmill stopped. Reed returned to the phone, huffing.

"Tell you what," Reed said. "Forget the New Year's Eve photos. We can buy some stock images and maybe a few video clips from Getty when you get back—" Asher tried to protest. "I know you hate that, but hear me out." Asher paused to listen.

"I've got an idea, but I need you to back me 100 percent," Reed explained. "Then, I need to go and work some magic."

CHAPTER TWENTY-FIVE
PLAN B: DUBLIN
SIBLEY

Everything happened so quickly. Before I knew it, Asher and I were on a plane to Dublin. Yolanda remained at the conference. Reed managed to smooth things over with Jack Vex in the most complicated way possible.

In his schmoozing, Reed was able to pitch a story that would be easy on Jack Vex's fragile ego and make him out to be the hero. Jack was pleased. The old story? It was expected that I would choose Jack as my Valentine's Day date, where he—being the gracious person that he is—would divide the prize money among the three "losers" (Bodhi, Theo, and Arran). £25,000 translated into more than ten grand per person. No telling at what point Jack would "let me down easy," but I'm sure that was in the clause somewhere.

The new story? Jack Vex, in his infinite wisdom, realized that I was still processing my emotions after my divorce from Thomas and clearly wasn't ready for commitment. He also discovered that he and his assistant, Harper, had more chemistry than at first blush. So, I was to spend a little time in Dublin and then drive out to Glendalough in County Wicklow, to visit one of the most spiritual and sacred places in

Ireland. The final piece to my chronicles, they decided, was my personal journey into healing. As such, no more planned dates or photo ops for me—save for this one. Asher was supposed to capture my "spiritual transformation" somewhere between the Glendalough Monastic Site and the Lower Lake in the Wicklow Mountains. Meanwhile, Jack and Harper were off to the Eiffel Tower and the newly restored Notre Dame for a romantic date.

All's well that ends well.

Somehow, for the first time on this entire trip, I felt a sense of relief wash over me. I fumbled with the blue stone necklace Asher bought me from Stonehenge. No more conferences, dates, managing people's emotions, defending myself against unwanted affection, or feeling like a small child "playing" at life. Most of all, no more trying to live up to everyone else's expectations.

For this leg of the journey, I wore stretch jeans, a thermal black shirt with a striped red T-shirt over it, comfortable boots (in case it rained), and no makeup. Take that, Reed. If he didn't like it, then he could edit, enhance, or cut the photos from the final article entirely. I was past the point of caring. They want spiritual renewal? They want authenticity? Then they've got it. But don't expect me to pander to the audience or keep trying to be someone I am not.

This newfound freedom was incredibly fun. Asher and I checked into the Clontarf Castle (separate rooms, of course) and immediately began exploring the grounds. I mean, it's not every day that one gets to stay in a medieval castle, reminiscent of the original castle of 1172 and once overseen by the Knights Templar. Jack Vex might be a jerk, I thought, but this was stellar. Or maybe it was Reed's influence. I couldn't tell anymore, and the "new" me was all about savoring the experience—outcomes be damned.

As such, Asher and I had a game plan. First, we would each procure a beverage from the Knights Bar, and then, starting at the top, review the art on each floor, with an Art Trail brochure in hand. It was difficult for me to find the words to describe Clontarf—contemporary art meets the medieval? Each cloister and sectioned-off private area housed high-backed purple upholstered chairs and thick hardwood tables against the backdrop of gray stone, or sitting areas across a balcony where one could stretch out on a long lounge chair and take in the ambiance. Long, decorated tapestries with historic scenes seemingly connected one floor with another. I can't speak for Asher, but for me, it was great fun—exploring an art gallery and a castle all at once.

Finally, after having our fill of lions, monkeys, and the odd flamingo, we decided to venture out to the nearby Promenade, taking the walking path alongside Dublin Bay. Unlike where I lived in Florida, most dogs here were off-leash, small and large, eagerly following the heels of their caretakers. A tall man bundled up with a coat and long scarf tossed a ball across the lawn. To our surprise, it bounced into the bay. His border collie friend eagerly jumped across us, landing (to my horror) in the bay with a splash. I thought we might need to assist, but two seconds later, the same dog seemed to bounce out of the water, shaking off the wetness and sending spray everywhere as he eagerly returned his ball to his master. I'd like to see Skinny do that.

"What did you think of Clontarf Castle?" Asher finally asked.

"Really cool, honestly," I answered. "I somehow expected it to be dreary and more … dungeon-like? I don't know."

"An intriguing place for sure," Asher agreed. "Hey, what's your energy like? Feel like heading into Dublin City Centre for lunch and a bit of sightseeing?"

I don't recall anyone asking about my energy levels before. And now that I thought about it, I felt a bit of a rush of excitement now that the weight of the chronicles was lifted. Certainly, I still had to submit my next installment for the chronicles—Christmas at Stonehenge with Arran (shudder) and New Year's with Jack at the conference and London Eye (shudder again). Given the feel-good nature of our journal, and not wanting to lose more sponsors or cause a lawsuit, I had to think of a positive spin on it. But

I had time to figure it out after I'd returned home. *Home.* Up until this very moment, I had been homesick every day. But not now? Why?

I realized my mind had been drifting again and steered it back to the conversation. To Asher's credit, he never did the annoying thing of snapping his fingers in front of my face or calling, "Earth to Sibley. Are you there?" He just kept walking, matching my pace, and waiting patiently for my eventual return.

"City Centre sounds perfect," I answered.

We made our way to the bus stop in the residential area where Clontarf Castle was located and, less than thirty minutes later, we had made our way to the Ginger Man, a local tavern and regular haunt of young people near Trinity College. It was surprisingly busy for an early Sunday afternoon, but we found space at a corner table. I ordered the fish and chips. He got the Beef Guinness pie, and we both ordered Guinness on tap.

Once the order arrived, I caught the scent of his beef pie, looking hopeful but forlorn at my crispy fish choice.

Asher knew me too well. "Wanna go halfsies?" he asked. "I have to admit, I'm envious of your dish. It smells fantastic."

Gratefully, I nodded, and we swapped halves of each of our dishes. Asher seemed to be observant about a lot of things with me. I wasn't entirely sure whether to feel grateful, suspicious, or both. There was a part of me that felt a little exposed. Arran was probably the closest I'd observed of anyone actually being mindful of me and my preferences. Unfortunately, he seemed to use that to his advantage.

But no. Asher wasn't at all like Arran. He'd been pretty consistently himself in the decades I'd known him. Kinda wish I actually had the chance to get to know him sooner.

"Sláinte!" We clinked our Guinness glasses in a toast.

While technically part of my chronicles, this wasn't essential to the dating adventure planned for me. As such, Asher was freed from his heavy camera equipment for the day. Instead, we asked the server for a photo souvenir taken with my phone.

"How's this?" she asked, showing the three she'd snapped of us.

There was a distinct pause before Asher answered, "Perfect, thanks!" The shots were off-center, and one was a little blurry, but despite Asher being a seasoned photographer, he was gracious.

After a quick bite to eat, we were off and running. We meandered through Merriam Square, capturing selfies with the Oscar Wilde statue before wandering the streets, listening briefly to buskers singing a combination of Elvis tunes and French songs as we made our way to St. Stephen's Green. We wandered through the Little Dublin Museum, bypassing the official tour and skirting upstairs to the "U2 Room," filled with memorabilia of the famous band, with a loud audio loop of their greatest hits. We climbed into the staged multicolor car in the center of the room to pose for more selfies. By the time we hit the Temple Bar an hour later, my energy was starting to falter.

"Tourist ride on the Hop-On bus?" I suggested. Asher nodded. We spent the next hour or so listening to the bus driver telling us some tall tales and other (mostly) true stories about Dublin.

By the time we made it back to Clontarf, we were exhausted, pausing for a meal at the Fahrenheit Restaurant at the hotel. Ever since my adventure in Cassadaga, I was trying to be more mindful of what I ate. Since we had a large lunch, I settled on a beetroot dish, and we split Wicklow Mountain Ice Cream … only fitting since that was the final stop on our journey tomorrow, the place of my "spiritual enlightenment."

"What did you like best about today?" Asher asked, curiously.

I didn't miss a beat. That was easy. "The company," I answered.

I could have sworn that Asher blushed a little. "I'm flattered," he smiled, dipping a spoon into our shared dish. Oddly enough, it hadn't even occurred to me to be concerned over germs or the intimacy of eating ice cream from the same bowl. Everything felt sort of natural with Asher. "Hey, so I have an idea about tomorrow," he added.

"Yeah? What's that?"

"Well," he pulled out his phone. "I looked up a map around the visitor centre, the cemetery, and the Lower Lake area." I waited, expecting another long itinerary with lots of photo ops and even more walking. I suspected I was the most fit I've ever been in my life, thanks to all the walking. Ah well, at least this leg of the adventure was nearing an end and had been the least stressful of all. "I vote we park at the visitor centre, perhaps get a photo of you in front of St. Kevin's Cross. Then, we drive to the Lower Lake parking area, get a shot of you looking all serene in front of the misty Wicklow Mountains, and then toss the camera in the car, explore a little, and call it a day."

"So, you mean, two staged photo ops and that's it?" Asher was a consummate professional. That seemed too simple.

"Well, I mean, we could get a couple of selfies or phone shots as fillers if you like," he paused for a moment. "I just thought, on your last day in Europe, you might prefer to actually get to do the tourist thing— explore—without feeling as if you're on display."

"I appreciate that, Asher," I felt a pang in the center of my heart. I was touched.

Then, a miraculous thing happened. We spent the next ten minutes eating our ice cream in silence. No one was looking at their phones. No one was talking. Occasionally one of us would glance at the other and smile, or notice something happening with the servers or other diners. There was no need to fill the silence with mindless small talk. And in that moment, being quiet was the most comfortable and natural thing in the world.

CHAPTER TWENTY-SIX
GLENDALOUGH
SIBLEY

Despite working for a metaphysically minded journal for so long, I still considered myself a seeker, never having quite figured out what I believed in. Though, I liked to think I was open-minded enough to acknowledge that there could be many paths to enlightenment and to whatever higher power one believed in. On this journey, I was quite surprised that Asher was far less jaded, cynical, and doubtful than I thought. To the contrary, for someone whose job it was to be the resident skeptic, he did due diligence and sought to be educated on a subject before—sometimes critically—shooting an idea down. That said, he seemed to have a soft spot for Glendalough.

"According to history, St. Kevin created this monastic settlement in AD 498. He was born into a wealthy family but gave it all up to live as a monk, largely in solitude. If you want, we can take the trail around the Lower and Upper Lakes after we wander through the cemetery and find his 'bed,' where he lived alone for years."

At the moment, we passed the round tower and were exploring the high crosses, the sanctuary stone, and medieval ruins along the Grave-yard Trail. But it didn't feel ominous in any way. A mist had fallen over the land, giving it an ethereal glow. I took a deep breath of fresh mountain air, feeling a deep sense of peace. My shoulders relaxed and my nerves settled. I hadn't realized how chronically tense I had been until this moment, when a sense of equanimity and awe washed over me. In the distance, I noticed a small bird shimmering. He had settled on St. Kevin's Cross. I'm not sure what possessed me in that moment, but I took Asher's hand. "C'mon," I said. "I want to get closer. I think that's a starling."

Sure enough, Asher's namesake, and the bird from my journey, sat quietly on the cross. After a shared moment of the bird looking at me and me gazing back at him, he took to flight. It was only then that I realized that minutes had gone by, and I was still holding Asher's hand.

"Sorry." I pulled my palm away. "I don't know what came over me," I blushed.

"I wouldn't mind whatever it was coming back," Asher answered softly. "I quite like holding your hand." I cast my eyes toward the ground. Attention was something I had still not gotten used to. Asher sensed that and changed the subject. "As it would happen, St. Kevin was supposed to spend so much time in prayer, with his arms outstretched, legend suggests that a blackbird built a nest in his hand and had time to raise her young."

"Not sure I buy that one," I confessed. "But seeing this place, and feeling its energy, I can see how one might choose this over a privileged life. Though, I'm not sure I could have done it myself."

"Well, perhaps that's why so few of us become saints," Asher joked. "Care to wander with me?"

We followed a walking path around the Lower Lake, ending at the Upper Lake. It had begun to rain as we gazed out over the Wicklow Mountains. And at that moment, I froze.

Asher saw my face. "Are you okay?"

I could feel my lip quivering, but I couldn't stop it. Nor could I stop the tears that followed. I'm not sure how to describe what happened next, just that I felt this overwhelming rush of sadness, relief, awe, love, and transformation. It was as if everything that happened in the last year—maybe longer—had finally come to the surface. As I stood there, sobbing in the rain, Asher did the only thing he could think of—he wrapped his arms around me in a tight embrace, while we both got drenched.

I'm not certain how long I stood there—maybe five minutes, ten, or longer. We both shuddered in the cold. Finally, I looked up at him, still wrapped in his arms. "Back to the car?" I suggested.

"I thought you'd never ask," he grinned. This time, he took my hand, as we half walked and half ran back to the rental car.

Once inside, Asher got the heat going, while I pulled a dry towel from a tote bag in the back seat, for just such an occasion. I handed it to him.

"You first," Asher said. I nodded, making a weak attempt at drying my face and hair before giving him a half-wet towel.

"Should have thought to bring a second one," I apologized.

"Well, given how often we've gotten caught in the rain, you'd think we'd both be better prepared by now," he smiled.

"What?" I pointed to the waterproof rain jacket that I was wearing. "I did my best!" Sure, I purchased it yesterday, while Asher and I were in Dublin, but still—better late than never.

After a moment of silence, Asher asked, "So, can I ask what happened back there? You okay?"

I nodded, slowly. "Yeah, I think so." Asher waited while I tried to find the right words. "It's just that, I don't think I ever had taken the time to just feel, you know?" I turned to face him—Asher in the driver's seat and me right beside him. "I was numb after things ended between Thomas and me. I never took the time to get angry, to grieve, or to process everything I was feeling. Then, I jumped into this stupid assignment where I was suddenly being matched up with people I didn't know and expected to find love again so easily ... Difficult as I wasn't sure what it felt like, exactly. I'm not certain what Thomas and I had was love—certainly limerence, in the beginning. But he quickly married me before my young hormones calmed and logic won out. By then, it felt as if it was too late."

"You never thought to leave him?" Asher asked. "I mean, even before the affair?"

"Perhaps that has been the hardest part of all," I confessed. "Somewhere, in the back of my mind, I think I told myself: 'you're not going to do better than him.' And I guess I believed that this was all I was worth."

"And now?"

"And now … I think I'm finally starting to love myself," I began tearing up again. "Go figure," I sniffed. "Maybe there was something to Reed's plan for my spiritual awakening."

Asher dug a tissue out of the tote in the back seat and handed it to me. "You chose the best place for it," Asher laughed, "with Glendalough being one of the most beautiful places in nature, with a long history of the Valley of the Two Lakes being a place for meditation and reflection."

I accepted the tissue, dabbing my eyes and nose. "How did we end up here, anyway?" I just realized that we were a far cry from the original plan of heading to Paris.

"I suggested it," Asher confessed. "I was here years ago on one of my many adventures. It struck me how serene it was and how peaceful I felt when I was here. Clontarf … well, that was Reed's idea. Said he had a connection."

"He seems to have connections everywhere," I whined. "And they all seem to be related to someone he dated at some point in his life."

"Well, in this case, it worked out," Asher grinned.

"I used to think that about you, you know?" I admitted.

"Me?" Asher was surprised.

"Yeah, with all the traveling you've done—being single and free. I don't know, to a married woman with almost no dating experience, it seemed you could be footloose and fancy-free."

Asher cleared his throat, somewhat awkwardly. "Well, I won't lie and say I haven't dated a fair bit—but I was always faithful in my relationships. And, truth be told, I've always envied my married friends who had someone waiting for them when they returned home from work, or accompanying them on a trip, or even just knowing someone's got your back."

"Well," I fidgeted with the blue stone ring around my neck. "As someone who recently ended a dysfunctional marriage, I can honestly say that you're the first man I've ever met who has consistently had my back—not just now, but over the years in working together. I appreciate that."

Once again, a silence fell over us. Only this time, it was different. It was as if the energy from Glendalough had seeped into our very core and was now passing back and forth between us. Without another word, we leaned toward each other, kissing softly before pausing to eye one another, making sure it was okay to continue. Asher wrapped one arm around my waist while the other holding my back. He cupped my head in his hand as he half-leaned me across his chest and lap. He kissed me again, more deeply this time.

I was lost in the moment. For once in my life, not feeling insecure about how I kissed or what he thought of me. My mind wasn't reeling or catastrophizing or doing any of its usual ruminating. I was fully present in the moment, exactly where I wanted to be and with whom I wanted to be. And it was magical.

It seemed our romance was short-lived. As we returned to Clontarf Castle, hand in hand, we decided to go to our respective rooms to freshen up. I showered and changed into a long-sleeve knit dress with the idea that Asher and I would share an early dinner, and then—who knows? I wasn't planning for intimacy at this point—not after what just happened with Arran—but maybe a few more kisses? Snuggling in a quiet corner of the castle with a nightcap and enjoying a roaring fireplace?

Just then, an email alert came on my phone. It was from Reed. Only, when I opened the message, I got halfway through it before realizing that it was addressed to Asher, but I was copied on it. Based on its contents, I would wager that Reed got foiled by Google's "Did you also mean to copy—" autofill. Either that, or Reed was playing games with us—again.

My face grew flushed and my skin hot. I could hear my heart pounding in my chest as I read the words … "seduce," "unexpectedly fall in love," "surprise ending to the entire story."

The long and short of it? Reed's new plan to recover from the matchmaking fiasco at the convention wasn't for me to reach spiritual enlightenment while Jack found Harper and the others were gifted consolation prizes. No, it was for Asher to make the moves on me and encourage a romance in a "true love was right in front of her the whole time" moment. Asher didn't have feelings for me … he was just following orders.

I was livid.

There was a loud pounding on the door. "Sibley!" It was Asher.

I threw the door open, angrily. In his hand, he held a cell phone. He didn't have to ask … "I can explain."

"There's nothing to explain," I spat out, feeling a sense of overwhelming rage. "You and Reed used me—"

"No," Asher pleaded. "If I could just come in for a moment—"

"No!" I stopped him. "We're done here, and as soon as I get back home, I'm giving Reed a piece of my mind—right before I quit. Let him come after me for my final two articles. I don't care!"

"At least read the rest of the email for context," he pleaded as I slammed the door on him.

But I was too angry. I couldn't hear him, and I certainly couldn't listen. I'm not sure how long I paced the floor before ordering room service. By the time it arrived, forty-five minutes later, I had begun to calm down—just a little. I did my best to eat. I wasn't hungry, but I knew I'd regret it if I waited until morning—particularly since we were checking out so early. I probably wouldn't have time for breakfast until we'd reached the airport, anyway.

At his suggestion, I reluctantly cringed as I read the entire email. I wasn't privy to the phone conversation that Reed and Asher were on, but from the gist of the email, I could determine that Reed wanted Asher to make a pass at me—and "make it convincing." He "sensed something between us" anyway. In the email Reed wrote, "I know you were against this idea, initially, based on our earlier call … glad you came round to see it my way. And, who knows? You two might just work out after all." It was the closing that got me: "The offer still stands," Reed wrote. "There's a cash bonus in it for your extra efforts, with my gratitude."

I felt cheap, betrayed, and angry. After packing everything I could, save for what few things I would need come morning, I curled into bed far too early and cried myself to sleep.

CHAPTER TWENTY-SEVEN

LEAVING CLONTARF CASTLE
SIBLEY

"Would you at least let me explain?" Asher pleaded with me.

"What is there to explain? It seems pretty damn obvious to me. Reed paid you a good bit of money to try and seduce me." I yanked all the drawers of the dresser out and slid the closet door open. I didn't want to accidentally leave anything behind.

"First of all, 'seduce' is a strong word," Asher followed behind me as I hoisted my suitcase onto the bed and unzipped it.

"The point is, he paid you to pretend to fall in love with me. How humiliating! And this from the guy who built a career out of uncovering slimy behavior such as this." And to think, I was actually allowing myself to start having feelings for this charlatan. I grabbed a short stack of mostly folded jeans and thermal shirts and haphazardly tossed them into the case.

"Did you miss the part where I turned him down?" Asher pleaded. "Could you stop packing for two minutes so we can talk about this?"

"But you lied to me!"

"How did I lie? I never said anything more about it."

"Guilt by omission," I paused, lifting my chin proudly. "You weren't transparent about your intentions."

"I don't think that applies in this case," Asher shook his head. "It wasn't my information to share. It was Reed's. And what would you have done if I had said, 'Reed tried to pay me money to hit on you for the grand finale, assuming that you were already interested in me. But don't worry, I turned down his sleazy offer.'" Sibley didn't respond. "It was only after I hung up the phone that—" Asher stopped.

I added a few pairs of socks and undergarments to my suitcase and zipped it closed.

"That … what?" I felt a tingle in the back of my neck and scalp.

"That I realized Reed may have picked up on something that had escaped my attention entirely," he finished, quietly.

"And what was that?" My voice softened as I dropped my chin down and tilted an ear in his direction.

"That I was falling for you." Asher rubbed his forehead. "And if I told you what he proposed, you might have quit and flown home right away—"

"I most certainly would have—"

"And I would have lost my chance," he confessed. "Even if you stayed, I'd worry that you'd spend the next three months wondering if it was an elaborate scheme for the sake of the story. Or worse—"

"What could make this, in any way, worse?" I sniffed, fighting back a few watery tears that were threatening to form.

"That you'd go along with it, and I'd be the one who ended up with a broken heart."

It felt as if the air had suddenly been sucked out of the room, and for the next minute, no one spoke. It was the longest minute of my life.

"Aren't you going to say something? Yell at me some more? I think I'd prefer that to silence," he smirked, in an attempt to lighten the situation.

"Just … go sit over there!" I motioned to a pub chair by the window. "I need to think!"

Asher obeyed. I felt under a microscope as he watched me grab my toiletries from the bathroom and pack them in a separate, smaller case. He realized he must have been making me nervous, because he began lightly fiddling with the edge of the bedroom curtain and gazing out the window.

My head was spinning.

Theadore, Bodhi, Arran, and Jack must have all been a part of Reed's elaborate scheme to turn my ongoing chronicles into more than just features for our humble magazine … he had aims to have this made into a reality dating show. Good old, poor, sad, bumbling Sibley Bloom was just the prototype. Were any of the men actually who I thought they were? What if Jack wasn't really a business Tycoon? What if Bodhi worked in IT and ate meat on the regular? I hadn't thought I needed to question Reed on this. Maybe they were well-paid actors. Consider Jack…of all the women he could have had in this world (as much as it pains me to say it), why on Earth would he go after me, and then be hell-bent on revenge when I rejected him?

And seriously? Theodore the shaman, Bodhi the Buddhist, Arran the Neo-Druid, and Jack the Tycoon?

Although, now that I was thinking this through, I can easily see why Jack was the sponsor for everything that was supposed to go down in Paris … not just because I was to stay at his luxury spa, but because, of the men I was introduced to, Jack was the most likely to be able to give any woman the life she dreamed of: travel to exotic places, access to the finer things in life, and a man who—to the outside world—appeared handsome, intelligent, spiritually evolved, successful … fabulous.

I could almost see Reed reeling with anger when I turned his friend and former lover (a detail he had conveniently omitted) down. *Who did she think she was?* he must have been saying.

No doubt that was when Krystal and Reed developed a new plan.

They left Phoebe out of it because of her loyalty to me, and the fact that she's actually a true and honest person … one of the few, next to Yolanda, who actually buys into the mission of *Positive Enlightenment*. Perhaps it would have been better if they had been at the helm. No, this had to have been kept between them and good ol' Bertram the sales rep. Bertram liked to promise advertisers anything they wanted just to make the sale, even if it was something he couldn't deliver. Maybe I was thrown into the sponsorship package, though I'm not entirely sure why Jack would have gone for it.

As for Reed, he must have promised Asher Starling a good bit of money to save the story by this newest plot twist … him "falling in love with me."

Not sure how this story could possibly get any worse.

Suddenly, there was a knock at the door.

"Sibley? You in there, darlin'?"

Thomas? What the heck was my ex-husband doing in Dublin?

Asher stood, alarmed, as I went to answer the door.

There stood Thomas, dressed in what appeared to be a new pair of jeans and a freshly ironed button-down shirt with a turned-down collar. What was left of his thinning hair was slicked back. In his hands were a dozen roses.

My least favorite flower, I thought. *But how could my ex of fifteen years be expected to remember something like that?* my inner voice snarked.

"I called the paper, and they told me where you'd be," he confessed, sheepishly.

It's not a newspaper, it's a monthly journal … Oh, never mind. "Why are you here?" I asked calmly, my heart beginning to thump loudly in my chest.

"Can we talk?" he asked, handing me the roses. "These are for you."

Frankly, it was strange to see Thomas with his bravado gone. What was happening? I pulled the door open wide and propped it open with the built-in doorstop.

"Well, it just so happens I'm getting ready to check out. Might be better if we took this conversation down to the lobby?" I suggested.

"Oh, okay?" It was then he noticed Asher. "Am I interrupting something?" he asked, curiously. There was a tinge of jealousy in his voice.

"Yes," I answered. "You're interrupting me leaving."

"No, I meant him," he pointed. "Who's—"

"Asher?!" Asher's on-again-off-again, but now just off, ex—whatever-you-wanna-call-her, Chloe, appeared beside Thomas wearing an overly tight dress that appeared two sizes too small and six inches too short. On her feet, she wore bright red stilettos. "I was just knocking on your room next door. Why are you over—" Her eyes grew wide and her lips and nose contorted into a sneer as she suddenly put two and two together and realized he was standing in my hotel room.

"Let me guess," Asher let out a huff. "Someone from *Positive Enlightenment* told you exactly where you could find me?"

"Well, yes. How did you—"

I shook my head. "When I get a hold of Reed, I'm gonna kill him!" I threatened.

"You'll have to get in line," Asher grumbled. Suddenly, his voice brightened. "Can I help you with your bags?" he offered with a cheerfulness that I know he didn't feel.

"Yes, please," I agreed.

"What about—" Thomas protested.

"Come with me," I ordered. "You can wait in the lobby while I check out. I should have a few minutes before my ride arrives to take me to the airport."

"But, I'm confused. I thought you were staying another two nights?" Thomas fumbled with the roses. "I was hoping . . ."

"I know you were, Thomas," I answered, as all the gears began to click into place. The four-car pileup that was me, Asher, Chloe, and Thomas was no accident. "But there has been a change of plans. I'll tell you all about it in a moment."

Asher grabbed my suitcase, lifted the handle, and began to roll it toward the elevator. I followed behind with my second, smaller case rolling behind, my purse strapped on the back.

"Don't they have hotel porters who do that, Asher?" Chloe complained as she struggled to keep up with him in her tight red dress and high-heeled shoes.

For someone with an MBA, she sure wasn't very bright.

Asher paused. "Chloe, would you mind meeting me at the restaurant downstairs? I'll join you as soon as I've seen Sibley off."

"There are two down there, which one—"

"Just pick one, and I'll find you," Asher grumbled.

Chloe was taken aback. Asher had never snapped at her before—not once. Her lip quivered as her expression bounced back and forth between anger and sadness. Finally, she nodded. "You guys go ahead," she said as the elevator arrived. "I'll catch the next one."

Thomas, Asher, me, my luggage, and several other guests from Clontarf piled in, making it a tight squeeze with my ex-husband just in front of me, Asher behind me, and me sandwiched in between. The air was hot as we made our final descent to the lobby. As if those around us could feel the vibe of our energy, the entire elevator cab remained silent.

After checking out and confirming that my ride to Dublin Airport was on the way, I met with Thomas, who was now sitting on a chair at a small table near reception. He stood as I approached and pulled out a chair for me.

"I'll get that," he said, then pulled my suitcase up to my chair and out of the walkway, so no guests would trip. I set my smaller travel case on the table. He pushed my chair in for me. He'd never done that, not in all the time I'd known him—except maybe for the first week of dating. Which begged the question: if he knew how to behave like a gentleman and show me that I mattered, why the hell had I never seen this side of him before?

"I was surprised to find you in Dublin," Thomas confessed. "I read your two articles in the paper"—again, not a paper—"they were real good, by the way. Sounded real professional-like."

"That's because I am a professional writer, Thomas." I pursed my lips.

"I know, I know," he waved a hand at me. "I just didn't realize how good. I didn't understand why anyone would pay good money to send you on such an extravagant assignment—"

"Gee, thanks."

Thomas blinked nervously before answering softly. "Now, I get it."

He looked defeated. I softened my voice. "Why are you here, Thomas?"

"I wanted to talk to you."

"A phone would have been easier than a transatlantic flight."

"The truth is . . ." he framed his words carefully. "I miss you, and I want you to come home."

"We're divorced, Thomas. I moved out months ago. Did you forget?"

"Of course not," he shook his head. In the past, that would have been enough to set his temper off. Now, he merely hunched his shoulders forward, a frustrated scowl on his face. "I just didn't realize what a good thing we had." I wanted to retort that we never had a "good thing," but I didn't have the heart. He seemed really beaten down. "Then, when I read your articles … goin' on dates with other men. Well, I got jealous. And, if I'm being honest, I didn't expect you to move on so fast." He put his arms on the table, clasping his hands together.

I touched his arm, gently. Thomas turned his chin up to me and smiled, hopefully. "Well, this was less moving on and more of an assignment."

Thomas's expression brightened. "Well, that's what I thought, and then I got an idea," he smiled at his cleverness.

"You'd fly here and whisk me off my feet again, and the Valentine's finale would involve me choosing you over the other men I was set up on dates with? We'd enjoy a kiss under the Eiffel Tower and it'd be business as usual."

"How'd you guess?" He was legitimately surprised.

"It wasn't hard," I replied.

"So, how'd you end up in Dublin?" Thomas asked.

"Long story," I answered, watching as a cab driver popped through the hotel entrance. "That might be for me." I flagged the man down and confirmed he was here for "Bloom." "I'm sorry to cut this short, Thomas, but I'm heading back to Florida."

"But," he protested. "I came all this way to see you!"

"Again, you might have called instead. Sorry, hon. But there's a business-class ticket and a complimentary glass of Prosecco with my name on it."

"Wow," was all he could say. "Fancy."

"Goodbye, Thomas."

I grabbed my bag, and the cab driver—a tall, stout man who immediately read my expression better than anyone I'd ever met before—snatched my larger bag and ushered me quickly out the door. It had me curious how many scenes such as this one he'd witnessed in the past. With the cab driver at my back, I felt safe enough not to bother looking behind me. And so, I boarded the taxi and headed to the airport.

Meanwhile . . .

Chloe's eyes shimmered as Asher made his way to the Knights Bar.

"OMG, Asher," she smiled from a booth, reaching a well-manicured hand with long red fingernails and several gold rings out to him. "Have you seen this place? Isn't it the sweetest?"

He slid into the booth across from her, without bothering to take her hand.

"Are you still mad at me?" She pouted. "I thought you would have appreciated my little surprise."

Asher was past the point of being angry. He had moved on to indifferent. He shivered. "It's a bit chilly, don't you think?"

"I've asked them to turn up the heaters," she winked. "Give it a few minutes."

"Why are you here, Chloe?"

"You don't seem very happy to see me," Chloe deepened her voice in what she had intended as sultry.

"I'm not," he answered, flatly.

"Asher!" She was taken aback.

At that moment, a server was headed in their direction with a pitcher of water but quickly turned on their heels and retreated.

"You made it very clear that you and I were finished," Asher explained. "I've accepted that, and moved on."

"To Sibley Bloom, you mean," her eyes darkened.

"To 'it's no longer your concern.'"

"Can I at least explain myself?" Chloe pouted again. Until this moment, Asher had never realized that she had a built-in stream of ready-made expressions, as if she'd practiced them in the mirror, perfecting them over time.

"If it would make you feel better, go ahead," he relented.

The server deemed it safe to return, pouring them each a glass of water. "Can I offer you any drinks to get started?" she asked, politely.

"I'll have the French Martini," Chloe wriggled, winking at Asher.

"And for you, sir?"

"Just the water, thanks," Asher answered. "I won't be staying long."

"Very good," the server answered. To Chloe, she asked, "So … one brunch menu, then?"

Chloe's head ticked a little from side to side. "Could you … give us a moment to decide? Thank you."

"Of course, madam." The server retreated.

"Asher, I must admit, I expected a slightly warmer reception from you," Chloe leaned back in the booth, her fingers wrapped around the glass of water. "But I understand. I invited myself along on this trip and then bailed at the last minute."

"Because you got a better offer," Asher pointed out.

"Because I was afraid of my feelings for you." She lowered her gaze.

Asher grinned before leaning in and whispering, "You forget, my dear. It's my job to uncover the charlatans and fake faith healers and psychics. I can spot bullshit a million miles away."

"Asher!"

"It just took me longer with you because your crap was wrapped in a very pretty package."

"So, you still find me attractive—" Chloe was hopeful.

"Goodbye, Chloe." Asher stood, just as the server deposited the drink.

"Well, wait!" she whined. "I don't actually have any place to stay in Dublin. I just assumed—"

Asher shook his head. "Well then," he answered, "you should talk to reception. Since Sibley checked out early, they might have the space. I'll be following, shortly behind her. But whatever you do," he finished, "please don't come knocking on my door."

With Asher and Sibley gone, and after the dust had settled, Chloe sipped her drink—her eyes darting nervously around the bar. It was awkward for her, dining alone. She liked to believe she was the kind of woman who should never have to.

Just then, she spotted him ... a slightly balding, tall man with a paunch. In his hands were a dozen red roses. He surveyed the pub, uncomfortably.

"Hey," she called out to him, sipping her martini. She twisted the lower half of her torso so her long legs dangled in plain view beneath the table. She crossed them demurely.

"Yes?" Thomas's eyes drifted from her legs back up to her face. He had taken the bait.

"You're Sabine's ex, aren't you?" She leaned forward, placing one arm on the table for emphasis.

"Eh, Sibley," he corrected.

"Whatever." She tilted her head. She scanned Thomas from head to toe. Not the most attractive man she'd seen, but not the worst. From the look of his clothes, he didn't have much money to speak of. But she hated the idea of being seen without a companion.

"Are those for me?" She winked, just as the server brought a single menu. Once again, they turned on their heels, this time to procure a second.

"Uh." Thomas thought a moment before catching her meaning. "Yes. Yes, they are." He beamed. Thomas slid in the booth across from Chloe, setting the flowers in front of her.

"Roses!" she squealed, delighted. "My favorite."

CHAPTER TWENTY-EIGHT
GASLIGHTING
VIDALIA

I took the day off and was happily doing a bit of grocery shopping for Sibley and me. She was arriving home from the Tampa airport today after her whirlwind assignment overseas. Given the time difference and my work schedule, we had very little time to chat. The last I heard was a text message that read, "Jack Vex is an ass."

"What happened? Zoom chat later?" I texted. But she and her team had to make a sudden pivot, it seemed.

"Text you from Glendalough," she promised. But then, nothing since, until her message that she'd touched down safely in Florida.

I didn't know what finally happened between her and Arran, but if my suspicions were correct, he was as big a cad as I first thought. And one only had to read the tabloids to have a thing or two to say about Jack. I really needed to have a conversation with Sibley about the dating red flags. I tried before she left, but everything happened in such a rush, I don't think any of it sank in.

"What the heck is limerence?" she asked me.

I tried explaining about the dopamine–oxytocin rush, the drop in serotonin, and all the things that led to infatuation without logic. "Basically," I told her, "your judgment is bound to be skewed when caught up in the romance of a European vacation."

"It's not a vacation," she insisted. "I'm working."

"I know, but—"

"Vidalia Oliveira," a voice called, pulling me from my thoughts, just as I was adding scallions and broccolini to my shopping cart. I looked up to see Rosaline Perdita sniffing the side of a cantaloupe. She set it down, adopting the snarkiest of walks as she sauntered over to me. "Surprised you're not in prison," her voice dripped with disdain.

This was Nadia Perdita's older sister. No doubt she was grieving over the loss, particularly with Nadia's death being questionable. I'd only met her once, the night she came to retrieve the last of Nadia's things following the divorce. She didn't say much as I handed her a cardboard box with her sister's belongings. I was told the breakup was amicable, but Rosaline still gave me the side-eye, as if I were "the other woman." By that point, Nadia and Tod had been "over" for nearly eight months. Today, I tried to give Rosaline the benefit of the doubt. After all, how could she know what kind of person I was … or wasn't?

"Rosaline," I began. "I am so sorry for your loss—"

"Save it, sweetheart," she spat, loud enough for others to hear and quickly double back with their carts. One lonely teenager stocking apples remained, looking decidedly uncomfortable. "I know it was you." Rosaline was a tall, bulky woman with heavy foundation and bright red lipstick that stuck to her teeth as she spoke. Her dark hair was dyed and tied back in a fierce ponytail.

"Rosaline," I moved toward her, secretively. She backed up, defensive. *What did she think I was gonna do, stab her with a bunch of limp broccolini?* I backed up as well, giving her space. "I'm still trying to make sense of what happened. The police have no idea what she was doing on the top of our roof in the first place."

"Oh, that's right," Rosaline was on a roll. "You and that slimy cop are trying to pin it on Tod."

"Wait, what?" I asked, surprised. Rosaline's eyes grew wide. She knew she'd said too much. "Have you spoken to Tod?"

After a long pause, she blurted out, "No, why would I?" She darted her eyes from side to side. I knew she was lying.

I sucked in my breath. Rosaline lived several towns over, so what was she doing in this neck of the woods? And did that mean that Tod was nearby too?

"Rosaline," I tried again. "I'm not sure what you've heard, but I've never even met Nadia."

"I'd," she corrected.

"What?" I was confused.

"Past tense. It should be 'I'd never even met Nadia.'"

Ah, right. Nadia had been an elementary school music teacher; Rosaline was a fifth-grade English teacher. Somehow, I felt she was missing the point. "So you're telling me you didn't know that she and Tod were getting back together?"

"What? No. That can't be true," I felt a sucker-punch pain in my belly. Something told me that what she was saying might be true.

Rosaline smiled, a sardonic smile. Suddenly, I was feeling less sorry for her loss.

"Word has it, they were going to reconcile and kick you to the curb." She tossed a melon into her cart with a bit too much force. It landed on a package of blueberries that crackled beneath the melon's weight. No matter—Rosaline removed the blueberries and set them back on the shelf, reaching instead for an undamaged package. "Did you think getting rid of her would make a difference?"

Alarm bells were going off in my head. "Rosaline," I told her, slowly and distinctly, "I've never met Nadia, and Tod may be dangerous. If you know anything about his whereabouts—"

"I don't," she waved a hand at me, "and you're boring me," she dismissed me as she brushed past my cart, purposefully knocking it slightly off to one side.

I didn't waste any time. I set my cart aside, hightailed it outside where I could get decent phone reception, and called Jameson.

"I think he might be nearby," I gasped, recounting my interaction with Rosaline.

"Stay calm," Jameson advised. "Where are you now?"

"I'm at the grocery store. Sibley is coming back today. I was trying to get some food in the house."

"Tell you what," he offered. "Finish what you're doing, and I'll meet you at your apartment in, say, an hour? In the meantime, we'll look into Rosaline Perdita's story."

I nodded. Then, realizing he couldn't hear a nod over the phone, I answered, "Okay. Sorry to keep setting off alarm bells. I know you have other, more important cases."

"I can't think of one more important than keeping you safe," he answered. "See you soon."

He hung up the phone as the weight of his words hung in the air. I suspected he might be thinking of me as more than just a case, a suspect, or whatever. But until this very moment, I hadn't been sure.

So there I stood, in the Publix parking lot, feeling a mix of fear, betrayal, and confusion, coupled with excitement, joy, and a sense of possibility.

Had Tod really planned on leaving me and getting back together with Nadia? Was he just stringing me along while I gave him money for the house? The only thing I knew for certain? I had no business giving Sibley, or anyone, romantic advice. I may have been gaslighted by a murderer.

CHAPTER TWENTY-NINE
BACK HOME
SIBLEY

I fumbled with the apartment key, jet-lagged and in need of a long shower. I had my suitcase and one additional travel bag behind me. I wasn't sure if Vidalia was at work or not. Honestly, I felt I could have done a better job communicating with her about my return home. But I was exhausted, embarrassed, and really didn't want her armchair therapy right now.

I had just dragged my bags back inside when Skinny leapt all over me, showering me with puppy kisses. I dropped my key on the end table and wrapped my arms around the mutt. I knew he was Vidalia's dog, but somehow, he now felt like mine, too.

"Excuse me," a man's voice called out from the hallway behind me.

Startled, I turned to see a tall, thin man wearing a white T-shirt, ripped jeans, and a red baseball cap. He had a small goatee, and bits of his blond hair crept out from under his hat. Skinny went crazy, leaping all over the man, excitedly.

"Wow," I commented. "He really likes you."

"Aw, shucks," he answered, scritching Skinny behind his ears and laughing. Eventually, Skinny got whatever it was out of his system and promptly sat on the man's foot.

"I'm so sorry," I apologized. "Skinny, c'mon inside."

"It's alright," the man said with a long Southern drawl. "I don't mind."

"Er, can I help you with something?"

"Yeah, I hate to bother you, seein' as it looks as if you've just returned from a trip. I'm Bobby. Just moved in down the hall." He motioned toward his apartment.

"Oh, well, welcome to the neighborhood," I offered, tiredly.

"I feel so silly," he grinned, sheepishly. "I've managed to lock myself out. Any chance I could use your phone to call my girlfriend to come by and let me in with her key?"

"Oh, of course." I really wanted nothing more than to crawl into bed for a long nap, but I couldn't very well leave him stranded. "C'mon in. I'll fish out my cell phone from my bag in a second."

The man grabbed the handle on my suitcase. "Let me," he smiled, helpfully.

Once inside, the man shut the door behind him, giving me an uneasy pause. But then I watched as Skinny happily jumped all over the man, yet again. *Can't be that bad, if the dog likes him.* And, with the door open, who knows at what point that darn dog was going to go running through the halls, down the steps, and potentially hurt himself—or my neighbors?

"So, Bobby, care for a bottle of water or anything?" I asked.

"If you don't mind. That would be amazing," the man sat on my couch and spread his long legs out in front of him. Hmm, oddly comfortable for a stranded neighbor.

Just then, the door handle rotated a bit. I could hear as the door opened. A shuffling followed. Then, dead silence.

I turned to face the living room, bottle of water in hand. "Vidalia, you're home!" I exclaimed, gleefully.

But then I saw the man and Vidalia exchange glances. Even Skinny was confused, darting glances between the two humans, undecided.

"Welcome home, Vidalia," the man echoed, eerily.

"Tod," Vidalia stated. "How did you find me?"

The hairs on the back of my neck stood up. *Oh shit. I never met Tod. In hindsight, I should have asked for a photo—something to keep a lookout for my friend. I'm so stupid.*

"I was disappointed how we left things," Tod continued, his voice smooth and calm.

"I need you to leave, right now!" Vidalia exclaimed.

My tired brain was trying to process everything, but it wasn't firing on all cylinders. Sleep deprivation does that.

Just then, Tod pulled out a Glock 19 from his back pocket. How on earth did I not notice the holster? He pointed it at Vidalia. "Have a seat," he instructed. To me, he called, "You too, Ms. Bloom."

How did he know who I was?

Skinny began barking and making a fuss. Tod pointed the gun at Skinny.

"Don't you dare!" Vidalia cautioned. "Or so help me—"

His gaze lifted, as if moving in slow motion. "Vidalia, kindly get a hold of your dog."

"Skinny," Vidalia's hand was shaking. "Settle now. Settle."

For once, Skinny listened. Unfortunately, he chose to hop on the couch next to "Bobby" and curl up beside him.

"Good dog," Tod praised, petting him with his free hand.

I sat on the couch opposite Tod and Skinny, next to Vidalia. Tod continued to point the gun at Skinny. It was genius. I knew for damn sure if it was pointed at the two of us, Vidalia or I, at some point, would have taken our chances and lunged at him. But Skinny? No, he was an innocent dog. Neither of us moved a muscle.

"What is it that you want, Tod?" Vidalia asked, carefully.

Asher knew in his heart that the timing wasn't right—they were both angry, disappointed, and jet-lagged. He scheduled his flight to arrive home sooner than originally anticipated. He grumbled a little as he chose economy, remembering how Chloe had said, "It's only one-way," and "whatever you can afford. Sorry, babes." Come to think of it, he realized, he'd become so consumed with the assignment—and Sibley—that he all but forgot about his ex-girlfriend.

And now, there was something in him that couldn't rest until the issue between him and Sibley was, at least, somewhat resolved. In all his life, he may have lacked clarity. But the one constant was Sibley Bloom … as a work colleague, a friend, and now? Who knows? He'd known her for more than fifteen years. And yet, it was as if he was finally seeing her for the first time. How had he managed to ignore what his heart had been telling him for so long?

He was jolted from his thoughts just as he arrived and buzzed the intercom of her apartment from the street below. There was another man there, at the exact same time.

"Sorry," Detective Jameson said. "You go first."

Jameson was dressed in a shirt and tie with black slacks, a holstered gun in obvious view. Asher eyed the gun, but thought nothing of it … this was Florida, after all.

To Jameson's surprise, Asher buzzed the same apartment he was about to, for Vidalia. His brow lifted a bit, with interest.

Asher coughed a little, as Jameson's looming presence did nothing to ease his nerves. After what seemed like an eternity, a voice answered.

"Hello?"

It was Sibley.

"Sibley," Asher began. "It's me … Asher, of course. I suspect you know that. Listen, I know you're tired from your long trip, but could we please talk? Even just for a moment?"

There was a weird shuffling sound from the intercom. Finally, she answered, "Asher, darling," Sibley began. *Darling?* Asher furrowed his brows—something that did not escape Jameson's attention. She continued, "I'm so sorry about our argument, love. But could we talk in the morning? I'm ever so tired."

Asher didn't know Detective Jameson any more than Jameson knew him. But their exchanged glances had a keen understanding that something was wrong.

"All right … *honey*," Asher answered, struggling to find the right words. "I'll ring you up tomorrow … Sleep well. And, for what it's worth … I'm sorry too."

The intercom went silent.

"Sorry, man," Asher apologized. "I'm tying up the line. Your turn." He moved aside.

"Erm . . ." Jameson began. "I couldn't help but notice that you rang the same apartment as I was about to."

Asher's face went pale. *Who was this stranger?*

Jameson recognized that expression from years of police work. "No, man. I was calling on Vidalia—Sibley's roommate. Though I'm concerned for her safety. Tell me, did that message seem off to you?" Jameson pointed toward the intercom, pinching his lips together, sourly.

"Completely," Asher replied, running a hand through his hair.

Jameson didn't waste any time. He phoned for backup but asked them to be discreet. If his fear was justified, then Vidalia was home too, and they weren't alone.

"What's happening?" Asher asked, concerned.

"Not sure yet," Jameson eyed Asher, suspiciously. "You wouldn't happen to know Sibley's roommate, would you? Vidalia Oliveira?"

"Only in passing," Asher answered. "During after-work happy hours she's served us on occasion. I know she is friends with Sibley, but not much beyond that."

"Right." Jameson buzzed the intercom. After a long pause, Sibley answered again.

"Asher, I told you—"

"Sibley," Detective Jameson interrupted. "This is Jameson. I'm supposed to be meeting Vidalia here. Is she home?"

There was another long pause.

"Uh, no," Sibley answered. "I just got home from a long trip. I haven't seen her yet."

By now, several unmarked vehicles pulled up in front of the apartment complex, while two additional police cars drove into the parking garage, and two more in the back of the building.

"Okay," Jameson answered calmly. "Now listen carefully, Sibley. If you happen to hear from a man named Tod Evans, I'd like for you to leave him a message for me, okay?"

Jameson waited an unbearably long time for a reply. Finally, the buzz of the intercom kicked in, and she answered, "Okay." He could hear her labored breathing on the other end. With all his years on the force, he could read this easily … fear.

"If you hear from Tod Evans," Jameson began slowly, "I want you to tell him … tell him I know he didn't kill his wife. I can help him, but he needs to talk to me."

The intercom buzzed. After a moment of heavy breathing, a man's voice said, "Ex-wife, Detective Jameson … Yeah, that's right. I know who you are, detective. Hooching up to my Vidalia as soon as I was out of the picture."

Jameson felt the heat rise in his face and neck. From Asher's perspective, it seemed the detective's brow broke out in a sweat. "Tod … I can help you. But I need you to let Sibley and Vidalia go."

"They're my security, Detective!" Tod yelled into the intercom. "How stupid do you think I am?!"

Jameson was wise enough to keep those thoughts to himself. Apparently, Tod was dumb enough to keep the intercom button pressed hard against the wall. Vidalia could be heard saying, "Tod, honey, please listen for a moment—"

"I'm tired of listening! While all you stupid women do the talkin'!"

Jameson waited for a moment. Vidalia continued, "Tod, if you let Sibley go, Skinny and me will stay right here with you—isn't that right, Skinny?"

She's letting me know exactly who's inside … human and otherwise.

Skinny let out a bark.

"Nah … nah," Tod sounded frantic. "Lemme think … okay. Okay. We'll do a trade. I'll let Sibley go, but you have to take her place, Detective."

"That's just fine, Tod. How shall we make the trade?"

"Come upstairs, leave your gun by the door. If you don't—"

"I will," Jameson reassured him.

"I'll let Sibley go and you come take her place … but no funny business!"

"No funny business," Jameson agreed. "Give me a minute or two to climb the stairs and remove my gun and holster. I'll knock when I'm ready for the trade, okay?"

"Okay," Tod spat, reaffirming, "And no funny business."

The intercom went dead. A moment later, the door buzzed, giving him access. He slid his foot in place to keep the door open while he made a call.

In a split second, Jameson phoned the head of his rescue team. He eyed Asher, who was now frozen in place with no idea how to respond. "Listen," he barked into the phone. "I'm going in. Tod is going to let one hostage out. I'll be inside, presumably with Tod Evans, Vidalia Oliveira … and her dog. When Ms. Bloom comes out, her partner, Asher—" He paused to confirm he heard that correctly. Asher nodded, repeatedly. "Asher will collect Ms. Bloom. Keep them safe until we've resolved this matter, okay."

He got the affirmative and disappeared inside before Asher had a chance to say more.

Jameson followed protocol.

Moments later, the door opened. "Greetings, Detective," Tod's voice dripped with disdain as he held a gun out. Had it only been Jameson, he was confident he could easily disarm him. But he dared not risk anyone else getting shot in the process. "Come inside."

"We had an agreement," Jameson reminded him.

"Oh, right."

Tod grabbed Sibley's arm, pulling her toward the door and pushing her back, essentially shoving her out the door.

"Go!" Jameson ordered, slipping inside the door before any other potential tenants could inadvertently be pulled into this mess.

Sibley, sleep-deprived, jet-lagged, yet hyped on adrenaline, ran past him—offering a sorrowful backward glance as Jameson disappeared into the apartment.

She took to the stairs at such speed that she had to routinely hang onto the rails for dear life, lest she fall headlong downward. When she reached the outdoors, she sailed into Asher's arms, all but toppling him over.

Sibley sobbed, uncontrollably, shivering.

"It's okay, I've got you," Asher hugged her in a tight embrace.

"But what about Vidalia?" Sibley sniffed.

"Ma'am," an officer approached, carefully, "I'm gonna need the two of you back near the police vehicles for safety."

Sibley clung to Asher until they'd reached one of the cars, where Sibley declined a blanket to offset the trauma. Fear or no fear, it was still Florida, and it was still hot. Sibley cast her gaze upward toward her apartment, saying a silent prayer for Vidalia, Skinny, and Jameson.

"He knows what he's doing," Asher reassured her about Detective Jameson. "Let him do what he's been trained to do. It'll be alright … I'm just glad you're safe."

Sibley sniffed, clutching Asher's arm. "I'm still mad at you!" she sobbed.

"I know," he rubbed her shoulder. "You can yell at me later, okay?"

Sibley nodded, her face tear-stained as she answered simply, "Okay."

Once inside, Tod quickly motioned for Jameson to take a seat on the couch beside Vidalia, while he sat next to Skinny, petting the dog haphazardly.

"Traitor," Vidalia whispered to Skinny. Skinny, not knowing the word, merely wagged his tail, happily.

"I can help you," Detective Jameson told Tod. "But I need you to be honest about what happened with your wife."

"Ex-wife," Tod repeated. "I told you."

After a long pause where Jameson and Tod exchanged long, intensely distrustful looks, Jameson answered, "I stand by what I said."

Vidalia sat upright, shifting her gaze between the two men. "What's he talking about, Tod?"

Tod, feeling defeated, deflated, and just plain tired, sat back—the gun still held haphazardly, resting on his knee. This time, it was pointed at Vidalia (something that didn't escape Detective Jameson's attention).

"Fine," Tod relented. "I'll tell you everything, but you gotta protect me!"

"I'll do my best."

"Okay," Tod began, pausing suddenly. "Damn, I need a cigarette."

"I can hold the gun for you if you like?" Vidalia smirked. The old Tod was beginning to resurface, and he wasn't nearly so scary.

"No!" Tod sat up. Vidalia sank back in the couch. "I'll be fine. Just let me think . . ."

They sat for an eternity before Tod began his story.

"You see," he said. "You're mostly correct, detective. Nadia Perdita and I are still—technically—married."

"What?" Vidalia eyed him in surprise.

"She got sick," Tod explained, kicking the edge of the end table, absentmindedly. He was so distracted that Jameson had thoughts of overtaking the man and pinning him to the floor while backup came barreling through the door. But it would have been different if it were just him—not with a civilian … someone whom he had begun to care very much about … and an innocent dog. I mean, really, Jameson thought. How big of a jerk do you have to be to threaten a dog? He remained seated.

"Cancer," Tod continued. "She thought she was gonna die … hell, everyone thought that."

Vidalia and Jameson didn't say a word; they just waited. He scratched the side of his head with his left hand, his right still firmly planted on the gun.

"We wuzz already having trouble … hell," Tod chuckled. "Nothin' could keep that woman happy … then she got sick. Said she was going to her family home up North. Promised me that she'd leave the house to me after she'd died, but didn't want us to continue the way we were . . ."

For the first time that Vidalia could remember, Tod seemed to be fighting off tears. She kept her guard up. After all, with Tod, how could you know if they were real?

"Then why did you tell me we had to buy her out, Tod?" Vidalia questioned. "Why'd you tell me that my paycheck was going to pay off her half of the house? Was that all a lie?"

"Shut up!" Tod picked up the Glock resting on his knee and fluttered it around, dangerously. Jameson put a hand on Vidalia's arm, a subtle warning. She fell silent. Tod placed the gun down, carefully. Beads of sweat poured down his face. "Got word from family that the tides had turned. She was gettin' better. Suddenly, she wasn't feelin' so generous." He eyed Vidalia, sorrowfully. "I pictured a life with you and me. I really did. If that bi—" Tod caught himself. "If that woman changed the rules, then that meant that Nadia and I would have to sell. Except that the deed was in her name—her house long before me. I coulda been left with nothing."

"But she was the legal owner of the house," Vidalia clarified. "Not you."

"Woman!" Tod's eyes grew red. He turned to Jameson. "You see what I have to deal with?"

"You and Vidalia would have had to find a new home. That can be stressful. I understand," Jameson offered, calmly.

"Exactly!" Tod eyed Vidalia as if to say, *Why can't you think more like him? More like a man?*

"How did you smooth things over with Nadia?" Jameson encouraged, gently.

Tod fell silent, deep in thought. One couldn't tell if he were grieving, planning … or deciding.

"All right," he finally said. "I'll tell you what happened … honest-to-goodness truth. But—" he added. "You promised to protect me, right?"

"I will do my absolute best," Detective Jameson confirmed.

After a long sigh, Tod's eyes seemed to glaze over, as if remembering a recent past . . .

CHAPTER THIRTY

WHAT REALLY HAPPENED
BACK IN JULY

"What in the hell are you doing, Nadia?"

"Nice to see you too, Tod," Nadia replied curtly, fighting with a tall steel ladder. Her small frame was struggling to stand it up against the side of the house. Tod, having just returned from work, was surprised to find his estranged wife at their home—the one he currently shared with Vidalia.

An expression crossed Tod's face. It was only for a split second. If you'd blinked, you'd miss it. It was the one that Vidalia had only recently learned to read, the one where he was about to spin a yarn to manipulate you into doing something you didn't want to do.

"Aww, I'm sorry, sweet pea," he answered. He wasn't very creative. This was the same term of affection he used on Vidalia, too. "Where are my manners? How are you feeling?"

Nadia paused, her long worn out sundress flapping in the breeze, revealing long black leggings underneath. The wind was picking up fast. With a bright smile, she rested one foot on the lowest rung of the ladder. "I'm cured!"

"What?" A flicker of disappointment crossed his face before he covered it up.

"Cancer's in remission! Thought I was going back home to die. Turns out, I wasn't! Maybe time with family was just what I needed—soothed my soul."

Time to turn on the charm, Tod thought. "That's amazing!" He rushed over to her small frame, lifting her up and twirling them both in a circle.

"Tod!" she squealed, laughing. "What's gotten into you?"

"Just happy, is all." He set her down.

Nadia smoothed her soiled dress with her hands and brushed her hair from her face. "I can see that. But why? Last I heard, we took a 'trial separation' to 'figure things out.' Didn't take long before you brought another woman home."

"Aw, it wasn't like that, sweet pea," Tod argued. "I just thought you were finished with me." He took a step closer. "If I thought we had a chance—"

Nadia rested her hand on her waist, foot tapping, unconvinced. "And here I thought you were waiting for me to die so you could inherit the house."

"What?" Tod feigned surprise. "I thought no such thing. Honest, I've been working extra shifts so if you did give up on me, maybe I could buy out your half."

That was a lie. It was Vidalia's earnings that Tod was collecting for such a purpose. But in his mind, he figured he just had to wait it out. Nadia would be dead, and he'd have extra cash to spare.

"Half wouldn't do me much good dead, now would it?" Nadia replied, sourly.

"I never believed you were going to die," Tod answered, a slight tremble in his voice that let on he was lying. Once again, a trait that Vidalia had begun picking up on, but Nadia never did. Or at least, she preferred to believe what she wanted to believe.

"Well, no matter," she waved her hand. "Now that I'm going to live, I've come to a conclusion."

"And what's that?" Tod asked, hesitantly.

"I want us to sell the house and split the profits."

"What? No…This is our home!" he protested.

"Really?" Nadia lowered her gaze. "'Cause last I heard, you and that bartender were in pretty tight."

"No … but wait a second. What are you doing with that ladder, anyhow?" Tod removed his red baseball cap to give his head a scratch and let his hot head breathe a little.

Clouds began rolling in as the wind picked up speed. Nadia struggled to keep her dress from flying up as the current got under the hemline.

"Don't know if you're aware, but we've got a hurricane coming," she eyed Tod, seriously.

"Only a Cat 1," Tod rolled his eyes. "Lawn chairs everywhere, beware!"

"You know as well as I do that the winds can pick up fast, and people die, even in a Cat 1 hurricane! Besides, our roof is not in the greatest shape."

"And your plan was?" Tod asked.

"I wanna climb up there and take a look," Nadia's jaw set in a determined way.

"What exactly would you be looking for?" Tod challenged.

"See if any shingles are loose. Maybe snap a 'before' shot in case we need to contact the insurance companies after the fact." She fished into a pocket in her dress for an old, outdated phone with a modest camera.

"You'll break your neck," Tod answered. "If you're so hell-bent on photos, let me do it."

"What do you care?" Nadia spat.

And there it was—a little quiver of the lip. A little bit of emotion. That was all the encouragement that Tod needed.

"I care a great deal," he told her, pulling her away from the ladder and wrapping his arms around her. Nadia resisted at first, but then relented. Tod held her in a warm embrace. "You and me are meant to be."

"What about the bartender?" Nadia asked.

"She's history. She could never replace you. In fact, she and I broke it off weeks ago. She's just staying here until her new apartment becomes available … which happens to be next week, by the way."

"That was kind of you," Nadia acknowledged.

"And now, who do I see trying to climb up on my roof?" Tod joked, brushing a piece of Nadia's hair away and gazing into her eyes. "But the person I was meant to be with, all along."

Just then, Tod's cell phone buzzed. He reached around their embrace to pull his phone from his pocket. "Speak of the devil," he said, nervously.

"What?" Nadia asked.

"Vidalia—she's on her way home." He pulled away from Nadia abruptly, all but pushing her.

"Well, if you broke it off, what dif—" Nadia began. Suddenly, her eyes grew dark. "Oh, I see."

"What?"

"Tod, you are the most manipulative so-and-so that I ever laid eyes on! Git out of my way while I check the roof and be on my way. I'm selling this house, and you and the bartender can figure out where to live on half the profits … unless you buy me out. Choice is yours."

While Tod contemplated how to stall Vidalia—maybe ask her to stop and pick up some Bud on the way home?—Nadia was already angry-climbing up on the roof.

And then it happened . . .

As she gripped the rooftop with her hands, her left foot balanced on the ladder's top rung, she struggled to plant her right on the roof–just as the ladder began to topple. Tod dropped his phone and rushed to steady the ladder, but it was too late—

Nadia lost her balance, her fingertips scraping the shingles as she struggled to hang on. As she fell, Tod—though his reaction time was limited—did his best to catch her. Her small frame fell, knocking him over as her head smacked the paved driveway when she landed. Nadia, Tod Evans' wife, was dead upon impact.

Tod scrambled to get up. Blood marked the driveway where she landed, the impact weakened by Tod as a buffer. "Shit, shit, shit, shit!" he cried out, shaking his wife's lifeless body, just in case she might reawaken.

She didn't.

Vidalia is on the way home, he thought, miserably.

He'd have to explain … or call the cops … and still have to explain.

Given his track record for past offenses (most nonviolent … most. But still—there would be questions).

Then a thought occurred to him … if he just hid the body and waited it out for a few years, he could legally acquire the house when his wife disappeared and never returned. In a way, it was no different from waiting for her to die of cancer. Either way, he'd still inherit—

With shaky hands, he texted Vidalia. *Can you stop for Bud, chips, and a few hurricane supplies?* He waited, momentarily, as a "thumbs up," emoji came in.

Tod quickly grabbed a shovel from the garage and started digging … a shallow grave under an oak tree at the edge of their secluded property . . .

~

When Tod finished telling his story, Detective Jameson spoke. "You're looking at some very serious charges, Mr. Evans."

"But I didn't kill her!" he protested, gun still at his knee.

"I believe you, but that still leaves failure to report a death, abuse of a dead body—"

"Abuse?" Tod questioned.

"Abuse," Jameson confirmed. "As in, burying her on the property to conceal evidence … tampering with evidence and possible obstruction of justice."

"Would I have suffered less with a murder charge?!" Tod whined, his face turning red and crumpling under the stress.

"Of course not," Jameson reassured. "But unless you cooperate, you could still be looking at fifteen-plus years in prison."

"That bitch!" Tod shook his head. "Ruining my life over and over again."

"The 'bitch' that you were ready to leave me for?" Vidalia couldn't help herself. "The one who ended up *dead*, in case you missed that little factoid."

"I was never planning on leaving you for her," Tod explained. "I just told her that so—"

"You could get what you wanted," Vidalia finished.

"Well, if you hadn't been on the way home at that very moment, things might have been different," Tod defended.

"So, somehow this is my fault?" Vidalia crossed her arms.

"Tod," Jameson tried again, calmly, "if you put the gun down and turn yourself in, I promise I will do my best to lessen the charges against you."

"Oh sure," Tod spat. "I bet you're doing this so you can have Vidalia all to yourself. Yeah! I see the way you look at her."

Jameson cleared his throat, slightly embarrassed. "If my aim were to get you out of the way, I promise you, I could plan a lot worse for you."

"Not if I shoot you," Tod threatened, holding up the Glock and pointing it in Jameson's direction.

Vidalia fought the urge to dive in front of it, in order to grab the gun and protect Jameson. She'd seen too many movies that taught her this was a bad idea.

"You could," Jameson agreed. "But right now, I have a swarm of undercover officers surrounding the place. You wouldn't get out alive."

"What of it," Tod sneered. "I'm done for, anyway."

"Not if you cooperate," Jameson explained. "I can't promise anything, but the evidence shows you didn't kill your wife. You were scared. That's understandable. You made a rash decision based on fear. The judge will understand that."

After much deliberation, Tod conceded, hesitantly turning his gun over to Jameson. Moments later, officers rushed in to cuff him and read him his rights. As they were escorting him toward the police vehicle outside, he turned his head.

"Hey, Detective," he called. Jameson looked up. "Seein' how I didn't kill her … does that mean I still get to inherit the property?"

Jameson gritted his teeth, stifling back a response as the officers stuffed Tod into the police cruiser. He turned to Vidalia, concerned. "You okay?" he asked, placing a hand on her arm.

Vidalia hugged herself and nodded. "I will be," she answered, quietly.

CHAPTER THIRTY-ONE
THE LAST CHRONICLE
SIBLEY

I sat in the conference room of the Positive Enlightenment office with a printed copy of the final chronicle in a folder in front of me on the table. It was for the February issue and included my adventures in Glendalough, a wrap-up of my "spiritual and romantic journey." Technically, Valentine's Day was still more than two weeks out and the only one of my pieces that preceded the actual holiday.

For once, I was the first to arrive—which did not go unnoticed.

"Oh, hey!" Yolanda was surprised. "I swung by your office to remind you of the meeting, but you're already here." Yolanda took a seat beside me. "Everything okay?"

"Of course. Why wouldn't it be?" I asked, quizzically.

"No reason," Yolanda countered. She pulled out her own copy of the article she'd written about the London conference and set it in front of her. I had no doubt that it was glowing—Reed would have made sure of it. I'll bet there's no mention of Jack's predatory behavior nor his loss of temper at not getting his own way. No, it would be all praise and smiles, I bet.

Phoebe arrived next. "Oh, you're here already," she said to me. "Are you okay?"

"Why does everyone keep asking me that?" I proclaimed. "It's not like I'm late to every meeting."

"Hmmm," Yolanda bit her lip.

Reed, Krystal, and Bertram entered next. As expected, Bertram's eyes were glued to his phone (so much so that he accidentally bumped into the conference table on the way to his chair), Krystal was tapping on an open laptop as she walked (one long-fingered key at a time), and Reed … well, Reed had his usual nose-in-the-air sort of glow with a small grin turning up the corners of his mouth. This was his "enlightened" face, the one that feigned humility and equanimity but was riddled with conde-scension.

Finally, Asher arrived. He looked a little … disheveled … if I'm being honest. Like he hadn't had a decent night's sleep in a while. He eyed me sheepishly before taking his usual seat across from me, eyes downcast.

Probably on to his next conquest, I thought, bitterly. *No*, I chastised myself. That's not entirely fair. I'm the one that shut him out. What did I expect him to do? Keep apologizing forever?

"Welcome back, travelers," Reed began, addressing Yolanda, Asher, and me. "Made it back in one piece, I see," he joked.

"Barely," Yolanda pressed her lips together and puffed out her cheeks. She eyed me, apologetically.

"Yes," Phoebe added. "We could have done a better job with trans-parency. You know that, right?"

"Ah, I see," Reed answered. "Dissension in the ranks. Can't say I'm surprised—"

"But you could say you're sorry," Yolanda pointed out. "We all should."

"Guys," I interjected. "It's fine." To Reed, I said, "I get what I think you were trying to do. I mean, this was more than just a good story, right? You were testing the waters on some type of dating show?"

Reed's face dropped in surprise. "How did—"

"Remember, this was part romance and part spiritual quest. I re-read the itinerary from start to finish when I returned home—my version and the versions you sent everyone else—the ones I wasn't supposed to see. Follow that with some quality meditation time and my roommate's nutty ex pulling a gun on me and—"

Bertram looked up from his phone, suddenly interested. "A gun?"

"Yeah," I answered. "But that's not what's important—except that everything suddenly clicked into place for me. Vidalia—my roommate —was being gaslighted by her ex, Tod. I was being manipulated by Reed—"

"For the greater cause—" he defended.

"If you say so," I finished. "But once I started looking at what everyone had to gain, it all pointed to an alliance between you and Jack Vex for some future business endeavor." I reached into my folder and pulled out a few more pages. "In addition to my article, I have here a few online clips I printed out on Vex's other business ventures—when he's not franchising out overpriced spas."

"Eh? What did you find?" Phoebe leaned in, with interest.

"He's pitched a few reality shows in the past … a bisexual partner-swap show, the 'find out who's cheating' program, and the 'behind the scenes at a spa' reality show—his partners didn't like that one—"

No one in the room spoke, not even Reed with a few platitudes. Even the tapping on Krystal's computer stopped as she lifted her fingers from the keys to listen.

"It was *Heartbreak on a Deadline* that sold 'em—"

"But that was my idea!" Phoebe cried out, half standing before catching herself and sitting back down. "Not that that's important," she shifted her gaze awkwardly in my direction.

"When were you planning on letting us in on this, Reed," Yolanda asked. "Or were you going to pull up stakes and go create a new reality show and leave us high and dry?"

"First of all," Reed pointed a finger in the air, "I'm offended that you would think that. Second of all, if it did get picked up by a major network after this experiment, I had roles for all of you—and the journal would continue as well."

I didn't like that I was now being lumped into an experiment, but none of this mattered anymore.

The only one not talking was Asher, who was now slumped in his chair, arms folded—an angry scowl on his face.

"Cat got your tongue?" Krystal asked, fanning the flames.

"Just feeling a little used, and very stupid, for the blatant manipulation that went on here, is all. And I'm embarrassed that I allowed myself to buy into it." He shot a sorrowful look in my direction. I quickly averted my gaze.

"Guys," Reed answered, staying remarkably calm. "If I told you everything up front, it wouldn't have worked. It had to seem real."

The old me would have been livid. But the new me could see everything with remarkable clarity.

"May I point out," I interjected, "that we still have a journal to run and a story to tell. Phoebe, I've emailed you my final piece for review."

"Thank you … wait. When you say 'final' you just mean the final piece of the chronicles, right?" She eyed me suspiciously.

"I'm afraid not," I stood. "Krystal, I'll send you an invoice for my final article and my leftover expenses from the trip. But I resign—effective immediately."

~

Excerpt from the Heartbreak on a Deadline Chronicles
I'd be lying if I said that this experience didn't change me. When I began my journey, I was freshly divorced with little dating experience and even less

knowledge about what I wanted in a partner. How could I know? I didn't even know who I was as a person and what I truly wanted in life.

I quickly went from living under my parents' roof and following their expectations of me, to marrying a man who never bothered to ask about my dreams. And so, my dreams were simply modified versions of everyone else's.

It took a series of blind dates and a travel itinerary spanning three countries for me to find myself. So, in the end, I chose me. But I will be forever grateful for the lessons I learned along the way. I figured out what boundaries were, why they are important, and how to set them. I learned how to know who to trust and to trust my decisions. I even discovered that to find love, I had to love myself first. This included taking care of all aspects of me—my health and well-being—through nourishing foods, meditation, and building self-worth. I became more self-aware, socially aware, and deeply attuned to the interconnectedness we all share in this universe.

I may not have found true love in the way that everyone expected. But in the end, I found … me.

CHAPTER THIRTY-TWO

VALENTINE'S DAY
SIBLEY

"You sure you're gonna be alright?" Vidalia asked.

It was sweet of her to worry about me, but I didn't need any sympathy.

"Of course," I answered. "Why wouldn't I be?"

Vidalia eyed me, curiously. "Because last month you were on the final leg of a romantic jaunt through England with promises of romance in Paris. And now, you're lying on the couch in your pajamas on Valentine's Day with a book, a cup of tea, and Skinny as your lap pillow."

Skinny raised his head at the mention of his name. I took his face in my hands and rubbed his ears. "Who needs romance when you have the love of a good dog? Isn't that right, puppy?" I scrunched my face as Skinny licked my nose.

"No offense, Skinny," Vidalia smirked. "But I choose romance."

"What time is Detective Jameson picking you up?" I grinned at her.

Who would have thought that a dead body could be the spark that brought two people together? Honestly, I think her story is a better one. If I hadn't resigned last month, I would have pitched it for *Positive Enlightenment* … adding a focus on mental health, of course.

"Should be any minute now," Vidalia caught her image in our hallway mirror, pausing to fluff her hair and pucker her lips. She turned to me. "Are you ever going to forgive Asher and give him a chance?"

"He lied to me," I reminded her. "And you yourself said that a relationship started with a lie is doomed from the beginning."

"And may I remind you, Miss Smarty-Pants, that you have told me on numerous occasions that I'm not a therapist. Since when do you listen to me, anyhow?"

"When it suits," I smirked.

"Well, I don't see it as a lie, strictly speaking. Personally, I believe Reed offered the money to poke the bear … anger Asher into a reaction. It worked, I think."

"He should have told me." I sighed.

"Maybe," she answered. "Perhaps that's what Reed expected … then you two would bond over a common enemy … Reed."

"I feel you might be giving my old boss a wee bit too much credit." I chuckled.

"I'm not saying his manipulation throughout this process was anything less than deplorable. What I am saying is, you weren't the only one being gaslighted."

"Asher," I sighed.

"Asher," Vidalia nodded.

Honestly, I hadn't thought of it that way. I was so quick to assume the worst of Asher because it made it easier for me to reject him before he could hurt me.

"Holy crap." I put my hands on my hips.

"What?"

"You might be right about that avoidant attachment style assessment."

"Why do you seem so shocked?" Vidalia's eyes lowered in feigned fatigue.

"Well, I'm sorry," I apologized. "I didn't give you enough credit."

"Damn skippy, you didn't!" She laughed, before waving a hand at me. "I'm just funnin' with you. Actually, it prodded me to go back to school."

"Really?" I sat up, wide-eyed. It's amazing that we were roommates, but rarely had time to chat given our opposing work schedules. "Vidalia, that's wonderful! Therapy, I guess?"

"Not exactly," she wagged a finger. "Detective Jameson suggested forensic psychology. I looked up a program online, and I think he might be on to something."

"Wow," I nodded in approval. "I'm really excited for you."

"Well, we'll see if I get accepted. It'll be a little rough working night shifts and going to school during the day. Hope I am up to the challenge."

"I'm certain you are," I reassured her. "And you've got me to help with household chores and looking after Skinny here." I put my forehead on Skinny's head, and he immediately began sniffing my forehead before licking my nose again. His tail was wagging a mile a minute.

Just then, the doorbell rang.

"Guess that's your date. Have fun!" I encouraged.

But when Vidalia opened the door, it wasn't her date on the other side. It was Asher. He was carrying something in his arms. I sat up, tugging at the collar of my pink pajamas self-consciously. I hadn't actually planned on seeing anyone today. I set my tea and book on the side table just in time, before Skinny leapt from my lap.

Vidalia put her hand out in a grand gesture, motioning for him to enter.

"Vidalia told me you were a little under the weather, so I brought you some homemade lentil soup and soda bread from the local bakery. I even got Irish butter, just as a reminder of our visit to—"

He paused when he saw the blank expression on my face. I didn't know what to say.

"How are you feeling?" he finally continued.

"Feeling?" I answered. "Why, I'm just fine, thank you. I don't know what Vidalia was thinking." I glared at her.

Before Vidalia could protest, Jameson appeared at the door with a small box of chocolates in the shape of a heart.

"Thank you, Jameson," she touched his cheek. "Why don't we leave these lovebirds be and head to dinner." She snatched the box and quickly shut the door, with Asher standing in our living room and me still on the couch. Skinny started panting, wagging his tail as he tried to jump on Asher's leg.

"Skinny, sit!" I ordered. Skinny sat, his tail frenetically flicking back and forth across the carpet like the windshield wiper on a car during a storm.

Finally, I stood. "Why don't we bring this into the kitchen?" Asher followed me past the bar-top granite counter and set the large insulated bag on the cutting board I had sitting next to the stove.

"It's still a little hot," he explained. Asher unpacked the bag, revealing the soda bread wrapped in a paper bag, butter, and a large glass bowl with a plastic lid containing the soup. "I assume you have utensils."

"Drawer on the right," I pointed. "I'll grab a couple of bowls for us … assuming you're joining me." It was only then that I remembered I was still in my neon pink pajamas sans underwear. "Uh, give me a second to get changed?"

"Don't go out of your way on my account," Asher protested. "I'm happy to bring you a bowl if you want to get comfortable. You should rest."

I leaned my arm on the counter. "What exactly did Vidalia tell you was wrong with me?" I asked, quizzically. "And where did you run into her, anyway?"

"Well, I stopped in the Bar Fly after work last night to grab a Guinness with one of my college buddies, and she happened to be working that night. I asked how you were doing, and she said that you had a little cold and were skipping Valentine's Day this year in favor of a rom-com movie and popcorn alone on the couch. I asked if she thought you'd be open to me bringing you soup, and her eyes lit up—"

"I'll bet they did."

"She thought that was a great idea." He paused, gauging my reaction. "Was it not a great idea?"

"It was very thoughtful of you," I acknowledged. "But she pulled one over on you. I'm healthy as a horse. I just wasn't feeling the vibe of Valentine's Day. And I did say in my final feature that I was going solo this year. But thank you for the soup."

"Oh, well … Did you eat yet?"

"Not unless you count the graham cracker I had with my tea." I made my way to my bedroom, the entranceway just past the kitchen. "Give me a second to change."

"Okay," he called. "But I fully support you being comfortable. The pink pjs look good on you," he joked.

When I returned moments later wearing a purple robe over my pjs, he laughed. "Well," I reasoned. "Since you support my comfort. There you go."

I grabbed a few placemats and put them on the small dining room table just beyond the bar-top counter. "I don't think I've ever had anyone cook for me before." I returned for the bowls, two spoons, and a butter knife as Asher popped the dish into the microwave to heat up the soup.

"You mean your ex-husband never cooked for you … not once?" He was surprised.

"Well," I gave it some thought. "I suppose he tried once or twice. But he was never very good at it, and had no real ambition to learn." I grabbed a small plate for the bread and a tea towel for the soup dish and set them on the table.

"Oven mitts?" Asher asked.

"Drawer to the left of the stove," I answered.

He found them, putting one on each hand before removing the newly heated soup. He set it on top of the tea towel and retreated to heat the bread up in the microwave. "Unless you prefer me to pop it in the oven instead?"

"Please," I answered. "You made me homemade soup … the microwave for the bread is just fine." I went to the fridge. "I have a half-open bottle of Bordeaux if you care to share. Probably go good with the soup."

"I'm just happy you agreed to spend Valentine's Day eve with me." Asher smiled.

"Oh, I kinda forgot about that," I cringed, setting out two wine-glasses and pouring the Bordeaux. I set the bottle down before Asher returned with the bread and butter, and the ladle he found in a porcelain jar on the kitchen counter.

We sat, each letting out a sigh.

Skinny came to the table, hopefully.

"Go lie down, Skinny. I'll take you out after we eat … and it's not your dinnertime yet."

Skinny's ears perked at the *d* word. I pointed a long arm at his cushion, and he reluctantly curled up like a fortune cookie.

"This is really good!" I acknowledged, after taking a sip. "You are a man of many talents."

"Glad you like it," he took a hearty spoonful from his bowl.

Then the awkward silence ensued. This wasn't the plan for the evening, at all. And I was supposed to still be mad at him. Now, I had no idea what to say.

"Why don't I put on some music," I suggested.

"That would be good," Asher agreed.

I fumbled with the Sonos and finally settled on a "piano dinner music" playlist before returning to my seat.

After an eternity, Asher spoke. "I'm sorry I didn't tell you about Reed's offer from the get-go. If I could go back in time, I would do things differently. But I can't now."

"It's okay." I relaxed my shoulders. "Honestly? Being angry takes an awful lot of energy. Besides, it doesn't matter now, does it? I resigned and have to figure out what to do for work … and soon."

"Funny you should mention that," Asher sipped his wine. "You have heard the news, haven't you?"

"No … What news?"

"This was Reed's last hurrah as publisher. Turns out, he and his partner found someone to provide seed money for the dating show idea."

"Well … there's karma for you!" I joked, half-heartedly. "Clearly fate is punishing him for being unscrupulous."

"I think he would argue he did you a favor."

"How so?"

"Because Phoebe and Yolanda are going in as partners and buying him out. And they want you back as head writer … with a pay raise."

"When were they planning on asking me? And can they afford that?"

"I got their go-ahead to put a few feelers out when I mentioned bringing you the soup."

"Ah, so this was a bribery soup!" I exclaimed, triumphantly.

"Sibley," Asher protested, quietly. "Not everything has an ulterior motive."

"Darn my avoidant attachment style," I mumbled to myself.

"I'm sorry … your what?"

"Just something Vidalia said … She claims that I was so hurt by Thomas that I now push men away to safeguard my heart."

"Do you?" Asher eyed me, seriously.

"I wouldn't have thought so … were it not for you." I set down my spoon.

After a dramatic pause, where I'm certain Asher clearly felt my anxiety, he changed the subject. "As for how they can afford it … well, you'd be surprised at the journal's budget when you divide Reed's, Krystal's, and Bertram's salaries among the four of us."

"They're leaving?" I was shocked. I knew Krystal was tight with Reed and Bertram, but enough to quit?

"Well, Reed was bought out, and Krystal and Bertram refused to take even a temporary pay cut to keep us afloat and pay the rest of us a decent wage. Honestly, had I known what they were making, I would have spoken up years ago. Some reporter I turned out to be, huh? The biggest scam was right under our noses."

"Well, I might have someone in mind for a new sales rep." My mind went to Shaman Theodore. "Aside from that, what do we do now?" I asked.

"Why don't you come to the office Monday? I'll give Phoebe and Yolanda the heads-up, and we can discuss it. Wouldn't do to keep the magazine running without the original 'magic maker,' now would it?"

Skinny began whining.

"Okay, boy." I relented. "Let me just feed him and run him out for a walk."

"Dressed like that?" Asher was surprised.

"It's Bradenton," I argued. "No one cares. But I tell you what—I'll get dressed if you care to go with Skinny and me on a longer walk through the neighborhood."

"I would enjoy that. You get changed, and I'll put the rest of this food away."

Asher had no problem finding his way around the kitchen following a few pointers. I returned a short while later wearing a light red cardigan and black jeans. I thought makeup would be too obvious, so I settled on a pair of heart-shaped earrings and called it done.

Asher's eyes lit up when he saw me. Funny, I swear it was the same look he gave me when I first met him in the office all those years ago.

I put Skinny's leash on, and the three of us headed out.

Asher stopped me at the door, while Skinny tugged impatiently from the hallway. "Just a moment, Skinny," Asher said quietly, never taking his eyes away from mine. Surprisingly, Skinny stopped tugging and just kept looking back at us and down the hall, wondering when we were going to get a move on.

Asher's gaze was unsettling but not unwelcome. My heart felt as if it would leap out of my chest, and my face was warm.

To me he said, "I promise not to rush you into anything, but it is my hope that you won't shut me out of your life again."

"I won't," I whispered back, touching his chest lightly with my hand, reassuringly. "Just give me a little time."

He nodded, leaning toward me hesitantly, pausing just long enough to be certain I wouldn't back away. I didn't. "Happy Valentine's Day, Sibley." Asher lowered his chin and gave me the gentlest of kisses on my lips.

I leaned in and kissed him back. "Happy Valentine's Day, Asher."

THE DATING COMPANION GUIDEBOOK
DANIELLE PALLI

Thank you to everyone who gave me the gift of your time and interest in *Heartbreak on a Deadline*. People who know me know that I am a hopeless romantic. As a relationship coach to singles and couples, I take great joy in supporting those navigating relationships, bearing witness as people learn about themselves and their partners through personal growth, empathetic listening, and introspection.

As I write this, I have been happily married for a very long time. I wouldn't change anything about my past because it has led me to where I am today. But given my experience in my younger years, I wish someone had shared with me the nuggets of wisdom I am about to share with you. My wish for you is that you enjoy happier, healthier, and more peaceful relationships.

This Companion section, while not therapy, is meant to provide general knowledge about dating, with journaling prompts for your own reflection. I highly encourage you to dedicate a journal specific to relationships and what you are learning about yourself and others throughout the dating process. If you are in a committed partnership, you can still use this as a litmus test to spot potential blind spots. This chapter won't dive deep into enhancing love and intimacy, and dialoguing or solving areas of disagreement, but there are still some good takeaways here about building trust, setting realistic expectations, shoring up healthy boundaries, and cherishing your partner.

RED FLAGS (and Some YELLOW Ones)

This is probably the first thing you flipped to when you picked up this book. I get it. The reality is that many people miss the red flags from the get-go, either because they are new to dating and don't yet know how to read the signs; they are infatuated (in limerence) with someone and have blinders on; they are lonely and making excuses for the person (making someone "fit" even if they are the wrong choice); or telling themselves that they are "too picky" and giving the other person the benefit of the doubt. I'm not suggesting that we never give someone a chance or expect perfection when we ourselves are imperfect. But if we notice a pattern of behavior that concerns us over time, that cautionary "yellow flag" could become a "red flag" if changes aren't made.

Here's a list of things to be mindful of when dating. If you notice these, proceed with caution:

1. Lacking Honesty & Integrity

a. Lying, secrecy, and lack of transparency: If someone leads with a lie, that is an immediate red flag, no matter the excuse. And while someone may not bare their soul on a first or second date, notice if they gradually let you into their world or keep a wall up. Do they talk about their friends? Their family? Their career? Their dreams? Keep in mind that some people may have sensitive areas about their past or their family; but if you're doing all the sharing and being vulnerable, and they never open up, that is something to be aware of.

b. Words and actions don't match: Examples of this could be "I want to build a life with you" but never taking steps toward actualizing that dream. Or "I will always be there for you," but they are always too busy when you actually need support. My favorite: "I'm not looking for serious commitment right now," but becoming possessive, overly affectionate, and critical when you take them at their word.

c. Lack of follow-through: If they never follow through on their commitments (e.g., showing up consistently on time, keeping promises), this derails the possibility of forming deep trust.

2. CRITICAL AND DISRESPECTFUL

a. Talking badly about exes: Yes, we might share about an ex as a relationship deepens so that a future partner can understand triggers, past trauma, attachment styles, etc. But if the first few dates are talking negatively about their past partners, you can bet they're likely to turn that criticism on you one day.

b. Disrespectful: If they are condescending toward you, or even kind to you but mean and judgmental of others, that's a red flag.

c. The Four Horsemen are present: This comes from more than three decades of data-backed research by relationship experts Drs. John and Julie Gottman. The horsemen are the negative characteristics that block healthy communication: *criticism* (e.g., "You always . . .!" or "You never . . .!"), *defensiveness* (e.g., "Well, I would, but . . ." or "How am I supposed to do that when . . ."), *contempt* (e.g., "You're a real piece of work, you know that?" or "You disgust me!"), and *stonewalling* (e.g., shutting down the conversation by doing your best imitation of a brick wall).

3. UNTRUSTWORTHY

a. Love bombing (and then ghosting): This person showers you with so much love, the kind you read about in romance novels. They want to connect—fast. They may be in limerence. They could be a narcissist. Who knows? The problem is, this type of love is surface level and often short-lived. Then the ghosting happens (only for them to resurface later at a time convenient for them), or their hormones level out and suddenly you and the relationship are not the perfect fantasy they have created.

b. Assuming trust without earning it: This person demands unconditional trust without time and consistency to prove they are worthy of your trust. If you question them or their motives, they will become angry and defensive. This is a big red flag.

c. Neediness & dependence: This person wasn't "complete" before you. You are their everything. Their happiness is 100 percent dependent on your love and attention. You will never have the energy to consistently meet this person's needs year after year (without them learning independence and trust in self).

4. Lack of Communication / Poor Communication

a. Inconsistent communication: This is the "love bomber" who can't get enough of you … then disappears. This is the person who texts and wants to see you often, only to ghost you and ignore your calls. This person uses the "busy" excuse and only makes time for you when it suits them. *Note: This person doesn't value you or your time.*

b. Conflict avoidant: They stonewall, make excuses, or say things like "Why ruin a good time by talking about our relationship? Can we just have fun?" They may also have trouble dealing with any negative emotion or discussing feelings. Feelings, to them, should be swept under a rug and never discussed.

c. Blame shifting: Be mindful of the person who never takes responsibility for anything in your relationship. This person never apologizes and somehow makes whatever it is your fault. Good communication is not about blaming. It's about coming to a mutual understanding that both people can feel good about and assumes that both people can be right—just with different perspectives.

5. Controlling and Manipulative Behavior

a. Unequal partnership: If you find yourself feeling like the "parent" in your relationship because your partner ("child") is emotionally immature, or as if your partner takes care of you and assumes you cannot make decisions and think for yourself … this is a big red flag. Good partnerships are equitable.

b. Isolation tactics: If this person wants you all to themselves because they "love you so much," and gets jealous of your interaction with friends and family … beware. This could lead to stripping you of sound outside feedback about your life and having only one person's voice in your ears as a means of support—theirs. This is a control tactic … a very scary one.

c. Manipulative behavior: This can include gaslighting, turning arguments against you so that you feel you are to blame, talking you out of doing what you want, and instead making the decision they want for you. It's any time reality gets twisted and distorted. And if they've done a good job at isolating you (see above), you may not even question it.

6. Emotionally Unavailable

a. Lacks empathy: This is someone who is unable to comfort you when you are grieving, in pain, or sad. To be clear, this isn't that the person cares but doesn't know how to express it (a different concern). It's that they cannot sympathize or put themselves in your shoes—nor do they care to. Most often, this is a person who is only concerned about one person's feelings … their own.

b. Avoids vulnerability: This is someone who never shows weakness and sees vulnerability, not as a way of building trust, but as a flaw to fix.

They put on great appearances for others and are embarrassed if you or anyone in their circle expresses anything other than perfection and strength. This person doesn't talk about their feelings, either out of fear of shame, rejection, or because they simply don't understand them.

c. Unwilling to invest in personal growth: "Love me or hate me. I am the way that I am!" this person exclaims, triumphantly. They will have a fixed mindset and believe that the relationship will naturally work … or it won't. But don't expect them to put any of the work in.

7. UNSUPPORTIVE

a. One-sided effort: If you feel that you are doing all the growing and changing, becoming exhausted by the eggshell walking and workarounds to make the relationship limp along, this is a huge red flag. If they are unwilling to take ownership and accountability for any part of the relationship, and you stay with this person, you're in for one stress-filled experience that drains you of all energy.

b. Does not honor your dreams: If someone tells you, "I support you," in words only, but does not seek to understand and help you actualize that dream, this is a half-hearted attempt. Even worse if they mock your dreams or tell you why whatever "it" is isn't possible. I'm not talking about a partner lovingly discussing the reality of a potentially unrealistic dream (e.g., "I will be ruler of the world next year!") because that partner will always seek to try to make some part of that dream a reality (e.g., "I will totally help you become HOA leader next season"). I'm talking about someone dismissive of what is important to you.

c. Only shows up when they need something: This may be a person who love-bombed and ghosted you. Or it may be someone you've had a longtime crush on (who knows it) and uses this superpower when they need a favor … only to get your hopes up and disappear again. And sometimes, this need isn't even tangible. It could be that someone broke their heart, they're lonely and need validation ... and so they randomly text the one person they know will answer—you.

8. An Unresolved Past

a. No introspection or personal growth: This is someone who may be well aware of their past trauma and hardship. But instead of working on it through counseling, self-help books, or talking with friends, they blame their behavior on their past ... and you just have to accept it—or not.

b. The blame game: Beware of someone who has NEVER had a positive past dating experience or an ex that they have at least SOME nice things to say about. Beware of the person who blames all their terrible ex-bosses for why they are not successful. This is someone who will never take responsibility for their part in your relationship or anything that goes wrong in their life.

c. Lack of ANY close relationships or support system: I recognize that there are people who have had traumatic past experiences (e.g., growing up in a cult, abusive family, etc.) and may be rebuilding connections after losing a toxic "support system." However, if this person has no one except for you, ask a few more questions. Possibly encourage them to talk to a counselor. YOU cannot be their sole lifeline. Additionally, WHY are you their only "savior"?

9. Aggressive, Abusive and Unstable Behavior

a. Verbally or physically abusive, aggressive, and belittling: This person shows contempt and is condescending. They may not actually be physical with you, but the fear may be there. They are verbally critical, mean, and overbearing. **WARNING:** This is someone who may be angry and lose their temper, only to apologize later, crying that it won't happen again. This is someone you tread lightly around, for fear of their reaction. Pay attention. If you are afraid or intimidated by this person, they are harmful and untrustworthy.

b. Demonstrates addictive or destructive habits: This can show up as addiction to a substance (e.g., drugs, alcohol, mind-altering substances), but it can also show up in habits such as driving recklessly, starting fights likely to lead to violence, self-harm, working all night and giving up on sleep, gambling, or ruminating (obsessive) thoughts that lead to unhealthy behaviors. There are varying levels of this, so be careful.

c. Financially irresponsible: We all place different values on how we spend our money (e.g., experiences vs. possessions). This is less about how much someone earns or spends and more about their ability to be financially stable. If you enter a long-term relationship with this person, do you trust that you will be able to make sound financial decisions together?

10. Poor Ethics, Core Values and Beliefs (and Lacking Shared Dreams)

a. Mismatch in values: If you value honesty and kindness above all else, you may have a hard time dating someone who is always trying to "beat the system" and thinks that "payback is a b****." They may lack your moral compass or simply don't share your religious or spiritual beliefs. This is where you must take a hard look at what is most important to you. For example, you may be okay if they do not share your spiritual beliefs, provided that they respect yours and demonstrate kindness. Just understand that if you happen to be a rule follower dating a rule breaker, this might not go well in the long term.

b. Mismatch in lifestyle, goals & dreams: In early dating discussions, you might discover that their dreams do not align with yours. Their political and spiritual leanings may contradict your core values (see above). Therefore, you may have a difficult time navigating deeper commitment where you each still seek independence while also supporting shared goals and dreams. For example, if your goal is to marry in the town you grew up in, have three kids, and go to church every Sunday, and their goal is to travel the world, never have children, and are agnostic—you might have conflicting dreams.

c. No dreams whatsoever (or a mismatch of energy): Last, be mindful of a person who never advances themselves or pursues personal or professional growth, and never questions anything outside of their contentment in this moment—not if you are ambitious, have dreams, and are constantly trying to improve yourself and your life. This gets back to values (see above). They may value simplicity and freedom. There is nothing inherently wrong with this, except that they may be unwilling or unable to support your dreams if you happen to be highly ambitious. Conversely, if you are much more of a "live in the moment" kind of person dating someone with a five-year plan, you may feel misaligned with someone who is always goal-oriented and future-focused, who never seems to stop and smell the roses. Finally, notice if you are highly extroverted and value a lot of time with friends dating an introvert who may find that much external stimulation stressful. These can be yellow flags turned green if the two of you consciously reach a compromise.

GREEN FLAGS (and BUILDING TRUST)

I promise not to recap all the red flags in reverse to create a "green flags" list (though there is some of that). Instead, consider green flags as signs of trust. Trust is a core foundation of any solid relationship and gives you confidence that your partner will be there for you in the way that you need (vs. what they THINK you need). This list will also help you trust yourself and your decisions with regard to your dating experience.

Here are the healthy signs to look for . . .

1. Honesty: You trust that this person will always tell you the truth, even if you don't like what they have to say. This is not "honesty with an iron fist" or "brutal honesty," but one delivered with care and your best interest at heart. You never have to second-guess that this person is telling you the truth.

2. Proof of Alliance ("I've got your back."): This is a person who will support you in the way that you need. If things go south in your life (e.g., you're sick and need chicken soup; their mother belittles you; or your boss gives you a crappy performance review, etc.), they will always let you know, even in subtle ways, that they are there for you.

3. Empathy: They are emotionally available for you and take time to listen to your feelings, hopes and dreams, and needs. For those for whom this is a challenge (i.e., they may not be naturally empathetic), they will seek ways to understand you better.

4. Accountability: They will follow through on commitments and take accountability for mistakes. Additionally, if the same "mistake" is recurring, instead of simply apologizing, they will show signs of actively changing their behavior (e.g., they always cancel your date at the last minute or show up late; they may clear their calendar one day for you or text you if they are running late, as a start).

5. Transparency: They WANT to let you into their world. They seek to be understood, and they are not shy about inviting you to meet family and friends (when appropriate).

6. Vulnerability: This is a tricky area because, as a relationship coach, I get asked, "How much is too much?" and "When do I know it's okay to be vulnerable?" While there is no magic number of dates, what I can tell you is that building trust takes time. You don't have to share EVERYTHING about yourself on a first date (e.g., your past trauma bonds and narcissistic father). More, this is a chance for each person to share—little by little—as they develop trust. In other words, if your date shares something sensitive about themselves, can you hold that space and be present without judgment? Can you discuss what's confidential and what's okay to share with others? Green flags are when you both feel emotionally safe and able to share things about yourselves that not everyone gets to know.

7. Ethical and Value-driven: This person shares your core values and treats others with kindness. One trap I think people fall into is when there's a surly person who is kind to us and irritable to others. We may attribute this to them being "misunderstood" when, in reality, they are on their best behavior. Understand that it takes an enormous amount of ENERGY to be ON … ALL THE TIME. Look for someone who is consistent in their treatment of everyone—preferably, kind.

8. Respectful of Boundaries: A good match will respect your physical and emotional boundaries. If you express discomfort in discussing a particular topic, they will honor that. If you need physical space or want to build more trust before intimacy, they will respect this. They do not test boundaries. They honor them.

9. Consistency: A green flag is someone who is consistently present; their mood and behaviors are balanced. There's no "Where did THIS person come from? I hardly recognize them!" Their words and actions align, and you know what to expect from them.

10. You Trust Your Gut: I can't tell you how many times I've heard in my practice, "I knew there was something off about them, but I thought I was being too … picky … judgmental … [insert explanation of choice]. Turns out, they were exactly what I thought." If you have a visceral reaction to someone—good or bad—pay attention. Your gut and subconscious may be processing information faster than your mind is registering it. If you get a good "vibe" from someone, that's something to consider.

11. Respectful in Words and Actions: This person respects you, your hopes, and your dreams. Even if they disagree with you, they are kind, curious, and flexible enough to talk through differences. They are kind to others; this includes people who have vastly different beliefs.

12. Willing to Grow with a Partner: This person understands that we are continually growing and changing. Those who have been in a committed partnership for a long time can attest to the fact that their partner is NOT the same person they knew eons ago (and that's probably a good thing). Is this person willing to grow WITH you? Are they seeking continual personal growth? This may not seem important to you now, but I promise you it will be decades down the line. Choose someone who chooses "I'm willing to learn" over "If it ain't broke, don't fix it."

JOURNALING PROMPTS

The following prompts are designed to encourage you to reflect upon your past and current relationships, the fictional (but relevant) relationships in this book, and what you've just read about the red and green flags. There are also thought-provoking questions about your goals and expectations for your future or current partner, how to show up authentically in a relationship, and how to establish and maintain healthy boundaries. Take your time with these. You may choose to journal about one topic per day or take several days to reflect on one important topic for you. And, if writing is not your thing, some people choose to draw, paint, play themed music, or collage their ideas instead. There's no right or wrong approach.

1. The Stages of a Relationship: This may vary, depending on the relationship expert. For simplicity, I'm describing three stages. *The first is the limerence (or "honeymoon") phase* where your body releases a hormone cocktail of dopamine, norepinephrine, serotonin, and more. You may feel euphoric, excited, and have overwhelming thoughts and feelings about the other person. This may last for a couple of months up to a year. This is the stage where we are sure we've found "the One" and it's "Love at first sight." We may create a fantasy of the person that may or may not be true, but we want to spend as much time with that person to find out. *Stage two is building trust and strengthening communication.* This is the "reality" phase where you start to see one another's flaws and have to test the waters to ensure you feel emotionally safe opening up to the other person. This is the critical phase where you're not driven by hormones, but by wanting to experience deep connection and compare long-term dreams and core values. It is the stage where you will end up getting closer—or breaking up. *Last, there is the long-term commitment stage.* This is the beautiful stage where you have developed the foundations of trust and healthy communication and are intentionally choosing the other person every day. You work together through problems instead of walking away. You create rituals of connection and cherish one another. It's the stage where you are essentially saying to your partner, "I trust you to be there for me, and I will always be there for you."

Journaling Prompt

Consider your past relationships. Have you experienced all three phases and been in a long-term relationship (generally lasting more than a year)? Or do you notice a pattern of relationships ending at a certain stage? What have you learned about relationships from your previous dating experience? What do you hope to experience in the future?

2. Expectations: Most of us have a set of expectations for our future partner that we might mistakenly assume is understood, while a handful of others may have no expectations whatsoever. It's a delicate balance. If you have NO expectations, you have no way of defining who is a good connection for you. There's no foundation for long-term growth. Conversely, if your expectations are so rigid, no one will be able to live up to them for long (or your partner will become exhausted and resentful trying).

The key is setting REALISTIC expectations and letting go of the more superficial "nice to haves." For example, instead of looking for someone who "makes a million dollars a year, goes to the gym to lift weights six times a week, and has blue eyes and a square jaw," a more realistic expectation could be ". . . is financially responsible and makes health a priority."

Journaling Prompt

Make a list of ALL your expectations (if you could wave a magic wand and create the perfect person). Now create a new list, including the "must haves," and refine the unrealistic expectations into ones founded in reality. (The goal is not to lower expectations, but to create healthy ones.)

3. Relationship Goals: One mistake people make in the early stages of dating is they feel they will eventually be able to change the other person's mind (or behaviors, etc.). This is not to say that people don't change, but they have to want to and they have to work at it. An example might be someone who definitely wants to have kids and the other person definitely does not. You are not likely to change this person's mind by showing cute baby videos and spending lots of time with your niece and nephew. Could they change their mind? Maybe. But I would suggest that when you begin dating, assume the other person is not about to change—at all. Can you live with the person in front of you, just as they are?

Journaling Prompt

Journal about your goals for being in a relationship. Be honest about whether it is simply for companionship vs. long-term commitment; if the plan is to raise a family; or maybe it's to have a travel partner to share adventures with. You might even write your vision for your future relationship and life.

4. Boundaries: Establishing healthy boundaries is critical for feeling emotionally and physically safe when dating. When a partner respects those boundaries, trust is deepened. However, when someone consistently ignores or pushes the boundaries, trust erodes. An example of this could be early in the dating stage where a person either makes an unwanted sexual advance or asks you about sexual preferences and deeply personal information before you've had a chance to determine how vulnerable you are comfortable being with this person. Not only is this a HUGE red flag, but it becomes worse if you say, "I'm not comfortable with this," and they continue to push against your boundaries. Other helpful boundaries might be more subtle, such as "I care about you, but I can't immediately text you back every time you reach out. However, I would love it if we could agree to send a 'good morning' text each day and another at night if we don't have time to talk on the phone." You would be surprised how many fights and misunderstandings are over text messages, how often to text, and the "What did you mean by that?" In general, in-person or video chats are best when trying to have a meaningful conversation.

Journaling Prompt

What healthy boundaries are important for you to set for your relationships? Reflect on a time when your boundaries were crossed—or perhaps you crossed someone else's boundary. What did you learn? Additionally, did you come across any "boundaries" that seemed unfair or unrealistic? What made you feel that way?

5. Know Yourself & Be Authentic: The first key to establishing a good relationship is learning to love yourself. Would YOU date you? Becoming self-aware, learning to love and accept yourself, and being whole and complete before finding a partner will set you up for greater relationship success. Yes, we all want love and connection, but if we rely on someone else to make us happy? Well, that's a lot of pressure on them to keep us happy and limits our personal resilience if we can't function independently. Additionally, if you don't know yourself, you may get lost in another person's dreams without having the opportunity to establish your own. Finally, when you do venture into the dating world, be authentic. That doesn't mean you have to show up "warts and all" on the first date, but if you're putting up a façade about your core values, beliefs, and behaviors, think about how difficult that will be to maintain over the long haul. And it will not allow the other person to love the real you. Last, honesty is a foundation for trust.

Journaling Prompt

Ask yourself, "How can I show up as my authentic self? What are my key strengths and values? What do I believe about myself, and what will I bring to a future relationship?" (Or, "What do I bring to my current relationship?")

6. Character Analysis #1: Sibley was set up on dates with Bodhi, Theodore, Arran, Jack, and, finally, Asher. Pick one character to focus on.

Journaling Prompt

What did you notice about this character? What red or green flags showed up? Are they reflective of a personal dating experience? What did you learn about yourself or what to look for in a partner?

7. Character Analysis #2: Vidalia, while seemingly relationship-savvy, had her own struggles with Tod and formed a connection with Jameson. There were also some troubled waters between Phoebe and Amir, along with a subtle reference to Yolanda's marriage. Last, we can get a small sense of what Krystal's, Bertram's, and Reed's relationships might be like. Pick one character or relationship dynamic to explore.

Journaling Prompt

What did you observe about this person or couple? What did they do well? What could they have done better? Have you experienced something similar? What did you learn (or validate for yourself) from these examples?

Conclusion

This wraps up the Dating Companion portion of the book. Please keep this section handy for future reference and return to these prompts as needed (possibly revising or choosing new characters to focus on). Wishing you a happy, healthy, and fulfilling relationship ahead. Love well.

ABOUT THE AUTHOR

Danielle Palli is a multi-genre author, a board-certified positive psychology and mindfulness coach, a relationship coach, and a multimedia content creator and book coach. She lives in Florida with her husband and a plethora of pets. She finds joy in nature, travel, music, theater and the arts, and is known for singing and dancing around the living room at any hour of the day or night. As a free-spirited outlier enamored with life, she finds that life is more exciting when you color outside the lines. Learn more: www.DaniellePalli.com.